BLOOD ON THE MONEY 2

Lock Down Publications and Ca$h Presents

Blood on the Money 2

A Novel by J-Blunt

Lock Down Publications
P.O. Box 944
Stockbridge, Ga 30281

Visit our website
www.lockdownpublications.com

First Edition December 2020
Printed in the United States of America

Lock Down Publications
Like our page on Facebook: Lock Down Publications @
www.facebook.com/lockdownpublications.ldp
Cover design and layout by: **Dynasty Cover Me**
Book interior design by: **Shawn Walker**
Edited by**: Jill Alicea**

Stay Connected with Us!

Text **LOCKDOWN** to 22828 to stay up-to-date with new releases, sneak peeks, contests and more…

Submission Guideline.

Submit the first three chapters of your completed manuscript to ldpsubmissions@gmail.com, subject line: Your book's title. The manuscript must be in a .doc file and sent as an attachment. The document should be in Times New Roman, double-spaced and in size 12 font. Also, provide your synopsis and full contact information. If sending multiple submissions, they must each be in a separate email.

Have a story but no way to send it electronically? You can still submit to LDP/Ca$h Presents. Send in the first three chapters, written or typed, of your completed manuscript to:

LDP: Submissions Dept
P.O. Box 944
Stockbridge, Ga 30281

DO NOT send original manuscript. Must be a duplicate.

Provide your synopsis and a cover letter containing your full contact information.

Thanks for considering LDP and Ca$h Presents.

Word from the author:

BLOOD ON THE MONEY 2 will introduce new characters. While Carl was getting money with Triple Beam Team, there was another young boss coming up on the scene named Drayez. This is his story. By the end of this book, you will begin to see characters from book 1 and the stories will combine and flow into book three. Sit back and enjoy!

Acknowledgments:

Miss Hendricks, you are an amazing blessing. Thank you to everybody that showed love and support during my fight with this injustice system.

A special thank you to the fans and supporters of J-Blunt. None of this would be possible if y'all didn't go out and buy and read my books. The reviews you leave on Amazon are golden. Thank you.

Connect with me on Facebook @ Author J-Blunt

Book I: Drive

TO FORCE. URGE ONWARD. PUSH FORWARD. TO IMPEL OR PROPEL AS MOTIVE POWER. CAUSE TO FUNCTION. TO MOTIVATE, INFLUENCE, OR DIRECT.

THE PLACE WHERE DESTINY, DESIRE, AND DESPAIR MEET.

WHERE THE BOUNDLESS “I WILL’S” KILL OFF THE WEAK SPIRITED “I CANT’S”.

WHEN YOU DECIDE TO CHANGE YOUR POSITION FROM A HAVE NOT TO A HAVE.

DRIVE DOESN’T OVERLOOK THE FAILURES, BUT USES THEM AS FUEL TO KEEP YOU MOVING FORWARD WHEN ENERGY AND RESOURCES RUN OUT.

only three, but she knew what she did. After using the bathroom and freshening up, I hit the kitchen to make something to eat. I was drinking from the orange juice when Rayna walked in to make Draya a bottle.

"Don't be drinking all my baby's juice. You know you ain't got no money to buy more."

I took a long-ass drink and threw the container against the wall. Juice splashed everywhere. "Man, why the fuck you always talkin' shit? You want a mu'fucka to beat yo' ass!"

She stepped in my face. "Do it then, nigga! If my babies go hungry, you ain't gon' get them no food. I gotta take care of *you* and them. It's like I got *six* kids instead of five."

"Bitch, shut the fuck up," I snapped, muffing her ass and smashing the back of her head into the cabinet. I wanted to put hands on her, but two of her little ones, Maya and Vontrez, walked into the kitchen.

"Put cho hands on me again, muthafucka!" Rayna screamed, grabbing a knife from the drawer.

Not wanting to end up in the hospital with stab wounds, I dismissed her and went to the room to get dressed. I scanned the floor for something to wear. I grabbed a black Nike shirt, blue jean Levi's that could use a wash, and a pair of black Air Max that had seen better days. I hit the front door and stepped out into the late morning sun. The May air seemed to relieve some of the stress that had built since I woke up. I hated living with Rayna and all her kids. Hated that I didn't have nowhere else to live. Hated I didn't have a job. Hated I didn't have no money. Hated I got Rayna pregnant. Shit, I hated everything about my life. And as much as I hated my situation, I didn't know what to do about it.

For as long as I could remember, my mama told me I wasn't gon' be shit. Now, at twenty-four years old, I had fulfilled the prophecy. I didn't have no education or the drive to go to school. I had been a bum for so long that I became cool with it. Don't get me wrong, I had dreams of being rich one day. When I watched Drake, Future, and Rick Ross videos, I envisioned myself in they shoes. They made being rich look easy. But I couldn't rap. Hell, I didn't even known nobody that could rap. And I didn't know the first thing about selling drugs. I didn't even know where to buy enough drugs to sell. The nigga I bought weed from was a small timer. Besides, even if I did find somebody that sold weight, I didn't have the money to buy it, which put me back at square one. I was broke.

As I moped down the sidewalk, drowning in my sorrows, wishing I could find a few dollars on the ground, I walked two blocks over to my nigga Vic's house. He lived with his baby mama and two kids. Like me, Vic was a bum. His girl was a nursing assistant and provided for their house. He was basically a stay-at-home dad. He played video games while his girl worked. I still didn't know why it worked for him but not me.

"Who is it?" Vic called after I knocked on the door.

"Drayez."

Locks clicked and the door opened. "'Sup, nigga?"

Vic figured out a long time ago that he looked good (no homo). Light skin, long dreads, light brown eyes, average height with a stocky build. When we were in the streets, females flocked to him like he was Chris Brown or Trey Songz. He had four baby mamas and five kids. Didn't support none of them. Let him tell it, he just doing what God created man to do: repopulate the earth.

"What it do? Renae here?" I asked, shaking his hand as I walked in the house.

"Nah, nigga. My bitch got a job. I ain't with that SSI shit. TC here. Lock the door," he said before spinning off and leaving me with security.

"What up, Drayez?" TC called, not looking up from the TV screen. My nigga TC was brown-skinned, short, and chubby. I met him through Vic. They were boys since way back. The thing that separated TC from us was he had a job. He worked at McDonald's and was proud to make minimum wage.

"Shit. What you niggas on?" I asked, plopping down on the couch next to TC.

"This that new Madden. Just got it yesterday," Vic said.

I checked the graphics. The game looked so real that at first glance it could pass for a real NFL game. "This shit bussin'. I got next. Where the weed at?"

TC finally looked up at me. "Nigga, what you got on some weed?"

"C'mon, my nigga. Don't start with that bullshit. I already got this bitch up my ass about not having no money. I just wanna get high and chill."

"She put yo' ass out again?" Vic laughed.

"Nah. I was about to beat her mu'fuckin ass, but I left. Bitch always talkin' shit."

"You know, McDonald's hiring," TC cut in.

"Yeah right, nigga," I laughed. "I'd rather be broke than flipping burgers."

"On the real," Vic agreed.

"Well, stay broke then, nigga. Keep ending up catching domestic cases."

"Whatever, nigga. Where the weed at?"

"It's a li'l piece in there," TC said, nodding towards the ashtray. "I was just about to spark that shit."

I looked in the ashtray and seen that "li'l piece" was more like a blunt roach, but I fired it up anyway. "This Reggie?"

TC looked annoyed. "You got some money on some loud, broke-ass nigga?"

I let him have the dig. Beggars couldn't be choosy. "Man, I need some money bad. I'm tired of being broke."

"I told you McDonald's hiring," TC repeated.

"Fuck that fast food shit. I need some real money right now. I got a baby that I can't even take care of. That shit be making me feel like a weak-ass nigga."

"'Cause you is a weak-ass nigga, weak-ass nigga," Vic cracked.

"You just like me, weak-ass nigga. You don't got no money either."

"You don't need money when you got hoes, nigga. Anything I need, my bitches provide. A.O.B, nigga. All On a Bitch."

I blew him off. "Whatever, nigga."

"My cousin, L-Dog, lookin' for niggas to ride wit' 'em," TC spoke up. "I can introduce y'all if you want."

"Who is L-Dog and what he be on?"

"One of my older cousins. He just did like seven or eight years. Only been out three months and ridin' in a Benz."

The mention of the foreign car tickled my ears. "Straight up?"

"Yeah. He asked me if I wanted to be on his team, but I told him I was good. I'm too fat to be runnin' from the police."

I ignored the part about the police. "What he do?"

"Robbing dope boys. Last time I seen him he showed me 20 G's. Cash money."

Hearing how L-Dog got money made me think about my sister. She was doing a bid for robbery and I didn't want to end up in her shoes. I had already done time and I hated being locked up. But I also needed the money. I had never seen $20,000. Just thinking about it made my palms itch

"And you saying he gon' put me down, just like that?"

"I don't know. I can call and holla at him. But I'm telling you right now," he said, turning from the game to look at me. "That nigga crazy."

The look in TC's eyes scared me a little, but 20 G's was too tempting. "What'chu mean he crazy?"

He laughed and shook his head. "Before he went to jail, he shot my cousin - his sister."

"His mama's daughter? His blood?"

TC nodded. "Yeah. Shot her in the leg 'cause she wouldn't tell him where her nigga kept his money. When she screamed, my aunty came outside to see what happened and he shot at her too."

I couldn't believe what I was hearing. "He shot his own mama?"

"Nah. Just shot at her. They didn't tell on him either. They knew he woulda killed they ass. Don't nobody in the family fuck with him. He too crazy."

I thought about what my nigga just told me. L-Dog sounded beyond crazy. Insane. He popped his sister and shot at his mama. Shoulda been under the jail. But on the other hand, if he could get me $20,000, I didn't care how many of his family members he shot.

"Call him!"

***

As luck would have it, L-Dog was in the neighborhood. TC called and told him about me and he wanted to meet. We hopped in TC's 2007 Monte Carlo and headed to a house on 26th and Hadley.

"That's his whip right there," TC pointed as he parked.

I didn't know much about cars, but I knew L-Dog's Benz looked good. Shiny black paint. Big chrome wheels. I pictured myself behind the wheel. "Man, that bitch look good!"

"Yeah, but remember what I said. This nigga crazy," TC warned.

We climbed out the car and walked upon the porch of a maroon and white two story house. TC rang the doorbell. A few seconds later, the door flung open and a female that looked like she just left the set of a rap video stood in the doorway. She had long black hair, dark chocolate skin, big eyes, and lips that looked like she could suck a baseball through a straw. She wore a tight bright orange dress that showed so much cleavage that it looked like her titties was about to spill out. She gave us irritated looks.

"Who is y'all niggas?" she asked with way too much attitude.

"L-Dog here?" TC asked.

At the mention of the name, her face softened and she lost the attitude. "You his cousin?"

"Yeah."

"Come in, baby. He waiting on you."

Damn. Just the mention of this nigga's name changed her whole attitude. L-Dog gotta be a beast! A nigga's name that commanded that much fear and respect seemed like a God to me.

As soon as I stepped in the house, I was slapped in the face by the smell of strong skunk weed. Two niggas was sitting on the couch in front of a table with a big-ass brick of weed on it. One of them was brown-skinned, short, bald-headed, and chubby. There were tattoos all over his face and neck. Something told me that was L-Dog. He didn't look intimidating at all. I was surprised that somebody so short and chubby could be so terrifying. The nigga that sat next to him was tall, dark-skinned, skinny, bald, and had a mouth full of gold teeth. On the other couch were two more females dressed like the one that answered the door. They had their faces in their phones and didn't even acknowledge me and TC.

"TC! 'Sup, you li'l bitch-ass nigga!" L-Dog smiled, happy to see his cousin.

"'Sup, L-Dog. What's good, Twan?"

Twan looked up and gave a nod.

"So dis da nigga you was tellin' me 'bout? Dray?" L-Dog asked, looking me up and down.

"What up, my nigga?" I nodded.

He stared at me like he was looking for a flaw. The stare was intense and uncomfortable, but I tried to act like it didn't faze me.

"You been to da joint, nigga?"

"Yeah. Been out a year."

"Where you was at?"

"RYOC."

His eyes lit up. "Oh, you was in gladiatin' school, huh? How long you do?"

"A year."

"Dat ain't shit. What'chu do?"

I couldn't tell him the lie I told Rayna about serving an undercover because he might see through it. And I couldn't tell the truth, because going to prison for stealing a couple X-boxes and flat screens was weak. So I lied. "A bitch-ass strong-armed robbery."

Surprise and excitement shone in his eyes. "Oh, you took a nigga shit, huh?"

"Yeah. Somethin' like that."

"Well, I see you already got mo' heart than my bitch-ass li'l cousin. So dat's cool. You niggas sit down and chill. Roll up somethin'."

I tried to keep my eyes on rolling the blunt, but the females on the couch across from us was so bad that I kept sneaking peeks. Then the Hispanic one got up to leave the room. The stretch pants and tank top she wore showed off the kind of body that was in the magazines I used to jack off to while locked up.

"Damn!"

"You like dat, huh?" L-Dog grinned at me. "Bitch ain't shit. Ratchet-ass hoe."

L-Dog's comment surprised me. I was also surprised that her friends acted like they didn't even hear the diss.

"Ain't none of dese hoes shit. Nigga get a whip and a bag, dese hoes come a dime a dozen. Dey jus wanna be in da presence of a real nigga. Too many pussy niggas out here lettin' dese hoes call da shots. Bitch know dat if she fuckin' wit' me, I run shit. Ain't dat right, bitches?"

To my surprise, they responded with smiles. "You crazy, L-Dog!"

Before I could digest what I saw, a little girl about the same age as I'Yanna came walking into the living room, rubbing her eyes. It looked like she had just woke up.

"What are you doing, Michelle?" the thick Hispanic chick said as she scooped up the girl.

"In 'bout ten or twelve years, dat li'l bitch right dere gon' be suckin' dick jus like her mama. Ain't none of dese hoes shit. Ain't dat right, Twan?"

Twan blew him off. "C'mon, my nigga. That's a baby."

L-Dog got mad. "Fuck dat li'l bitch! You tellin' me she ain't gon' suck dick when she grows up? All hoes suck dick, nigga."

"I ain't sayin' that she ain't. I don't know. But she a baby right now, fool-ass nigga."

L-Dog waved him off. "You niggas just soft on dese hoes."

TC was right. His cousin was crazy. No, fuck that. He was insane. He needed to be in the same mental hospital Gucci Mane did time in. I was out of words to describe what I just seen, so I stayed quiet, just like the girl's mother. I lit my blunt, took a puff, and almost coughed up a lung.

"Look at dis weak chest-ass nigga!" L-Dog laughed. "Slow down, Dray. Dat ain't no Reggie, boy. Dis 500 an ounce."

I only heard bits and pieces of what he said because I couldn't stop coughing. And by the time I finished coughing, I was high as fuck.

"Now listen, Dray, I got a move planned. Couple days. 50, 60 G's. Easy. Lil cuz say you good, so I'ma put chu on. But know dis, lil nigga," he said, giving me a serious look. "I don't fuck around. And da one thang I don't play 'bout is my change. Secondly is snitches. Third thang is a bitch-ass nigga. You ain't no snitch or bitch, is you?"

I shook my head. "No snitch or bitch in my blood."

He tossed me a cell phone. "Put cho numba in dere. I'ma get at chu."

After putting my number in the phone, I tossed it back.

"I like you, Dray. I don't know why you kick it wit' my bitch-ass cousin, but—"

We got interrupted by a loud knock on the door. L-Dog gave the chocolate chick a nod. I watched her body parts jiggle as she went to answer the door.

"Hey, Man-Man!"

The chick with the baby shot to her feet like she got pinched on her big-ass booty. She looked scared. Like something bad was about to happen and she wanted to prevent it. But before she could get to the door, Man-Man walked in the house. He was tall, 6'5" or 6'6". He didn't carry a lot of weight, but was in good shape. When he seen us sitting around smoking weed and Twan and L-Dog bagging up, his nostrils flared like a bull. Whatever ole girl was trying to prevent from happening was about to happen.

"Fuck is this shit, Tasha?" he screamed at the chick with the baby.

"Don't do this right now, Man-Man. Let's go outside."

"Fuck you mean don't do this right now? Why you got these niggas in here smoking and bagging up weed while my baby in here? Fuck wrong with you, bitch?"

While Man-Man snapped on his baby mama, I glanced over at L-Dog and Twan. They looked ready to do damage. Man-Man's anger didn't allow him to see that his life might be in danger.

"Man-Man, just step outside and let me talk to you real quick," she pleaded, grabbing his arm.

He snatched away from her and walked further into the living room. "You niggas gotta get the fuck outta here. I don't know what she told y'all, but my baby lay her head up in here."

I agreed with Man-Man. We were disrespecting his daughter's house. When I looked at TC, he was already standing, ready to leave. I looked at L-Dog just in time to see him pull out a big-ass chrome pistol. Man-Man's eyes got big as a dopefiend that just took a hit. Fear replaced the toughness he displayed. L-Dog ran up to him and swung the gun like it was one of them little Louisville slugger bats. When it connected with Man-Man's jaw, bones cracked and he went down.

"Bitch ass nigga! Fuck you think you talkin' to?" L-Dog yelled, stomping Man-Man. Twan joined in and they stomped him in and out of consciousness.

"Stop, L-Dog! Stop!" Tasha screamed, holding her crying baby as their provider and protector got his ass beat.

TC nudged my arm. "Let's go."

He didn't have to tell me twice. I didn't know how that situation would end, nor did I want to be around to find out. We laughed all the way to the Monte Carlo.

After starting the car, TC looked at me. "Didn't I tell you that nigga was crazy?"

Chapter 2

It had been two days since I met L-Dog and he still hadn't called. I checked my government phone religiously to see if I had a message or missed a call. Nothing. I thought about L-Dog's car. Now I wanted a Benz. I thought about all the weed he had, which was the best I ever smoked. I still had a piece of the blunt. One hit and I was good for a couple hours. I wanted some more of that. And I thought about how all those fine-ass females were letting him say whatever he wanted. He even called Tasha's baby a dick sucker. They knew not to say nothing to him about it. L-Dog had money, power, and respect. I wanted that. But I didn't have a clue how to get it.

Keys jiggling the lock on the front door made me look up. Rayna stumbled into the house, tripping over kids' toys. She flopped down on the couch next to me, smelling like perfume and a liquor store.

"How was the concert?" I asked.

"K. Michelle is my bitch," she sang, lifting her hands in the air and snapping her fingers. "What you still doing up?"

"I just put Draya to sleep."

"That li'l bitch cry too much and she be getting on my nerves. But she love her some you. I don't know why. She came out my mu'fuckin' pussy."

I mugged my baby mama. "Stop callin' my daughter a bitch."

"I can call her whatever I want. Bitch. Hoe. Slut. I take care of her. That's my baby."

"You betta watch yo' mu'fuckin' mouth, Rayna. I ain't playing."

She laughed. "Is you mad or not? Huh? You mad, Drayez?"

I didn't feel like catching a domestic battery, so I went to the room and got in bed. Rayna followed behind me, staggering and bumping into the walls. "I can't believe I went for that bullshit about you being a baller when I met you. You's a lyin'-ass nigga," she slurred, falling onto the bed.

"Go to sleep, nigga. You drunk."

"So? I can get drunk if I want. I'm grown," she said, falling silent for a moment. "Why you lie to me, Drayez?"

I envisioned myself knocking her ass out. One punch. Right on the chin.

"You hear me talking to you, Drayez?" she yelled.

"Shut the fuck up before you wake up Draya."

"Who gives a fuck about Draya? I'm the mama. This my house. And don't be tellin' me to shut up. You shut up," she said, slapping me on the back.

The hit wasn't that hard, but that shit pissed me off like she punched me in the face. I rolled over and pushed her ass off the bed. She landed on the floor hard. Then she started laughing. She sounded like a witch at a haunted house.

"Yo' punk ass!" She laughed. "That shit didn't do nothing but turn me on and make me horny. Eat my pussy."

"Go to sleep. Leave me alone," I mumbled, rolling over.

"Go to sleep. Leave me alone," she teased in a whiny voice. "I'm horny, Drayez. I want my pussy ate."

I ignored her. Fuck that bitch.

Then I felt her hands rolling me over. She was kneeling on the bed naked.

"Eat my pussy or get out," she threatened.

"Man, you trippin'. Move."

She held me down and climbed on my chest, putting her pussy in my face. I could see lust and anger swirling in her eyes. This was going to be good. I stuck my tongue out and she climbed on top.

"Yeah, baby. Stick yo' tongue in me so I can ride that muthafucka."

I opened my mouth and stuck my tongue out as far as I could.

"Mmm! Yeah, nigga. Yeah!" she moaned, sliding her pussy all over my face. She wanted more of my tongue inside her and started grinding on my face harder. It felt like my teeth was about to break

"Wait," I mumbled, pushing her off. "That shit hurt."

She looked down at me with lust-glazed eyes. "Eat me from the back."

I looked at her like she was crazy. I had never ate pussy from the back, but I knew I would have to stick my face in her ass to do it and I wasn't sticking my face in nobody's ass.

"C'mon, Dray," she whined, getting on her knees, face down, ass up. "My pussy so wet, baby. Eat it. I wanna cum."

As much as I didn't want to do it, seeing that ass in the air got my dick super hard. So I said fuck it. I got behind her, shoved my face in her ass and stuck my tongue out as far as it would go. I eventually found her pussy and she started rubbing her ass all over my face while I licked her.

"Oh, shit! That feels so good, baby!"

I liked hearing her pleasure and started getting into it. "Oh yeah, Dray. Oh shit! Lick my ass, baby. Lick my ass."

I moved my face. "Hell nah!"

"Please, Dray," she begged. "I wanna do everything with you. I never had my ass licked. Please."

I didn't wanna lick no ass. Fuck that shit. But I also didn't want my baby mama feeling like I don't meet her needs. What I didn't do, the next nigga would. So I spread those cheeks, exposing her asshole. It was black as hell and wet. I stuck out my tongue and licked circles around it.

"Oh my God! Ah! That shit feel good, baby," she screamed, bucking and moaning.

Seeing how she reacted made me want to go harder so I started licking her ass like it was a pussy.

"Oh God! Oh my God! Oh shit!"

I continued doing my thang, licking her ass and clit. When she came, it gushed out, dripping on the sheets. Now it was my turn. I got up to strip and lay back on the bed. Rayna crawled over to me, looking at me like I was a sex symbol. I wasn't an ugly nigga by far, but I wasn't a pretty boy either. 6'2", 185 pounds. My hair was cut into a small Philly fro. Dark brown eyes, bushy eyebrows, a small nose, straight teeth, full lips.

"Mmmm," Rayna moaned, grabbing my dick and shoving it into her mouth like she was hungry.

"Oh shit!" I groaned, grabbing the back of her head.

My baby mama handled my tool with skill. She sucked hard, taking as much as she could down her throat, using lots of spit. What she couldn't get in her mouth, she jacked off. She moaned like she was making love to my dick. Started licking down the sides of my shit and jacking me off before allowing my dick to touch them tonsils again. My nut built up quickly. I grabbed two fistfuls of the sheets as she milked my dick. Nut poured down the side of my dick and was all over her face, hands, and sheet.

"Wait! Hold up!" I winced, tensing up. The pleasure and pain had me sucking in deep breaths and clenching my ass cheeks so tight that the sheets gave me a wedgie. But she still didn't stop sucking. Kept going until I was drained. When done, she stood up to admire her work.

"That's how a real bitch do!" she bragged.

My nut was everywhere. On her lips, dribbling from her chin, covering her hands, in my dick hairs, and on the sheets.

"Damn, yo' real ass did that, baby," I breathed.

"You crazy," she giggled, grabbing one of Draya's shirts from the floor to wipe her face and hands.

I was about to comment on her wiping sperm on my baby's shit until she bent over and shook that ass for me. I forgot about the dirty deed as I looked at her greatest asset. The view of her ass was amazing. Not a blemish, wrinkle, bump, or spot on them cheeks. I never seen an ass so perfect. That's how she got all the kids.

"Let me see if you know what to do with this," she said, twerking a little bit before getting back in bed. She lay on her back and began playing with her pussy. The lips were a shade darker than her skin, and they were fat and already wet. Her pink clit was swollen and juice dripped from her pussy hole. When I couldn't take watching no more, I got between her legs and slipped inside.

"Ssss! Mmmhhh!" she moaned, putting a hand on my chest to stop me from going all the way in.

I moved her hand, pushing all my weight down and going deep.

"Wait! Stop!" she gasped, using her hand to push my stomach again.

I didn't wait or stop. I grabbed her hand out of the way and slipped in deeper.

"Oh, Dray!" she moaned, sliding across the bed.

I slid with her and beat that pussy up like my dick was a jackhammer. We ended up against the headboard in a fucked-up position, like she was sitting on my lap. But I still didn't stop hitting it.

"Oh, Dray. Easy. Please. Slow. Down."

That shit sounded like music to my ears. I continued to dig her out until I was about to bust. "Lemme hit it from the back."

She spun around, looking over her shoulder. "Okay. But go slow."

When she assumed the position, I admired that ass for a moment. I jiggled, rubbed, and smacked it. When I stuck my dick in, I didn't give her time to catch her breath. I started beating that pussy up.

"Oh shit, Dray! Oooh! I feel it in my stomach!" she moaned, trying to get away.

I stayed glued to her ass. We went to the floor then ended up in the corner between the wall and dresser. She stood up, holding onto the dresser. I squatted down and kept drilling. Her ass cheeks jiggled like crazy as I tore her shit up. Then she started making noises I never heard before. Like a wounded animal.

"Grrrrrr! Ah, Dray! Oh, damn, nigga! Grrrrrr!"

Hearing the noises got me so geeked that I couldn't hold off any longer. I plunged deep into her pussy and busted my nut. Shit felt so good, I almost passed out.

***

The early morning spring air felt cool against my skin. It was 8:00 in the morning and I was hot. Me and Rayna had just finished arguing and I needed to get out of the house and cool down before I whooped her ass. I didn't have nowhere to go, so I just started walking. I had been walking for almost ten minutes when I stopped at another crazy woman's house. I walked up on the porch of a yellow and white duplex and rang the doorbell for the lower unit. It took a moment, but I heard someone behind the door.

"Who is it?"

"Drayez."

In between the locks clicking, I heard cursing. "Boy, what the fuck is you doing knockin' on my damn door this early in the muthafuckin' morning?"

When the door opened, I was standing face to face with the woman that gave me life. Marie Ashley Alexander was a feisty forty-three-year-old woman that didn't take no shit from nobody. She was kinda tall for a woman and had a body type some people described as sturdy. She wasn't fat and wasn't skinny, but a little bit more than thick. She cut her hair ten years ago and never grew it back, rocking a low cut with brushed waves. Her face was round with plump cheeks, almond-shaped dark eyes, small nose, full lips, and the exact same smile that I had made up her mouth. My mama wasn't beauty queen fine, but she looked good. She also had a quick temper and was always ready to give a left/right combo to anybody that offended her.

"Boy, what the fuck is you doin' knockin' on my damn door this early in the muthafuckin' mornin'?" she repeated.

"Hey, Marie. It's good to see you too," I said sarcastically as I slid past her. None of her kids called her Mom. She didn't play that. You came out the pussy calling her Marie or got slapped.

"Well, it ain't good to see you. I don't got no money. No, you can't use my car. And if you touch my cigarettes, I'm knockin' yo' ass out."

I plopped down on the blue pleather couch, eyeing the pack of Newports on the table. Suddenly I had the urge to smoke.

"Touch 'em if you want!" Marie threatened, appearing in front of me, head cocked to the side, hand on hip.

"You gon' hurt yo' son over somethin' that's killin' you?"

"I hurt a muthafucka for less."

I believed her.

"So what you doing over here this early? Yo' girlfriend kicked you out again?" she asked, grabbing the cigarettes and tossing me one.

"Nah. We had a li'l argument and I left. Wasn't that serious."

She gave me the "yeah, right" eye. "So what ch'all argue 'bout?"

I thought about lying to her, but I wasn't a fan of lying to Marie. Plus, I don't think she ever lied to me, even when she probably should. "I tried to get some while she was asleep. She got mad."

She gave me a "nigga, is you crazy?" look. "You tried to fuck her while she was sleeping, Drayez?"

I nodded.

"I wish a nigga would try to stick his dick in me while I'm getting my beauty sleep! You lucky she didn't try to cut yo' dick off. That's what I woulda done. Keith bet' not ever try no shit like that. I'll fuck his ass up! Now if Keith was a real man and had some real money and didn't depend on me for everything, like you do Rayna, then I wouldn't mind. But all he can do is wake me up wit' his tongue on my pussy. Now that, I wouldn't mind."

"Thanks for giving me way too much information."

She laughed. "Boy, you grown. You can handle it. So, how's my grandbaby?"

"She good. Gettin' big. I think she gon' be a daddy's girl."

Marie gave an unimpressed "hmph". "How you gon' support this daddy's girl is what you need to be working on. You need to get a job. I don't know why you won't help Keith. He don't make a lot of money, but he got more than yo' broke ass. Hell, that's why that girl won't give you no pussy in the morning. 'Cause you broke. Don't no bitch want a broke nigga."

And these was the moments when I felt like Marie should lie. Her honesty was brutal. "Thanks for making me feel like shit."

"I ain't making you feel like shit. You ain't shit. And you probably need to whoop her ass so she'll know you run shit. Rayna like me in some ways. Bitches like us need to be put in our place from time to time. Slap the shit out of her. Stick a foot up her ass."

"I ain't with that domestic shit, Marie. I ain't tryna go to jail, and I remember how Chris used to do you."

"The twins' daddy hit me 'cause I needed my ass whooped. Only way I was gon' stay in line. He knew that."

"That ain't how relationships work, Marie."

"Well, boy, I don't know what to tell you. Go get you a white girl then, 'cause they the only ones that'll probably put up with yo' bullshit."

And with that, she was gone.

I thought about Marie's words. Some bitches needed to been hit? That didn't sit right with me. When I was little, I felt sick and scared when I used to see my mama's bloody and swollen face. Seeing Marie with ice packs on her lips made me not want to hit girls, which is why I gave Rayna so many passes. Now she was telling me to put my hands on my baby mama or get a white girl. Shit was crazy.

"Hey, bum."

I looked up and saw one of my little sisters, Tikka. She was the older twin by three minutes. At seventeen, she was the spitting image of Marie, but younger and prettier. She had long curly hair, light brown skin, almond-shaped eyes, a nice smile, and somewhere along the way, she started developing curves, which she kept hidden under loose-fitting clothes.

"Who you callin' a bum, buster?"

"You, bum," she laughed, sitting down next to me. "Why you here so early? Rayna put you out?"

"Nah. We argued and I left."

She gave me the same "yeah right" look as Marie. "Right. She put you out."

I hit her with a couch pillow. "Shut up! Where Tina?"

"I don't know. We twins, but I ain't her damn shadow," she snapped.

"Damn. What's wrong with you?"

"I don't know. I'm tired of Marie. She keep talking about putting me and Tina out when we turn eighteen. Like she did you and Tracy. I'm not ready to leave yet. I'm still in high school."

"Well, you betta figure somethin' out 'cause Marie ain't playing. I thought she was bullshitting about putting me out until July 21st came and she took my key. Even though I seen her to it do Tracy two years before me, I didn't think she would do it until she did it."

"Can I come live with you and Rayna?" she asked, hope filling her eyes. "I want to go to college and become a lawyer so I can help get Tracy out of jail. I won't be able to do that if I'm homeless and broke."

I wanted to be able to comfort my little sister and tell her everything was going to be okay, but I couldn't. "Man, li'l sis. I'm almost on my way out. Rayna 'bout tired of my shit."

"Can you at least talk to her about it? I don't wanna end up like Tracy, in prison for the rest of my life for messing with a no-good nigga. And I don't wanna be like Tina, fucking everybody in the neighborhood."

When Marie kicked our big sister out, Tracy went to live with her nigga and they started robbing people. He used her to set niggas up until they ran up on an off-duty police officer. He killed her boyfriend and they charged my sister with party to a crime for the murder, saying her actions got him killed.

"Did you talk to Marie and see if she would let you chill a li'l longer?"

"Yeah. She said she can't afford it because her SSI only covers her until we turn eighteen. Plus, she talking about she don't want no grown bitches running around her house while her man is here."

Sounded just like Marie.

"I don't know, man. We still got a couple months. I'ma try to figure something out."

Tikka smiled and gave me one of the warmest hugs I'd had in a long time. "Thank you, brother. You still a bum, but I love yo' bum ass."

"Fuck you, too."

Chapter 3

Four days had gone by since I met L-Dog and he still hadn't called me back. I lay in bed playing a kissing game with my daughter, wondering when my luck would change. They said every dog got his day. And the good ones got two. I was still waiting for one good day. I had people depending on me too - not only my bright-eyed slobbering princess, but my little sister. Tikka was gifted with brains and the drive to get our big sister out of prison. She had five months until Marie gave her the boot. It was up to me to catch Tikka when Marie punted her off the front porch. I had to figure out something.

The vibrating of my government phone pulled me away from my daughter's kisses and thoughts of Tikka. I didn't recognize the number.

"Hello?"

"Dray?"

I couldn't place the voice. "Who dis?"

"L-Dog. Where Dray?"

Hearing his name made my heart beat fast and eyes pop. This was the answer to all my worries. "This me. What's good?"

"'Sup, li'l nigga? 'Member what we talked about?"

"Yeah. I been waiting on you to call."

"Good. It's goin' down tonight. Gimme yo' address. I'ma swoop you tonight."

I thought fast. I couldn't let this crazy nigga know where I lay my head at. So I gave him the address to the house next door to Vic.

"A'ight, li'l nigga. I'ma hit chu when I'm on my way. Wear all black."

I laid my phone on the bed and sat staring at the wall in front of me. I was about to get some real money. About to show Rayna and Marie that I could take care of business. I was done being a bum-ass nigga. I was about to be Young Rich Nigga Drayez!

I lay around the house all day, waiting for night. As soon as the sun went down, I was out of the house and I went to Vic's.

"Who is it?" a female called after I knocked on the door.

"Drayez."

When the door opened, Vic's girl smiled at me like she couldn't wait to tell a joke. Renae was by far the worst-looking girl on Vic's bandwagon. She was short and round, every bit of 250 pounds. She wore a bogus wig that couldn't pass for real hair in the dark. Her complexion was somewhere between root beer and Pepsi soda. And she had freckles. How God came up with that combination was a mystery. Her eyes popped behind coke bottle glasses that were too big for her face, her nose was so wide that cocaine tooters wouldn't go near her, and her lips was so big that she could blow out a hundred candles with one breath. And she had the nerve to be rocking purple scrubs.

"What's up, Drayez? Yo' bitch kicked you out?" she asked, laughing like she told a good joke.

"Shit wasn't funny, nigga." I mugged her. "Standing there looking like a big-ass grape with that purple shit on. Where Vic?"

Her face went sour. "He right here," she managed, stepping aside.

The house smelled like chicken. Vic was sitting in front of the TV with a plate full of what looked like KFC extra crispy.

"'Sup, nigga?"

"Shit. Just came to see what you was on. Gimme some chicken, nigga," I said before snatching a leg from the plate.

"What happened? Rayna put you out?"

"I just asked him that." Renae laughed.

"Man, why er'body keep sayin' that? I left because I had some business to take care of, soft-ass nigga."

"'Cause she always puttin' yo' ass out." Vic laughed. "And when you get some bidness, nigga?"

"I gotta meet up wit L-Dog. He s'posed to be callin' in a minute."

Vic stopped eating and gave me a serious look. "Brah, you really fuckin' wit' that crazy-ass nigga?"

"Shit, what else I'm supposed to do? I need the money. I'm tired of this broke shit."

"You know you finna fuck around and be in a shootout? That nigga probably got like ten bodies, easy."

Vic's words stirred something inside of me. But it wasn't enough to stop me from going through with my plan. "He said it was gon' be easy. Fifty or sixty G's. I can't pass this up."

"A'ight. Hard head makes a soft ass. Just don't bring the police to my house. And that crazy-ass nigga ain't coming in here either."

"I didn't tell him where you lived. He think I'm coming out the house next door."

I chilled with Renae and Vic until I got the call from L-Dog. I walked out the back door and came from the neighbor's yard looking for the Benz. Didn't see it. A horn blew. I looked across the street at a dark-colored old school car that looked big enough to be a boat. L-Dog was driving. Twan was the passenger. Both of them wore black and looked serious. My stomach rumbled as I got in the back seat. Too late to turn back now.

"'Sup, li'l nigga?" L-Dog nodded.

I was nervous, but I tried not to show it. "I'm good. Ready to get this money."

"Dat's what I'm talkin' 'bout, nigga. Dat's what I'm talkin' 'bout. We got us one right here, Twan."

"We'll see," Twan said before turning to look at me. "'Sup, Dray?"

"Ready to make it happen."

"You ever rob a nigga before?"

I stuck to the lie I already told. "Yeah. Some strong arm shit."

"Well, check this out, li'l nigga. You gonna need a banger for this move. These niggas got money and ain't scared to buss that thang. You ain't scared to clap a nigga, is you?"

I looked in Twan's eyes to see if he was serious. They were stone cold and dark, like shooting and killing was part of his everyday life. Vic's words about being in a shootout echoed in my head. I never even shot a gun before and all of a sudden I was being thrown into some heavy shit. Damn. And I thought this shit would be easy. For who? Them?

"I'ma do what I gotta do," I managed.

Twan studied my face. "You sure you good, nigga?"

"Yeah. I'm good."

L-Dog looked at me through the rearview mirror. "If you scared, say sumthin'. I'ma let chu out right now."

I needed that money. "I'm good. Just tell me what to do."

"You and Twan goin' in. Dem niggas know me, so I'ma be in da car. Dis my baby mama new nigga. Dey runnin' it up. It might be like a hunnit G's in dere. And some work. Dese niggas'll buss dat thang so y'all gotta go in dumpin' shit. Make dem nigga give dat shit up and get up outta dere. Here." He passed me a pair of black leather gloves, a winter mask, and a pistol with a clip in it as long as a ruler. The gun was heavier than it looked. And it was cold. It felt like I was touching death.

"Know how to use that?" Twan asked.

"Yeah. This the safety, right?"

He nodded. "Up is safe. You got thirty-two shots. Use all them mu'fuckas if you got to. Follow me and do what I say. You good?"

A lump formed in my throat, making it hard for me to talk. And my mouth was dry like I had smoked fifty blunts. "I'm good."

The drive was short. We ended up on 47th and Villard. It was a white house in the middle of the block. L-Dog parked a house away. Nobody was outside. Me and Twan put on the mask and gloves and crept up to the house. Bushes lined the front. We hid in them and peeped through the front window. Two niggas was playin' a video game on a big-ass TV. Both wore designer clothes and jewelry flooded with ice. On the couch across from them was two bad bitches with faces in they phones. We crept around to check the rest of the house. Music came from a room at the back. A fat nigga wearing boxers was sitting on a bed. A brown-skinned chick with a crazy body was dancing for him.

"C'mon, nigga," Twan whispered, going back to the front. "Stay in the bushes til I get the door opened. Then we goin' in bussin'."

I knelt in the bushes, praying to God they didn't open the door. I didn't want to shoot anybody and I didn't wanna get shot. Twan pressed the doorbell. I could hear the chime.

"Hold on!" one of the niggas called.

I gripped the butt of my pistol, clicking off the safety. "Please, God, don't let him open the door," I whispered.

God wasn't listening. I could hear locks clicking and the door open. No asking who was outside or nothing. They had to be the stupidest d-boys alive. I never sold drugs, but even I knew to ask who was outside before opening the door. But he didn't, and that was his mistake.

Twan pulled his pistol and shot twice before running in the house. I ran on the porch and seen a nigga laying in the doorway bleeding. Two more shots rang out and a female screamed. I looked back towards the car and saw L-Dog waving for me to go in the house.

Fuck!

I spun back around and looked at the nigga on the floor. He was bleeding from holes in his stomach and chest.

"Don't kill me, fam!" he cried, reaching for his pocket.

I lifted the gun, about to blow his shit back.

He pulled out a bankroll. "Here. This all I got. Don't shoot!"

I took the money and ran in the house. I couldn't find the other nigga that was playing the video game, but both females was lying on the floor. One of them was bleeding from a bullet hole in her back. Before I could decide what to do next, more shooting came from the back room. That's where I went. The dancer was laying on the ground bleeding. The fat nigga was laying on the bed, Twan standing over him with the gun pointed at his head.

"Where the shit at, nigga?"

The fat nigga was calm. "It's in my pants pocket. They on the floor."

I went for the Balmain jeans and found a fat-ass knot.

"Where the real money at, nigga? Quit playin' wit' me before I off yo' bitch ass," Twan threatened.

"I told you it's in my—"

Twan moved the gun to his stomach and squeezed the trigger.

"Aaaah!" the fat nigga screamed.

"Where that shit at, nigga?" Twan yelled, pointing the gun at his head.

"It's in the dryer! Laundry room next to the kitchen. Work in a Tide box!" he cried, pressing a hand against the bleeding hole in his stomach.

Twan gave me a nod and I went to find the shit. I found the wash room and opened the dryer. There was a duffle bag inside with stacks of money. Seeing that much cash damn near made me faint. On the shelf was the box of Tide. Inside was a white brick wrapped in plastic and a brick of compressed weed. I threw them in the bag and went to the room.

"I got it, Twan!" I yelled, realizing the mistake as soon as I made it. I said his name. Shit!

Twan mugged the shit out of me right before he shot the fat nigga in the head. I thought he was about to shoot me next but he ran past me and out of the room.

"C'mon, nigga!"

I followed. We was almost to the front door when the other nigga that was playing the video game popped out of the closet with a big-ass black revolver. It happened so fast that we couldn't react. He shot Twan twice in the chest. Twan shot back. They both stumbled and fell. I kept moving, jumping over the nigga that was still at the front door bleeding. I never ran so fast in my life. I got to the car and dove into the back seat.

"Go, go, go!" I yelled.

L-Dog looked towards the house and then back at me. "Where Twan?"

"Dude shot him! They got guns! We gotta go!"

L-Dog looked like he wanted to kill me. "Bitch-ass nigga, go get Twan!"

I wasn't going back in *that* house. "They got guns, brah."

"Li'l bitch-ass nigga!" He mugged me, pulling a pistol identical to the one I had. "If Twan dead, I'm killin' yo' bitch ass. And you bet' not touch my money."

I watched L-Dog hop out of the car and run in the house with the same bravery as a firefighter running into a burning building to save a baby. Gunfire sounded. And then it hit me. L-Dog was probably going to kill me when he came back out. I bitched up and

Twan got shot. Plus, with all the shooting, the neighbors were on the phone with the police already. This big-ass ugly car was hard to hide. My best chance was to get away. Right now.

I grabbed some of the money from the bag and the brick of compressed weed before fleeing. I stopped in an alley to throw away the mask and gloves and kept running all the way home. As soon as I walked in the house, Rayna was in my face with Draya on her hip crying.

"Where the fuck you was at, nigga? Why you wasn't answering the phone?"

I bypassed her to peek out the window. "Not now, Rayna. Watch out."

"What the fuck wrong wit'chu? Why you peeking out of windows and shit?"

I ignored her, going to the closet to hide the brick of weed. When I came out, I went to the back door to make sure it was locked. When I spun around, Rayna was in my face again.

"Hel-looo! I'm talking to you, Drayez! What the fuck is wrong with you?"

I snapped, grabbing her by the face and muffing her ass to the floor with my daughter still in her arms. "Bitch, shut the fuck up and leave me alone!"

She lay on the ground for a moment, staring up at me with wide eyes. I knew I went too far, especially since she was holding my baby.

"Leave me alone right now," I mumbled, flashing the gun as I went in my pocket to get some money. I threw it at her before walking away.

She got up and went to the room. My phone began ringing. It was TC. I cut the phone off and went back to watching the windows for L-Dog. About thirty minutes later, I was standing in the kitchen checking the back windows when somebody knocked on the front door.

Shit! L-Dog found me!

I pulled the pistol from my waist as Rayna was coming from the room. When she saw me with the gun, she stopped, her eyes growing wide. “Who at the door?”

“I don’t know,” I whispered, tiptoeing across the living room.

Rayna clung to my arm. “I’m scared, baby!”

I shook her off and checked the window. TC’s Monte Carlo was parked out front. Him and L-Dog was cousins. I had to be careful. “Who is it?”

“It’s me. TC.”

“You by yo’self, nigga?”

“Yeah.”

“On what?”

“On everything I love. Open the door, nigga.”

I opened the door, keeping the gun in my hand and looking around.

When TC seen the pistol, his eyes bugged like Wendy Williams. “What the fuck y’all do, nigga?”

“Come in, man. That nigga crazy,” I said, locking the door and looking out the window again.

“Who crazy? What happened?” Rayna asked.

A part of me wanted to fill her in but something in my gut told me to keep my mouth closed. “I’ma be right back. Let’s hit it, bro.”

“Wait, Drayez. Where you going?” Rayna asked, worry and fear lighting her watery eyes.

“I gotta step out. I’ma be right back.”

I carried the gun in my hand all the way to TC’s car, watching every shadow and hiding place. When we got to the car, I kept the gun on my lap.

“What happened, nigga?” TC asked.

I told him the story of the robbery, leaving out the part about me taking the weed. Surprise and awe shone on his face.

“L-Dog called me a li’l while ago and said he killing you.”

“Did Twan die?”

“He didn’t say. Just called you a bitch-ass nigga and said he killing you.”

“Did you tell him where I lived?”

"He didn't ask. And he hung up before I could ask questions. I tried to call you, but you didn't answer yo' phone."

Damn. Having a certified killa looking for me was crazy as fuck. I had nowhere to hide. The best thing I did was act like I lived at Vic's neighbor's house. "Fuck it. Let's go get some liquor. I need to calm my nerves.

I pulled out some of the money and counted it while TC drove. 2,300 dollars. The most money I ever had. And all of my other pockets were still stuffed with money I hadn't counted. I was going to count it when I got back home. I peeled off 500 dollars and gave it to my nigga.

"What's this for?" he asked.

"For nothing."

"Good looking."

We got quiet again. I looked over and seen TC watching me.

"What's up?"

"Didn't I tell you that nigga was crazy?"

Chapter 4

It felt like I was having a wet dream, but I wasn't even asleep. I had my eyes closed, staring at the back of my eyelids, enjoying what was happening below my waist. When I heard the moan, I opened my eyes a little and seen Rayna's mouth going to work on my pole. I closed my eyes again, enjoying the bomb-ass head. And then she stopped. My eyes shot open.

"Mornin', baby!" she purred, crawling up my body.

I was surprised by the morning head. I couldn't remember the last time I woke up to getting my dick sucked. It had to be around the time I first moved in - before she got pregnant with Draya and found out I was broke.

"Hey, baby. You in a good mood."

"I am. Do you like yo' present?"

"What present?"

"Me." She smiled, leaning down and exploring my mouth with her tongue. "And you can have me any way you like!"

After a round of some of the best morning sex we'd had in a long time, I sparked a Newport and lay back. Rayna lay on my chest, running her fingers through my public hairs.

"Damn, girl. I know today ain't my birthday, but I loved you as a present."

She laughed. "Last night you seemed reel stressed. I just wanted to make you feel better."

I had a flashback of gunshots, bodies on the floor, the fat nigga trying to stop his stomach from bleeding, and the look on L-Dog's face when he threatened to kill me.

"You okay, baby?"

I came out of the flashback. "Yeah. I'm good. Last night was just crazy."

"So, is everything good? I was so scared the way you was looking out the windows. Where you get a gun from?"

I looked into her dark watery eyes and saw concern. Worry. Even love. I wanted to tell her what happened, but knew I couldn't. "Everything good, baby. I went out last night and tried to make some shit happen. Shit didn't go as planned, but I'm here. We good."

I could see the questions in her eyes. She wanted to know more. But the look on my face let her know that was all she was getting so she leaned over and kissed me. "You sound like Ja'Shawn. He never told me how he got his money, but I knew. After a while I just trusted him. Guess I gotta trust you too, huh?"

Even though I didn't like being compared to her dead baby daddy and oldest son's father, I knew what she meant so I didn't trip. "Yeah, bae. Trust me."

"So, do you got plans today? Because I wanted to see if I could use the money you gave me to buy a car."

"How much I give you?"

"1800 dollars."

Damn. I didn't know I gave her that much. "Yeah. Let's get a car. Matter of fact, I'ma put some more money with that so we can get a nice car. And I'ma take you and the kids shopping."

Her eyes lit up like Christmas lights. "For real?"

"Yeah, baby. You can have whatever you like!"

***

I stayed true to my word and took the family shopping. Everybody got new shoes, outfits, toys, and video games. I bought Rayna a couple dresses, heels, and one of those waist wrap things Kim Kardashian advertised. When she stepped out of the dressing room wearing a blue Dior dress and red bottoms, she was looking as good as a model on the cover of a magazine. For myself, I bought a couple pairs of Air Max and couple pair of Rockstar jeans and T-shirts. I was a simple man. It didn't take much to impress me. I left the mall about 10 G's lighter in the pockets, but the looks on Rayna and the kids' faces made it all worth it. Best money I ever spent.

After leaving the mall, I dropped Rayna and the kids off at home. I planned on taking her out and we needed a babysitter. Twenty minutes later I parked in front of Marie's house feeling like new money as I stepped out of our new 2010 Buick Envoy. Paid eight G's cash for it. After climbing from the truck, I pulled out 200 dollars, folding it in the palm of my hands as I rang the doorbell.

"Who is it?"

"Drayez."

The door opened and Marie was mugging me. "Boy, what you want?"

I held up the money. Her eyes cut to the bills. "What's this?" she asked, snatching the money from my hand.

"It's for you."

She unfolded the money, a smile spreading across her face. "Where you get this from?"

"I got lucky last night." I laughed as I walked in the house.

"You giving away money and got on new clothes. Boy, what the fuck you do?" Marie asked, locking the door.

"I told you I got lucky last night. Tikka here?"

"She in the room reading one of them big-ass books. Hope she know that damn book ain't gonna pay no bills or put food on the table."

I had no comeback. Marie didn't realize the books would pay the rent and put food on the table. It would just take a while. Instead of wasting my breath trying to explain that, I walked down the hall and knocked on Tikka's door.

"Come in."

Tikka was lying in bed on her stomach with her feet in the air, her nose in a book big enough to be a dictionary. "What the hell you reading?"

"A Black's Law Dictionary. Tracy sent it to me a couple months ago. What you doing over here, bum?"

"Came to check on you, buster. See if you wanna babysit for us tonight. Me and Rayna wanna go out."

She cocked an eyebrow. "Is Rayna paying me?"

I went in my pocket and pulled out 500 dollars. "Nah. I'm paying you."

Tikka looked at the money like it was a deadly snake. "Where you get that from?"

"Don't worry 'bout it. Do you want it?"

She took the money slowly, looking me over. “You got on new clothes, too? You sellin’ drugs?”

“Nah, girl. Just take the money. And send Tracy a hunnit.”

At the mention of our big sister, Tikka lit up. “Ohh, she asked about you in her last letter. I told her you still being a bum. Guess I’ma have to change that ’cause now you a bum with some money,” she laughed.

“Fuck you, buster. Get what, you need and c’mon.”

“Okay. Did you talk to Rayna about letting me stay with y’all? I can help with the kids and get a part time job.”

“Nah, not yet. But I will. I’m just waiting for the right time. Rayna kinda like Marie. Never know when they gon’ joke with you or curse you out. But I got you. In the meantime, put that li’l money in a bank account or something. Try to make it last ’cause I don’t know the next time I’ma have some more.”

She looked at me crazy. “Shoot, you thought I wasn’t? I ain’t finna spend my money on stupid stuff. It’s real out here in these streets, boy.”

***

“Oh my God, Drayez! I’m so full. I can’t eat no more,” Rayna said, pushing the empty dessert plate to the middle of the table.

We were at Prime Quarters, the best steakhouse I ever been to. It was Rayna’s idea to come here. I would’ve been cool with grabbing some McDonald’s and going home to drink, smoke, and fuck. But Rayna insisted on steak.

“That shit was so good, I feel like driving over to Marie’s house and slapping fire from her ass,” I joked.

Rayna laughed so hard that she slobbed a little. “You crazy, boy!”

After we stopped laughing, I decided to test the water with my little sister’s situation. “What you think about Tikka movin’ in with us?”

Rayna gave me a stank look. “S’cuse me?”

"Marie kickin' her out when she turn eighteen and she ain't got nowhere to go. She did it to me and my older sister and now she about to do it to the twins."

"You know we only got three rooms. One for the boys, one for the girls, and our room. Where she gon' sleep?"

"On the couch, I guess. She could get a part time job and help you with the kids. You know she wanna go to college, but she ain't got nowhere to live."

She didn't look convinced. "I don't know about this, baby. I need some time to think about it. When she turn eighteen?"

"In five months."

She sighed. "How about we talk about it another time? I had fun with you tonight and I don't wanna do no hard thinking."

I had to accept that. At least she didn't say no. "A'ight."

"And thank you for buyin' that stuff for the kids. You know you didn't have to."

"Yeah, I know. But ever since I met you, it's been all on you. You feed all six of us. At least I can finally help out. Don't none of they daddies help you. Since I'm yo' man, it's on me."

Rayna smiled at me like we were living in a fairy tale, like I was the knight that rescued her from a fire breathing dragon. "I don't know what I was thinkin' 'bout gettin' pregnant by them niggas. I knew they weren't shit. Except Ja'Shawn's daddy. That was my nigga."

"How you get from Ja'Shawn to the rest of them niggas? Where they come from?"

"When big Ja'Shawn got killed, that shit fucked me up and I lost myself. Started fuckin' niggas to erase the pain of being lonely. Shit didn't work. I just kept gettin' pregnant. Guess I been tryna find somebody to love me the way Ja'Shawn did. He accepted me for who I was."

"I accept you for who you is, baby. Whatever you did, it don't matter to me."

Her watery eyes were rimming with tears. "Aw, Drayez! That is so nice. I love you so much."

"I love you too."

Mischief spread through her eyes like a tidal wave. "Why don't you show me?"

We spent the rest of the night at a hotel. And I spent most of the night using my dick and tongue to show Rayna how much I loved her.

Two days later, we were back at home and I was lying in bed blowing smoke rings up at the ceiling. I finally felt like the king of my castle. I was the man of the house. Whatever I said was law. No questions asked. And all Rayna's kids were treating me like I was they daddy. Rayna treated me like royalty. Pussy whenever I wanted. Head any time of the day. Matter of fact, the next time she walked in the room, I was going to make her assume the position. Turned out I didn't have to wait long.

"I was just thinkin' about you."

Rayna licked her lips as she sat on the bed. "Funny. I was just thinkin' about you too."

Watching her lick her lips got my dick hard. I snatched off the sheet. "Why don't you do something 'bout that?"

"Mmmm," she purred, leaning over and grabbing my meat. "And how about you take care of something for me after I take care of you?"

"You know I got you, baby."

She knelt on the bed and licked me from my balls to the tip of my dick. "I need 500 dollars. Rent coming up."

"I don't got it right now," I said, wanting to feel her tongue again.

"When you gon' have it?" she asked before sucking the head.

"Mmmhhh! I don't know."

Her voice became harsh and the sexual energy disappeared. "What you mean you don't know?"

"I mean, I don't know. I don't got no more money."

Rayna shook her head from side to side like she was coming out of a trance. "You mean all yo' money gone? You broke?"

"Yeah. I just spent almost twenty racks on you and the kids. What's wrong?"

She mugged me and flung my dick to the side like it was a piece of trash. “What’s wrong? What’s wrong is you broke. The rent is coming up. What you gon’ do about it?”

She had been my sex kitten and down-ass bitch. Now she changed up on me like 2-Pac did when he got the gun in the movie *Juice*. “Why is the rent on me all of a sudden? You get a check. Pay that shit.”

“’Cause you my man. You acting like you was gon’ take care of everything so I spent the money on a washer and dryer. I’m tired of going to the laundromat. You around here rapping T.I. like yo’ ass was a baller so I figured you had a couple more dollars. I didn’t know yo’ ass was broke.”

Damn. My loving girlfriend that let me have my way was gone. “Well, what you want me to do?”

“I want you to grab yo’ gun and get cho ass back out there and get some money.”

She said it so easy. Like just owning a gun meant I could get money whenever I wanted. That money cost blood. And I’d be damned if I was about to risk my life just to pay the rent. “It ain’t that easy, bae.”

“How come it ain’t? You already did it.”

“I don’t wanna do it again. People’s got shot over that shit. I almost got killed. I ain’t tryna go through that shit again.”

“Niggas die er’day, B.”

She quoted the line from the movie *State Property* with ease. Like she didn’t care if I lived or died. Like her rent being paid meant more than my life.

“I know you ain’t serious.”

The look on her face showed how disappointed she was. Because I didn’t jump up and show foolish courage by risking my life to pay her rent, she lost the little respect that she had gained.

“I don’t wanna get kicked outta my house ’cause you scared to go get some money.”

I looked towards the ceiling and mumbled, “I’ma figure something out.”

***

The walk to Vic's house was long, lonely, and confusing. Twenty minutes ago, I was the man. King of my castle. Head of my house. Now it was over and I was back to being a bum. I kicked myself in the ass for not taking more money from the robbery. Fear made me leave a big-ass bag of money with a nigga that didn't lift a finger to take it. That was my money, but I gave it away.

"Drayez, what up, fool-ass nigga?" Vic grinned

"Shit," I sulked.

"Damn, nigga. What's wrong wit'chu?"

"Everything, brah," I grumbled, stepping past him and flopping down on the couch. Vic's six and seven year old sons, Tray and Vic Jr., were sitting on the couch playing a video game. They took their eyes off the screen long enough to say "what's up?" before getting back to it.

"What happened?" Vic asked as he sat down.

"I ain't got no money. Rayna trippin' 'bout bills and shit."

"You just pulled that move wit' L-Dog. Where yo' money?"

"I thought if I spent it on her and the kids, shit would be good. Well, it was until I ran outta money."

"You sucka-ass trick-ass, lame-ass nigga!" Vic busted out laughing. "You's a sucka, busta, and hoe trusta, my nigga. She played yo' ass. Shit was all good when you were having shit. You callin' the shots. Head in the morning. But as soon as you fall off, shit sour. That's how hoes like her do niggas when they fall off or get locked up. Shit good when a nigga stickin' dick in they ass and buyin' 'em shit. But as soon as a nigga go up north, that same hoe he took care of leave his ass high and dry. Suckas, bustas, and hoe trustas. That's why I would neva trust a bitch."

Damn, Vic was right. I heard stories like this when I did my li'l bid. Niggas thinking they got a winner until it was too late. Same for Rayna. When we first met, she treated me good because she thought I was a money getter. Then she found out I was a bum and shit changed. Same shit today. I was about to get blessed with some head til she found out I couldn't pay the rent.

"I gotta figure out a way to get some more money."

"Why, so you can give it to Rayna?"

"Fuck you, nigga. I need some money so I won't feel like a bum. I got a daughter. Plus, Tikka gon' need somewhere to stay when Marie put her out."

"Yo' mom's cold, dog. Heartless. You got some more weed?"

I pulled the sack from my pocket and threw it to him. That's when it hit me. I never told my niggas about the weed I took. "You know somebody that wanna buy some weed? Like, some ounces?"

Vic looked at me funny. "You got some ounces of weed?"

"Maybe."

He frowned. "How much weed you got, nigga?"

"I don't know. A lot."

"Pounds?"

"Maybe. Do you know somebody that will buy it?"

Vic looked like he wanted to fight me. "Nigga, weed sell itself. You can be the weed man, dumb-ass nigga."

I felt stupid as fuck. I was sitting on money and didn't even know how to get it. "Damn. I can, huh?"

"Yeah. Just fatten up the sacks and take Dino action."

I smiled. "Yeah. I just need somewhere to re-up."

"Cross that bridge when you get to it. First you gotta get the money."

A knock on the door got our attention.

"Get that for me, Dray?"

I went to answer. It was TC. He walked in smiling like he just got some pussy.

"What you so happy about?"

"Just got paid. 'Sup wit'chu?"

"Shit. Coming up with a plan. You wanna buy some weed?"

"I just grabbed some from Dino," he grinned, pulling out a sack. "I heard from L-Dog."

Hearing his name was like a cup of coffee to a tired a nigga. I was instantly alert. "What he say?"

"That he killin' you. Twan died. And his baby mama other nigga died too."

I panicked, ready to run home and get my pistol. "Fuck! He still in Milwaukee?"

"Nah. He wouldn't say where he was at, but I know he not here. He probably down south somewhere laying low. Everybody know Twan was his nigga so they know L-Dog had something to do with it. I think you good. For now." TC said all of this with the calm of a father telling his son a bedtime story.

"Thanks for the warning," I said sarcastically.

"I told you not to fuck with that nigga," Vic said.

"And I told you that nigga was crazy," TC added.

I fired up a blunt. "You know where I can buy some weed from?"

TC held up his sack. "I told you I just got this from Dino."

"I know. But I need more than that. Some weight."

"My cousin Van might know somebody. Why?"

"This nigga been holding out," Vic said. "He got plenty weed."

TC looked like he wanted to try me. "On what, you got some weed?"

I blew off the question. "If I can get up the cheese, you gon' call yo' cousin for me?"

"I got you, brah."

"This nigga ain't crazy, is he?"

TC laughed. "Nah. Van is smooth. Shit, a li'l while ago, he was the man."

"What you mean?"

"He was the plug."

"And what happened?" I asked, wondering why he wasn't the plus no more.

TC shrugged. "You gotta ask him."

I was about to get up and leave when another question crossed my mind. "Ay, how come you got family members that's gettin' money but you still working at McDonald's?"

TC laughed and shook his head. "More money more problems. I'm cool with being a simple nigga."

Chapter 5

Selling weed was hard work. I started from the bottom, working long hours like it was a real job. I posted up in front of gas stations, liquor stores, and corner stores advertising my product. Morning, afternoon, and night. Never taking a day off. The compressed brick of weed turned out to be a half pound. I bagged the whole thing up in twenty dollar sacks. Took me a couple weeks to sell it all. TC's cousin, Van, hooked me up with a nigga named Smitty to be my connect. Since I didn't know much about hustling, I didn't stack my money to buy more weed. I made enough to buy a pound and was cool with that. I spent the profit as soon as I got it, mostly on Rayna and the kids. That kept her happy. I was happy that she was happy. And as long as I kept enough to re-up, I was good.

A month had gone by since I jumped in the game and I felt good. I was lying in bed, bouncing Draya on my lap, when the bedroom door opened. Rayna walked in carrying a plate of food. The smile on her face told me she was in a good mood. Had been since the money started coming on a regular. She was back to being my sex kitten and down-ass bitch. And this morning she wore another hat: personal chef. She walked in the room carrying a plate filled with breakfast food.

"Damn! That shit look fire as a muthafucka!" I said, laying Draya on the bed and grabbing the plate. Cheese eggs, grits, bacon, and four big-ass pancakes covered in syrup.

"Here you go, baby."

"Damn, girl. I might not be able to eat all this."

"Don't matter. Long as you happy. You keep me happy and I'ma keep you happy." She smiled, picking up Draya and leaving the room.

As I dug into the food, I replayed what Rayna said in my head. Keep her happy and she would keep me happy. I was a simple nigga. All I needed was a place to stay and some pussy. The catch to getting my needs met meant meeting hers. And she was a simple woman. Only wanted one thing: to be taken care of. The exchange seemed fair. Give what you had to get what you need.

"How does it taste?" Rayna asked, coming back into the room without Draya.

"You did yo' thang, baby," I mumbled between bites.

She crawled onto the bed and kissed me on the cheek. "Good. Because I wanted you do something for me."

"You know I got you, baby."

She lifted my plate and tugged at the sheet, revealing my nakedness. Then she grabbed my dick and started stroking it. "I was wondering if you could do me a favor," she said before leaning down and sucking my dick in her mouth.

Breakfast and head. Damn. Why didn't I think of this before? I chewed on the bacon, watching as she chewed on me. Then she stopped, looking into my eyes while jagging me off.

"Can you buy me the new iPhone? I'm tired of my phone dropping calls. Can you do that for me later today?"

"Yeah, yeah. I got you, baby," I said quickly. "Now finish doing what you was doing. I think you just gave a new meaning to breakfast in bed."

***

I left the house later that morning and hopped in the Buick truck and went to make a few deliveries. Sometimes my hustling conflicted with Rayna's errand running so I was planning to get my own car. I had 2,000 put to the side for my ride, but now that Rayna wanted a new phone, it kinda fucked up my plan. But somehow I was going to make it work. I had to. Keeping her happy meant keeping me happy. Win-win. After making some serves, I went to the phone shop and grabbed her the phone. After dropping it off to Rayna, I went to Vic's house.

"What's good, nigga?"

"Shit. Just came from copping my bitch the new iPhone. You ever get head while eatin' breakfast in bed?" I half-bragged.

"Only cost you 500 dollars," he laughed.

"Fuck you, nigga. That's my bitch. It ain't trickin' if you got it."

"T.I. and Lil Wayne lied to you niggas. Trickin' is still trickin'. You niggas just some suckas, bustas, and hoe trustas. Now trick off on yo' boy and fire up some weed."

I pulled a blunt that I already rolled up and tossed it to him. "Roll with me to this car lot. Need to snatch up somethin' to get around in."

"You ain't got no license or a job to prove yo' income. Fuck you gon' get a car?"

I hadn't thought that far ahead. "Damn. I need all that?"

"Yeah. Proof of income, license. And you gotta get insurance too."

"You know somebody sellin' a car? I just need a li'l trapper to get from A to B."

"Holla at TC when he get off work. Fat-ass nigga always know something about something."

For the rest of the afternoon, I used Vic's house as my headquarters while I hustled. TC showed up after he got off work.

"You know somebody sellin' a car, nigga?"

"Uh, I think Van was sayin something 'bout selling a car awhile back. Want me to call him?"

"Yeah. I need a li'l trap."

TC made the call. "He said he got a 2002 Lumina. He want 2,500 for it."

"Tell him I got 1,500 for it right now."

"He said 1,800."

"Tell him we on our way."

Van lived in Brown Deer, a Milwaukee suburb. Back in the day, it was rare to see black people in this neck of the woods. Today it was filled with everybody from the business owner to the dope boy. Van lived in a big-ass house that didn't have a sidewalk out front. In the driveway was a silver Lexus, blue BMW, and black Chevy Lumina.

"'Sup with you niggas?" Van smiled. He was taller than me by a couple of inches and in good shape. Not swole, but cut up. He wore a dark T-shirt that I'm guessing was an extra-large because it showed off ripped arms. His complexion was somewhere between yellow and red. He had "good hair" like he was mixed, cut low with a taper. And every time he opened his mouth, the sun reflected off his diamond and platinum teeth.

"What's good, Van?"

"You got it, Drayez. See you gettin' to that money, huh?"

"I'm a'ight. No complaints."

"That's what's up." He smiled, blinding me. "That's my baby right there. This where it all started for me. Highways and all. Runs good."

"You said you was gon' let me get it for 1,500, right?"

He laughed. "You funny, Drayez. I left that old life alone, so all my money is accounted for now. I hate to let her go, but the fam got needs. This car was supposed to be a reminder. Every time I look at it, it reminds me of the life I left behind. But like I said, I got a family. Need that 1,800, lil brah."

I pulled out the money and gave it to him. "Shit, after hearing that, take this money."

He pocketed it without even counting. "Here go the keys. Title in the glove box. Might as well sign it and get it outta the way. You got L's, right?"

"Nah."

He gave a concerned look. "Get them license, li'l brah. Without 'em, you won't last long. I'ma give you 30 days with them plates. After that, it's on you."

"Cool."

"A'ight, my nigga. Holla if you need anything. And next time you get up wit' Smitty, tell him I said get at me."

***

The sound of my phone ringing woke me up. I wanted to leave it and go back to sleep, but I needed the money. I was almost broke. All I had was re-up money. Well, most of it. I was still a few dollars short because I bought the car, but a couple runs should get me what I needed. After wiping the sleep from my eyes, I reached for the phone. "Yeah."

"Dray, this Smurf. I need a cutie. You got me?"

Everybody knew I only sold sacks. But since he asked, I decided to test and see how much I could get. "My nigga, you know I only got them sacks. I need 1,500 for a cutie pie."

"1,500?" he asked, sounding like I asked to fuck his mama.

"Yeah, my nigga. I don't normally do this, but I'ma do it for you this one time."

"C'mon, Dray. Yo' shit fire, but you on one."

I stuck to my guns. "That's what it is."

"Damn, Dray. You fuckin' me up, my nigga. I got some action from up north. Fuck it. It ain't my money. Let me get it."

I couldn't believe he agreed, but I was happy that he did. "Okay. Gimme a minute to get up. I'ma hit you when I'm on my way."

The thought of making a couple extra dollars took all the sleep from my body. I needed the money. I only had two ounces left. I was going to get that 1500 and combine it with what I had to get a fresh pound. I called Smitty. He didn't answer so I left a message. I got dressed and waited twenty minutes before calling Smitty again. Still no answer. Damn. I left another message, hoping to get the money before it slipped through my fingers.

An hour went by and I still hadn't heard from my plug. Smurf called twice and said if I couldn't come through, he was going to look elsewhere. Another hour passed. When I realized Smurf's money was gone, I went on with my day. Got back on the grind and waited for Smitty to hit me back.

"Look at this bum-ass nigga. Done went from super broke to gettin' a li'l money," Vic teased.

I was at Vic's house and something like a get together had happened. Me, TC, Vic, Renae, and two of her friends sat around kicking it and smoking. Desiré wore her hair in some kind of crinkle curls piled atop her head. She had skin the color of a brown paper bag, deep set dark eyes that looked like they had a story to tell, and big pillow-soft lips. She was about 5'5" with some big-ass titties and a body type I called juicy, somewhere between thick and chubby with a lot of curves. The other friend was Chantele. She was tall with an athletic build and shade lighter than Desiré. She had gray eyes, hair in a short natural afro, high cheekbones, and a small gap between her top front teeth. Both of them looked good. And they was watching me.

"C'mon, you fake-ass Future. Quit with them weak-ass jokes, nigga. Put on that Kevin Hart comedy. Least we can get some real laughs," I shot back.

Chantele and Desiré laughed way harder than necessary. TC chuckled. Renae tried to hide her laugh.

Vic looked wounded. "That's how you do me, brah?"

"You started that shit, nigga. I just wanna watch a movie."

"Yeah, a'ight. How 'bout you just fire some weed up, nigga? 'Cause yo' jokes is super lame."

I went in my pocket and pulled out the last of my weed. I had twelve sacks. Smitty still hadn't called me back and I was starting to get worried. Since I started hustling, I had never run out of weed and Smitty never went this long without calling back. It was almost 8:00 at night, twelve hours since I left the first message on his voicemail.

"You gon' let me get two of them and leave me yo' number, right?" Chantele asked. The look in her gray eyes told me it was about more than weed.

"Fa sho'. Gotta give the people what they want."

"Why don't you give the people fatter sacks?" TC cracked.

"Fat-ass nigga ain't neva satisfied." I laughed, tossing him and Chantele sacks of weed. "Roll this up and gimme Van's number. Smitty still ain't hit me back and I wanna seen if Van knows somethin'."

While TC rolled the blunt, I called Van.

"Hello?"

"What's good, Van? This Drayez."

"Dray, what's good, family? How the Lumi treating you?"

"Man, no complaints. Like you said, she a runner. I'm calling to see if you heard from yo' boy Smitty. I been tryna get at him all day, but he ain't hit me back."

"That's my wife's cousin. Let me make some calls and get back to you. This yo' line?"

"Yeah. Hit me."

After hanging up, I went to piss. While I drained the snake, my mind roamed. Since I started having a little money, I noticed the way people were looking at me and treating me. Clean clothes, a car, and the weed had bumped my status from bum-ass nigga to up and coming player. The looks I got from females, the respect from Rayna, and the way my niggas spoke to me told that I was on the right track.

I was shaking the dribbles from my dick when the bathroom door opened. I locked eyes with Chantele briefly before she looked down to see what I was holding in my hand.

"Oops. Sorry," she apologized before closing the door.

She didn't look sorry. After washing my hands, I opened the door and found Chantele in the hall. "Like what you seen?"

She licked her lips. "I gotta no li'l dick policy and you measure up fine."

I laughed. "I ain't met nobody that could handle me."

"That's 'cause we ain't fucked yet. Just make sure I get yo' number before I leave. Excuse me. I gotta pee."

She gave me a seductive look before closing the door. I thought about busting in on her ass like she did me, but my phone rang. It was Van.

"What's good, brah?"

"Dray, it's all bad, my nigga."

I heard the doom in his voice. He was about to drop some bad news. Shit. "What happened?"

"Smitty got knocked last night. I think they said it was the Feds. Might wanna chill out for a minute 'cause them Feds will book yo' ass just for knowing a nigga that's gettin' it."

I closed my eyes and sank against the wall. "Damn. That's fucked up."

"I hear you. Be smooth, my nigga. Holla if you need me."

I let the phone dangle at my side as I stared at the wall in front of me. My plug got knocked, I was out of weed, and I only had three G's to my name. I had a family to support, a girlfriend to keep happy, and a li'l sister that needed my help. Just when it seemed like things were going my way...

I didn't even hear the bathroom door open. I just felt somebody watching me.

"If I didn't know no better, I would say you stalking me." Chantele smiled.

I just stared at her blankly. Her words didn't register. Sounded like she was saying, "Blah, blah, blah, blah, blah."

"You okay, Drayez?"

I didn't have words to describe what I was feeling, so I didn't respond. I just walked through the house and out the front door.

***

I woke up the next morning to the sound of my phone ringing. Normally that was a good thing, but not today. I had no product. A hustler with no product wasn't a hustler. He was a... Shit, I didn't even know what a hustla with no product was. Just a man. Or a bum. I reached over and cut the phone off, hoping the ringing didn't wake Rayna. I didn't know what I was going to do the next time she asked me for some money. One thing I couldn't do was tell her no. Since I had been getting money, we hadn't argued once. Not even a little debate. What I said went. If I told her I needed to save money to find another plug, my hold on absolute power might slip, and I couldn't let that happen. The only way to make sure I stayed in charge of the house was to find another plug.

I left the house around 11 o'clock on a mission to find some weed and drove down on Dino. The chubby redheaded albino was in the usual spot outside the corner store.

"Dino, what's good, nigga?"

"'Sup, Dray?" He nodded, staring me down.

I knew what the look was about. I was the competition and I had better product and fatter sacks. I put a dent in his pocket and nobody liked losing money. But I ignored the hostile look. "I need a favor, brah."

"Niggas in jail wanna get out."

"I need a pound. You know where I can cop?"

He looked me from head to toe and then right in my eyes and smiled. "Nah," he lied.

He knew where I could get some weed, but he didn't wanna help. Me not having weed meant more money for him. McDonald's didn't help Burger King and Dino wasn't helping me.

"C'mon, my nigga. We can put our money together and sew up the whole hood. The whole 27th Street can be ours."

He let out a chuckle. "If you ain't tryna cop a sack, beat it, fam."

I mean mugged the shit out his bitch ass. I wanted to hit that nigga in his shit. "That's some bitch-ass shit, nigga."

He turned up. "What's up wit'chu, nigga?" he barked, reaching a hand under his shirt.

I wasn't strapped so I took a step back. "It's good, Dino. We good."

Chapter 6

One day turned into two, two into a week, and a week into two weeks. I still hadn't found a plug. And I was also down to my last 800 dollars. I never told Rayna about my plug getting knocked because I didn't want to lose my hold on the power in the house. So when she asked, I gave, hoping that I would find a plug soon. Two weeks later, I was still outta my hustle. I killed the last sip in the bottle of Remy Martin before getting out of the car and stumbling into the house. The kids ignored me and Rayna gave me a sideways look. I went to our room and laid in bed. Rayna came in a few seconds later.

"You okay, baby?"

"Hell nah," I slurred.

She sat down next to me. "What happened? What's wrong?"

I decided to keep it real. "I'm damn near broke and I need a plug."

"You almost broke?" She asked, sounding like she didn't believe her own words.

"Yeah. Down to my last 800 dollars."

"So, what you gon' do about it? We got kids."

I let out a long breath. "I don't know."

"You betta come up with somethin', nigga. We got bills."

I woke up the next morning still fully dressed, lying in the same spot that I fell in bed last night. Rayna wasn't in bed. I sat up and immediately felt the effects of a hangover kicking in. My mouth was dry, lips cracking, and I was thirsty enough to drink toilet water. I went to the kitchen and downed a glass of water. Rayna walked in a few moments later carrying Draya. I could tell she was mad because she didn't look at me.

"I just need a li'l time to come up with another way to get some money."

"Well, you need to think of something fast because I don't get my check for a couple days," she said, fixing Draya a bottle.

"I think you should let me get yo' check so I can flip it."

She finally looked at me. “Why don’t you just get a title loan on your car?”

“’Cause I never went to the DMV and put the car in my name. And them bitches want too much interest. I can get a half pound for 1,500 and flip it.”

She searched my face for a moment, like she was judging my worth. “Did you find somebody to buy from?”

“Nah. But I will.”

She stared at me again. “Okay. I’ma do it this one time.”

I felt my self-worth rising. “I got’chu, baby. I’ma take care of everything.”

Rayna’s SSI check couldn’t come fast enough. As soon as she put the money in my hand, I hit the door like I was tryna catch a Black Friday Sale. I went against my better judgement and drove through a few hoods to see if I could ask around for a plug. I knew I was taking a big risk pulling up to niggas I didn’t know asking for weed, but I was desperate. I was driving down 19th and Vine when I spotted some niggas standing on the porch of a green and white house. They looked like they were hustling so I pulled up and rolled down the window.

“Ay, y’all got that bag?”

A dark-skinned nigga with dreads spoke up. “Who dat?”

“Drayez. Y’all got that loud?”

The men said a few words amongst one another before the nigga with the dreads and a light-skinned nigga with a nappy ’fro walked to the car. Dread head bent down to look inside. “What you wanted?”

I didn’t want to let them know how much money I had so I went low. “What you want for a quarter pound?”

The dread head stood and had a couple words for his boy. “He want a QP.”

“Eight hundred.” I heard the nigga with the afro say.

Dread head bent down again. “800. But we gotta take a ride.”

I looked in Dread head’s eyes for a sign of distrust. A gleam in his eyes, a lip twitch, not able to hold eye contact. But he stared back at me with a patient look, like he was waiting for me to make up my mind.

"A'ight. Get in."

Dread head got in the passenger seat. The other nigga got in the back.

"Hit the corner and make a left," Dread head said.

I followed the directions. When I pulled to the stop sign, I looked to my passenger for further directions. And that's when the nigga in the back seat put a big-ass silver revolver to my head.

"Where that bread at, nigga?" Dread head asked as he began searching my pockets and waist.

"Man, this some bitch-ass shit!" I cursed.

"Yeah, I know. We Savages, boy. Fuck you doing riding down on niggas you don't know tryna catch for?" the nigga in the backseat asked.

"This all you got?" Dread head asked, taking the 1,600 dollars.

"Yeah. C'mon, my nigga. I need that. I got kids and shit."

The nigga with the gun laughed. "You hear this nigga?"

"If you looking for us, come back wit' an army," Dread head said as they got out the car.

"But this li'l shit ain't worth yo' life, Drayez," the gunman said.

I pounded my fist against the steering wheel, wishing I would've brought my pistol. They acted like they didn't have a care in the world as they walked away with my money. I had heard about the Savages. They were a group of jackboys that terrorized Milwaukee. But I didn't give a fuck who they was. I was going to get my shit and pop they bitch asses. When I got home, I ran past Rayna and into our bedroom. I was searching the top shelf when she walked in.

"What happened?"

"Bitch-ass niggas robbed me!"

Her watery eyes showed a mix of emotions in an instant. Hurt, anger, disappointment, and then rage. She jumped on me like she was mixed with a leopard and started hitting me.

"Go get my fuckin' money, Drayez!"

I abandoned looking for the pistol and pushed her off me. "Move out the way, nigga!"

She jumped on me again, scratching me in the face. I grabbed her in a bear hug.

"Let me go!" she screamed and bit me on the arm.

"Ahhh, shit!" I yelled, picking her ass up and slamming her. A big boom shook the floor as her body crumpled. If she was hurt, she didn't show it. She was on her feet in an instant, showing a quickness I didn't know she had. She took off out of the room. I walked over to the mirror to check the scars on my face. And that's when I saw Rayna out the corner of my eye. She ran back in the room with a big-ass butcher knife.

"I'm killin' you, bitch!" she screamed.

I had nowhere to run. I wanted to go for the pistol in the closet, but knew I wouldn't be able to reach it before she stabbed me. My only option was to dodge the knife swing and move fast. She came high, aiming for my chest. Bitch was really trying to kill me! I jumped back as she swung, the knife missing me by a few inches. Her momentum made her lose balance. I took off from the room. The closest door with a lock was the bathroom. I just got the door closed when Rayna crashed into it. She grabbed the knob, but I was stronger and faster. I locked the door and took a step back in case she tried to break the door open.

"Open the door, bitch!" Rayna screamed.

"Put that muthafuckin' knife down, bitch!" I yelled back, checking my face in the mirror. There were scratches on my cheek.

"Nah, nigga. You wanna putcho hands on me and slam me? Do it again, nigga!"

"I swear to God, I'm beating yo' ass when I come out this bathroom," I promised.

"C'mon, nigga. Bring yo' ass out here. I dare you."

"Put that knife down. I ain't coming out til you put it down."

"Do you got my money in there, bitch?"

"I just told you I got robbed."

"Open this door and go get my money, Drayez!"

"You gon' put the knife down?"

She was quiet for a moment. When she spoke again, her voice was calm. "Okay. Yeah. I put the knife down. Open the door."

I didn't like her tone. She got way too calm way too fast. I knew she was on some bullshit, but I couldn't stay locked in this bathroom. I pressed my body against the door and unlocked it, opening it slowly. Rayna stood there with her arms behind her back. Her face was flat but her eyes burned with anger.

"What you got behind yo' back?" I asked.

"Nothing. Open the door and come out."

There was an eagerness to her voice that let me know to be on point. I opened the door a little more, and that's when she made her move. The knife came from behind her back fast, like she was a swordsman in a karate movie. I barely got out the way before the knife stabbed the door.

"What the fuck wrong with you, bitch?" I yelled, slamming the door before she could get off another swing.

"Yo' bitch ass is what's wrong with me! Get the fuck out my house, Drayez. And I want my fuckin' money!" she screamed, banging on the door again.

I knew I had to get the fuck out her house if I wanted to live to see another day. But she wasn't about to let me walk out in one piece. My only option was the bathroom window.

***

"Damn, nigga! What happened to yo' face?" Vic asked, looking at me like I wasn't human.

"Me and Rayna had a fight. Bitch tried to kill me," I said, shaking my head and sitting on the couch as an image of her swinging the knife at me played in my head.

"You bullshitting?" Vic asked, his eyes wide with surprise.

"Bitch scratched me and tried to stab me with a butcher knife."

"What? That bitch is a fool, my nigga! Fuck y'all fighting for?"

"I got her check and went to look for a plug. Got robbed by them bitch-ass Savage niggas."

His eyes got bigger. "You got robbed, my nigga? Damn, you having a fucked up day."

"I know. I gotta find a way to get this money back."

Vic shook his head. "I don't know what to tell you, my nigga. But I hope you done fuckin' with that bitch. Can't be fuckin hoes that's tryna kill you."

"Yeah, that shit a wrap. She tried to kill me, for real. Tried to stab me in the chest," I said in disbelief.

"Yeah, that's some bullshit. You can chill here for a couple days if you need to. 'Til you figure something out. I got some weed. Wanna smoke?"

I looked at him like he was stupid. "Hell yeah, nigga! Fire that shit up."

***

I barely slept that first night on Vic's couch. I kept thinking about the look on Rayna's face, in her eyes. She actually tried to kill me over a bitch-ass SSI check. I had spent thousands on her and her kids. Did it without hesitating. But it didn't mean shit to Rayna. Had I been a little slower, she would've fucked me up. I couldn't forgive her for that shit. I loved Rayna with everything inside of me but it was obvious she didn't feel the same way. I should've seen the writing on the wall, but I was blinded by good pussy.

I ended up sulking around Vic's house for two days. Didn't go nowhere. Didn't do nothing. Just lay on the couch and got my bum on.

TC popped up with Van and surprised the shit out of me.

"Vic, Dray! What's good with you niggas?" Van smiled, his teeth blinging.

"'Sup?" I mumbled.

"Van, fuck you doin' in the hood, nigga?" Vic asked.

"You know I show my face in the hood from time to time. Gotta check on my people," he said, looking to me. "Is it that bad?"

I shook my head from side to side. "I can't remember a time when it was worse."

"The sun don't shine forever, my nigga. We all have bad days. But this how you show the world what you made of. Gotta make that bounce back special, baby boy."

I didn't have a comeback. My thoughts were gloomy and so was my attitude. I didn't wanna hear that positive shit.

"I been tellin this nigga that shit for two days. Nigga got a serious case of depression. Probably need to see a shrink," Vic joked.

Nobody laughed.

"So that's it? Hustle gone? It's over?" Van asked, giving me a pitiful look.

"Shit, what I'm s'posed to do? I'm broke and I don't got nowhere to live."

"But that don't mean you quit, nigga. You still breathing. You come up with anotha plan and make it happen. If at first you don't succeed, dust yo'self off and try again."

My comeback was weak. "That shit sound slick in a song."

Van shook his head. "Man, when you came and got the keys to the Lumi, I thought you was on yo' way. I seen a little bit of me in you. But this?" He waved a hand in my direction. "This sad. You don't gotta start with a lot to become great. Behavior comes from belief, my nigga. You do what you believe you can do. You think small, you gon' be small. You supposed to use challenges that life throw at you to make stairs to move you to the next level. You don't give up when shit get hard. That's not what a man do. You a man, right?"

It was more of a challenge than a question. And the way he was staring at me, all serious, no smiles, let me know he wanted me to take it as a challenge.

"Yeah. I'm a man."

"Then act like one. TC told me about yo' situation. I was really just askin' 'bout you to check up on yo' hustle. I wanted to see how you bounced back after what happened to Smitty. I love to see niggas eating. But when he told me the state you was in, I had to see for myself. And I'm glad I did. This ain't what real niggas do. Real niggas use trials to make us bigger and better, not smaller and bitter.

Yo' outlook on life is what's gon' determine yo' outcome in life. If you say you can't, you won't. When you say you can, you will. Simple as that."

We were all quiet, thinking of Van's words. He sounded like a motivational speaker or preacher.

"That was some of the realest shit I ever heard," TC said.

"If by real you mean true, I agree," Van said before turning to me. "So, what's it gon' be Dray? What you gon' do?"

Being under the stares of my niggas made me nervous. It felt like they were waiting on me to step out on a rope 100 feet off the ground with no safety net to catch me. I knew they had love for me and wanted to see me win. Van's words came from that same place.

"I gotta get back up and try again," I managed.

"My nigga!" Van celebrated. "You gotta crawl before you can walk. Walk before you run."

Vic stared at Van in awe. "How you be comin' up with that shit?"

Van's response surprised all of us.

"Books. It's a sayin' that goes something like this: 'If you wanna hide something from a nigga, put it in a book.' It ain't no secret that street niggas don't read. That's why we filling up the joints wit' petty-ass crimes that get us over-sentenced. If niggas read, studied, planned, and stuck to they guns, we would have more success. But most niggas move without thinking and pay for it later. Sometimes that shit cost more than niggas can afford."

He left us to chew on those words. I understood what he was saying. And I also realized that I needed Van. I had jumped in the game late, without a good teacher or learning the rules. I needed guidance. He was sharp, and I needed what he knew. I needed the rules to the game, its principles, and way of life. I needed the lessons he learned and the wisdom he gained from those lessons.

"Van, can you teach me the game?" I asked.

He stared at me for a moment, searching - the same look I got from L-Dog and Twan. He was looking past my skin and bones and into my soul, measuring my worth. My value. My strength.

"I'm retired, lil brah," he said before looking away.

I didn't know if Vic or TC caught it, but I did. There was a gleam in Van's eyes, a yearning for the life he retired from. That's why he looked away. He didn't want us to see the truth. But I did. He missed the money. The fame. The overgrown ego that came with success. And shit, if he really was the plug, than he tasted the power that lots of money gave you. Now he was just an ordinary nigga, and it was killing him.

"I just need somebody to show me the ropes. I jumped off the porch late. I just started hustling when I met Smitty. I'm behind the curve, but I gotta do something, my nigga. I can't go back to being a bum. I'm twenty-four and ain't got shit. Not a pot to piss in or a window to throw it out of. I ain't askin' you to get back in the game. I just want you to teach me what you know."

TC and Vic watched Van the same way they watched me when he was kicking that motivational shit. At first, Van didn't show a reaction. And then he smiled.

"If you serious 'bout this shit, I'll mentor you. But you gotta do what I say, when I say. A'ight?"

I smiled for the first time in two days. This is where I got my drive.

Book II: The Game

A CONTEST INVOLVING RISKS AND REWARDS. MONEY AND POWER. PLEASURE AND PAIN. LIFE AND DEATH.

THE ULTIMATE GOAL IS SUCCESS. TO MAKE IT OUT OF WHATEVER PROJECT OR HOOD YOU COME FROM.

TO PLAY THE GAME, YOU HAVE TO KNOW THE RULES AND THE CONSEQUENCES OF BREAKING THEM.

THE BASIC RULES ARE:

NEVER KEEP MONEY OR PRODUCT WHERE YOU SLEEP.

NEVER LET PEOPLE KNOW HOW MUCH MONEY OR PRODUCT YOU GOT.

NEVER UNDERESTIMATE YOUR ENEMIES.

NEVER TELL YOUR BITCH WHAT YOU DO IN THE STREETS.

LOYALTY OVER EVERYTHING.

MONEY OVER BITCHES.

DON'T SNITCH.

DON'T BITCH UP.

RIDE FOR YO' NIGGAS.

TRUST YOUR GUT. IF SOMETHING DON'T FEEL RIGHT, IT AIN'T RIGHT.

YOU CAN ALWAYS ADD TO THE LIST AS YOU LEARN AND ADVANCE, JUST LIKE AMERICA DID WITH THE AMENDMENTS TO THE CONSTITUTION. WHEN YOU LEARN THE RULES, LIVE BY THEM AND PROSPER.

OR BREAK THEM AND DIE.

Chapter 7

Van wanted to see how serious I was about success. He wanted to test my drive to see what I could do when my back was against the wall. The task was to gather as much money as I could and call him in three days.

I sat around with Vic and thought of ways to get money that didn't involve robbing or stealing. Vic's answer stayed in line with his lifestyle. Get it from a female. I didn't know many females that would give me a loan. The only ones that had ever given me money was Rayna and Marie. Asking Marie for anything was out of the question. But maybe, if I got on my knees and begged or did some other desperate shit, I could get Rayna to look out for me one more time. If that didn't work, I would hit up Tikka to see if she still had some of the money I had given her. When I was hustling, I dropped her money a few times. Since she never went out or did anything fun, I figured she was saving the money for when Marie gave her the boot. If I couldn't get money from my little sister, my final resort was to go scrapping with Marie's boyfriend, Keith.

When I left Vic's house, I hopped in the Lumi and seen the gas gauge was past E. I ignored it and drove two blocks over to Rayna's house. A tan Porsche truck was parked out front. I got a sinking feeling in the pit of my stomach as I walked up on the porch. Thoughts of another nigga in her house three days after I left crept into my head. "Nah, she wouldn't do that," I told myself as the front door opened.

A nigga that I had never seen before stepped outside. He was in his mid-30s, six feet tall, a slim build, light-skinned, trimmed facial hair. He wore a gold and white Rockstar 'fit, an iced-out TBT chain, and a watch that cost more than all the money I ever had.

"Who is you?" I asked, the sting of jealously burning my chest.

He paused, looking me from head to toe in an instant. "Fuck is you, nigga?" He mugged me, hand moving close to the bulge at his waist.

"This my house, nigga. Who is you?"

Recognition flashed in his eyes and he smiled. “I think you and shorty got some talking to do.”

He walked away without another word. My heart hammered inside my chest cavity, filling my body with pain. The anger boiled inside of me as I rushed in the house. Rayna was standing by the front door wearing one of my T-shirts. When she seen me, fear shone in her eyes.

“That’s how you do me, bitch? I’m gone three days and you already fucking another nigga?”

She backed up a little bit. “I’m done, Drayez. Where my money?”

“So that’s it? I lose the money and you bringing other niggas in the crib?” I asked, moving closer. I wanted to beat her ass.

She took another step back. “I’m tired of yo’ shit. We through. I got rent to pay and kids to take care of. And I want my money.”

I kicked the table and sent it flying across the living room. “Fuck that bitch-ass money! This how you gon’ do me, for real?”

Rayna put some more distance between us. “I’m not finna argue with you, Drayez. Can you just leave? I ain’t tryna fight you.”

I didn’t trust myself to talk or move, so I just stood there and stared at her. Fear and uncertainty swirled in her eyes. I looked deeper, hoping to see remorse, sorrow, or love. She gave me nothing and that pissed me off even more. I drew my arm back and flinched at her. She jumped back, tripping and falling on her big-ass booty.

“You’s a weak-ass bitch! One day you gon’ get yours.”

I hopped in the Lumi and drove aimlessly, thinking about the last year and a half I spent with Rayna. I loved her. Gave her my seed. Didn’t matter that she had four other baby daddies. I accepted her for what she was. But all I ever was to her was a hustle. She needed a provider.

And as long as I played my part, shit was good. Soon as I stopped giving her money, it was over. She never loved me and I was too stupid to see it. Sucka, busta, and hoe trusta. Somehow I got out of my chest long enough to realize plan A was awash and I had to move to plan B.

I pulled up to Marie's house a few minutes later. I parked, about to pull my key from the ignition when the car cut off. I tried to start it again, but the engine wouldn't turn over. Er-a-er-a-er-a. Click. I did that three times before giving up.

"Sounds like you outta gas," Keith said as he walked to his beat-up gray F-150.

I checked the gas gauge and seen the light blinking. Fuck. I got out of the car, not bothering to lock the doors, and walked in the house. Tina walked into the living room as I plopped down on the couch. Although she and Tikka were twins, they were as different as night and day. Tina was wild and free. Tikka was reserved and humble. Tina was ratchet, wore revealing clothes, and dabbled in drugs and liquor. Tikka was guided by morals, dressed in clothes that covered her body, and swore off anything that would alter her mind. The only thing they had in common was their looks.

"'Sup wit'cho bum ass?"

"Where Tikka at, hood rat?"

"Bitch probably at school. I don't know. Can I use yo' car? I need to catch a check."

"Ain't no gas in it. It just cut off on me."

"Thought you was gettin' money, bum. How yo' car run outta gas?"

"Ran outta money. Marie here?"

"She in her room. Talkin shit as usual. Talkin' 'bout kickin' me and Tikka out. Like I give a fuck. I'm a bad bitch. Ain't shit to me. I got somewhere to go. She think somebody want Keith li'l dick ass. Nigga can't do nothin for me but eat my pussy and buy me a Birkin bag."

I looked at Tina like I was seeing her for the first time. She sounded like Marie and Rayna. Always wanted a nigga to buy them something. "All y'all hoes just alike. You, Marie, and Rayna. Always want a nigga to buy y'all something. Bitches ain't shit."

Tina wasn't fazed by my words. "I know I'm a bitch. But I'm a bad one. Yo' mama and Rayna just alike, lettin' niggas nut in them and hit it on they stupid ass. Not me. Ain't no nigga hittin' this pussy for free. And I ain't having no nigga's kids. Love ain't real. The only thing that's real to me is money."

And with that, she was gone. I thought about my little sister's words. How were she and Tikka so different? When did they grow up? And when did Tina become so materialistic? Was love real? Was life really all about getting money?

"What you doing over here?" Marie asked, popping up in the living room.

"My car ran outta gas and I don't got nowhere to go."

She stopped in front of me and took a long puff of her cigarette. "What happened to yo' money, boy?"

"It's a long story, but it's gone. I'm broke."

"So what'chu gon' do about it?"

"I'm tryna figure that out."

"Don't Rayna get a check?"

"I fucked that off too."

She gave a hmph. "So I take it you can't go back home?"

"Nah. Ain't been there in a couple days. She already moved on."

Marie laughed. "Really?"

"Yeah. Ran into the nigga leaving right before I came over."

Marie laughed again. "Hurt, don't it?"

I didn't respond.

"Let this be a lesson, Drayez. Fuck love. Get you some money. Ain't nothing in life free, baby. And you gotta pay the cost to be the boss. I don't love Keith's ass and he knows it. I love what he can do for me. And as soon as his ass stop doin' it, he gone. That's how Rayna is, was, and gon' always be. That's how most bitches is. We want providers. That fairy tale love shit ain't real. The sooner you realize it, the better you gon be. I'ma let you sleep on the couch for a couple days. After that, it's on you." Marie walked away, laughing and shaking her head.

I was going to show her and all the bitches that thought like them what I was capable of. Fuck love. MOB. I sat on the couch for three hours until Tikka came home.

"What you doing over here, bum?" she asked, dropping her books on the table and sitting next to me.

"I'ma be here for a couple days, buster."

"What happened? Rayna put you out?" she cracked.

"We broke up. For real this time. Bitch tried to stab me."

Her eyes popped. "For real? What happened?"

"I don't even want to talk about it. But listen, I need to borrow some money."

She gave a look. "I only got a little bit. And I need it."

"I'ma give it back in a couple days. I need this for real, sis. I don't even got no gas money. I can't even start my car."

She was quiet for a moment. "How much you need?"

"How much you got?"

"Almost a thousand dollars. 957 dollars, to be exact."

"Gimme 900 and I'ma give you back 1,800. But I need a couple days."

"You gotta take me to the bank. But how you gon' do that if your car won't start?"

"Don't worry 'bout that. We gon' go tomorrow. And thank you, baby girl. You saved my life."

***

"I do scrapping. Drive around and look for any metals that will sell. On the slow days, I might have to do some can collecting. Whatever I get, I take to the junkyard and they pay me cash on the spot. From the look in yo' face, I can tell you don't like what I do. But it's mostly an honest job and I make my own money."

"You do this every day?" I asked, kicking an old beer can under the seat.

"Seven days a week," he nodded.

"Why not get a real job?"

He thought on an answer. "Yo' mama."

I didn't understand. "What Marie got to do with this?"

"You young right now so you might not understand this," he said, turning into an alley and cruising slowly. "Don't no woman want a broke man. Now I ain't never been much of a criminal or drug dealer, but every now and then I do what I gotta do to make ends meet. But the criminal life ain't for me. I did three years in '96 for a petty robbery and I hated every day of it. Some niggas act like goin' to prison ain't shit. Like it's a natural part of life. Well, it wasn't for me. Muthafuckas watchin' you shit. Lookin at yo' nuts and in yo' ass. Niggas fuckin' other niggas. None of that shit was normal to me. Plus, I missed getting pussy. Never knew how important it was until you go without it. And yo' mama, she got——" He paused, realizing he went too far. "I decided that I was gonna turn my life around when I got out. And I did. Met a nigga that showed me how to scrap. When he first explained it to me, I looked the same way you did. Now, twenty years later, I can't see myself doin' nothin' else. C'mon and help me put this stove in the back."

The stove was next to a garbage can overflowing with trash. It was a big green metal thing. Didn't look like it was worth much and it was humiliating digging through somebody's garbage. But Keith didn't seem to mind at all. He looked at the stove like an art collector appraising a painting. After we loaded the truck in the back of the stove, I continued the conversation.

"But that don't explain why you ain't got a 9 to 5."

"Yo' mama ain't the kinda woman that wanna wait two weeks for nothin'. On my good days, I make 4 or 5 hunnit. Especially when it's warm out. Long as yo' mama happy, I'm happy."

Sucka, busta, hoe trusta.

We drove down more alleys, picked up more junk, and talked some more. Spending time with Keith allowed me to see what I didn't want to be. I could never spend my days going through garbage just to please a money-hungry female, even if that female gave me life.

When the back of the truck was full, we drove to the junkyard and unloaded. Got 200 dollars. Keith split it down the middle and then we went to collect more junk.

"Do you love Marie?"

Keith popped a cigarette in his mouth, taking his time lighting it. "Love her like Prince loves them jeans with the ass cut out," he laughed.

I didn't know what he was talking about so I didn't find the joke funny. "You think she love you?"

He lit the cigarette and blew out a cloud of smoke. "I know she don't. But when you get to my age, you take what you can get."

Sucka, busta, hoe trusta.

Spending the day with Keith got me 175 dollars and valuable lessons on life, love, and work. I learned that Keith was a simple nigga. Didn't want shit but some pussy and a place to lay his head. Dignity and respect were words with no meaning. That would be me in twenty years if I didn't do something about it. I also learned that falling in love was over. It wasn't real. People used loved to take advantage of others. Like Marie and Rayna. I couldn't let that happen again. And finally, I learned that never in my life would I pick through somebody else's garbage. I hit rock bottom. The only place to go was up.

I used the money I got from working with Keith to gas up the Lumi and take my ass to the DMV to put the car in my name and sign up to get my license. From there, I grabbed Tikka and went to the bank. After getting the money, I also took out a title loan on the Lumi. I was pulling up to Marie's house when I noticed the candy blue Chevy on 26 inch chrome parked out front.

"Who is that?" I asked Tikka.

"Manny. One of Tina's friends."

I eyed the donk as I climbed from the Lumi, picturing myself behind the wheel. Manny seen me looking and gave a nod. I nodded back.

"'Sup, bum-ass nigga?" Tina called as she walked out the front door in an outfit that flaunted everything that Marie gave her.

"Yo' ratchet ass is what's up. So that's what it's all about?" I asked, nodding towards the donk.

"And you know it!" She smiled, breezing by.

And then I got an idea. "Ask him if he wanna buy a pistol."

Tina spun around. "What?"

"I'm sellin' my pistol. Ask him if he wanna buy it."

When she got to the car, she and Manny exchanged words. "How much you want?"

"400."

"What kind is it?"

"Glock wit' an extendo."

"You got it right now?"

"Nah, it's at Rayna house."

"He said he'll give you 300 for it tomorrow."

***

I drove by Rayna's house later that night. My plan was to pack my shit, kiss my baby, and get out. No words. In and out. I parked behind the Buick truck and took the door key off my keyring. After I used it one more time, she could have it back. I walked upon the porch and tried the door. It was unlocked. When I walked in the house, what I seen made my blood boil. Rayna was ass naked, sitting on the couch. Standing in front of her was the nigga with the Porsche truck. Rayna had his dick in her hand like she had just pulled it from her mouth. The nigga looked annoyed, like I had interrupted something. Rayna looked unsure what to do. I didn't know what to do either so I stood there for a moment. I wanted to leave, but I needed my pistol. I also wanted to snap, but I noticed the black handgun sitting on the table. I looked from the gun and back to the nigga. He smiled before pushing his dick back into Rayna's mouth. She started sucking.

I walked onto the front porch and let out an angry gust of air. I couldn't believe this bitch! She really just sucked a nigga's dick in my face. I wanted to scream. I wanted to fight. I wanted to kill. But I knew that wasn't going to solve nothing. Rayna's bitch ass wasn't worth killing, dying, or going to jail for. Fuck that bitch. All I needed was my pistol, and I wasn't leaving without it. I checked my feelings and walked back in the house. I tried not to look at Rayna and the nigga, but they had changed positions. She was on her knees, face in the pillow, moaning like he was killing her. The nigga had picked up the pistol, fucking her from behind while wearing a smirk. I walked to the room and pulled the Glock from the back of the closet, having a vision of going out there and leaving both of they brains on the floor. Nigga was tryna rub that shit in my face. And Rayna was stroking his ego screaming like he was killing her. Li'l dick-ass nigga (no homo). I knew how she really screamed and ran from the D.

"Fuck 'em," I told myself, waisting the pistol. I walked past Rayna and her nigga, dropping the key on the floor as I left.

I spent the night tossing and turning on Marie's couch. Visions of the woman I loved fucking and sucking another nigga played continuously in my head. That shit burned in the middle of my chest like a hot-ass fire that I couldn't put out. I could feel the love I had for her turning to hate. I never wanted to feel these feelings again and I would do everything in my power not to.

The next day I sold the pistol to Manny and called Van. He told me to come over after he got off work. I pulled up to his house at 6 o'clock on the dot.

"'Sup, nigga?" Van smiled, blinding me as he got in the passenger seat of the Lumi.

"Shit. Anxious. Ready to get to it."

"So, what you come up with?"

"I pulled out the money. "1,700."

He blinded me with his smile again. "That's what I'm talkin 'bout, Drayez! When a real nigga back against the wall, he find a way to make something happen. You did what you was supposed to do. When life give you lemons, you squeeze the juice out that bitch and go get a bottle of gin."

"What you want me to do with this?" I asked, holding out the money.

"That's you, my nigga. You earned that. I just wanted you to see what you could do. I knew you could get money, but you didn't. Sometimes people see more in us than we can see in ourselves. And that's a shame. It shows that you don't know who you are. And knowledge of self is important. That's how you know what you will and won't do. What you can and can't do." Then he paused. "I want you to read up on this nigga, Supreme Understanding. He wrote some of the best books I ever read. Helped me on my journey to knowledge of self. You got a month to read one of his books."

"You for real?" I asked, unable to see how a book was going to get me some money.

"Yeah, I'm serious. You can read, right?"

"Yeah. I got a GED. But what a book gotta do with gettin' money?"

"We gon' talk about that after you read the book. You got thirty days. And here," he said pulling a cell phone and bag with an off-white powder in it from his pocket. "This yo' new line. Only give this number to action. Keep yo' other phone for personal calls. You got ten names programmed in here. That's yo' clientele. Get to know them. They already got yo' number and they gonna be calling. This yo' product. Heroin. Diesel. Dog food. Boy. 25 grams. This ain't the best shit, but it's good. 80 a gram. I want 1500. I already cut it so all you gotta do is serve it. Weigh it up on this." He scooted up in the seat and pulled a digital scale from his back pocket. "Did you get yo' license yet?"

"Nah. But I signed up to take the test next week."

"Good. Make sure you get on that. They givin' Fed time for this shit. Without them L's, they can search the Lumi without consent. Yo' career gon' be over before it start."

"I'm on it," I said, taking the drugs, phone, and scale.

"The name of the game is longevity. Getting greedy will get you killed or put in a cell. Fly under the radar and stack yo' chips. Fuck tryna live like them rap niggas. But if you do get greedy, you gotta say fuck longevity and run it up and get out. I'ma give you the game, but I got plans with the family. Call me on yo' regular phone if you need anything. Get at me when you get that shit off. Love, boy."

Chapter 8

One month later

I made a thousand dollars the first night that I got the work and phone from Van. The following week I got my license and paid my debts to Tikka and the auto loan company. I had even read *Hustle and Win* by Supreme Understanding. Even though the author's name sounded like something out of a 1970's Blaxploitation movie, the information inside the book was A-1. It challenged everything I was taught and not taught about a man and his role to his loved ones. And once I started applying the information and talking about it with Van, I could feel my self-worth and self-esteem rising. Sometimes I would sit in the Lumi, smoke blunts, and read. The weed seemed to make what I was learning seem way deeper than it was. I would sit back for an hour thinking about one sentence. Now, a month later, I knew the old bum-ass Drayez was gone, replaced by a man on a mission to get money and never be taken advantage of again.

"See, a lotta niggas lie to they self, saying the reason they hustle is to feed the fam. That's almost as big a lie as the Europeans told our ancestors about the forty acres and a mule. Niggas don't hustle for they kids. They hustle for money, power, and respect. Yeah, the kids and family might reap the benefits of hustling, but I know from experience that hustling is about the hustler. The hoes that'll do anything to be wit' a nigga having gwap. Driving foreign. Poppin' bottles. Makin' it rain. The jewelry. Fashion. That's what it's all about, my nigga. 'Cause if it really was about taking care of the fam, niggas wouldn't be so quick to spend Twenty G's on a watch.100 G's on a car. Ten G's at the club just to have a good time. If it was about the fam, niggas would be puttin' up for they kids to go to college. Investing in shit that appreciates in value so they can pass it down through generations. Goin' to business class to learn how to handle finances. But how many niggas in the streets do that?"

I took a moment to think about niggas I'd ran across that was getting some kind of money. Dino, the weed man, had been hustling on the same block for years. Looked like he was going to be there until he got locked up, killed, or tired of hustling. I didn't know much about Smitty, my old plug, but he probably didn't invest or put away money. L-Dog could barely talk and he shot his family members so I was sure he robbed to support himself.

"I don't know nobody that think on that level," I admitted.

"I met two people. But these niggas was really eating and left the streets alone. But you look at these other money gettin' niggas - Black Mafia Family, Triple Beam Team, Zo Pound… them niggas was gettin' money and living that fast life. They had money, power, and respect. Even fear. And they couldn't see past that. Most niggas hustle because it's quick money, and we spend it as soon as we get it. Make you wonder if niggas really love money as much as they say. Think about it. If you really love money, why would you spend it as soon as you make it? How many niggas you know been hustling for years and still on the same block doin' the same shit?"

I thought about Dino.

"The only thing they probably did was change cars, clothes, and jewelry. Niggas hustle like it's a job. Like it's legit. Takin' penitentiary chances for a few G's. But you gotta ask yo'self if that little money and a few stories is worth five or ten years locked up?"

I did a year in prison for a three thousand dollars' worth of electronics. Hell nah, that wasn't worth it. But if I was ballin' like BMF, I might think twice. "How much money is we talkin' 'bout?"

Van looked like I just asked him what was 2 plus 2. "And that's the problem, my nigga. Listen, Drayez, and listen good. Time is more valuable than money."

I tried to connect the dots. Van seen my struggle.

"Bill Gates is paid, li'l brah. Billionaire. Money so long that he could spend a hunnit G's every day for the rest of his life and still have plenty money. The nigga's money is unlimited. But his time ain't."

Silence filled the car as I drove and thought about Van's words. We only had so many years until we died. I understood that I couldn't get back the year I did in RYOC. But if I had a billion dollars, a year in prison wouldn't be shit. "Yeah, I hear you, brah," I nodded.

"But you don't agree," he said, reading my mind. "And that's cool. You still young. Ain't really seen or did much. But before it's all over, it's gon' be a time in yo' life when you wish you could go back and do it all over. Just think about yo' daughter. Do you think she care about how much money you spend on her, or how much time you spend with her?"

I hadn't seen Draya in a month. A baby didn't understand how important it is to get money. She was happy in my arms playing the kissing game. "It don't matter to her how much money I got. She cares about the time."

"Exactly!" Van smiled.

The car got quiet again. Thinking about Draya opened a wound in my chest that ached for her. I needed to see my baby. I turned to Van to share how I felt, but the look on his face made me pause. "You good, brah?"

When Van looked at me, I seen a pain in his eyes that was hard to describe. He looked like the world that he held on his shoulders had crashed to the ground and exploded. Then he blinked a couple times and shook his head, and the look was gone.

"Fuck you talkin' 'bout, nigga? I'm good." He smiled. "Where the rest of that weed at?"

I tossed him the sack I had on my lap.

"Yeah. That's that good shit. C'mon, nigga. Let's hit the mall up and get you fitted."

I went shopping for the first time in months, spending most of the four G's I had stashed away. Van told me not to go for flash, but conservative. I ended up buying khakis, polos, and button up shirts. I even spent a few dollars on my baby since I planned on seeing her later. After the mall, I dropped Van off at home. He was a working man with a family, so he never stayed out late. I hated when my nigga left, but I understood. His family meant everything to him, and I respected that.

From Van's house, I drove over to Rayna's. I searched for her new nigga's truck as I parked. I didn't see it, but I called just to be sure.

"What, Drayez?" she answered with an attitude.

This was the first time I talked to her since I seen that nigga's dick in her mouth. I knew she would be bitter, but I didn't expect her to have an attitude. If anything, I should be mad. But I kept cool. "I wanna see Draya."

"Why, nigga? You can't do nothin' for her. You ain't seen her in a month, and—"

"I bought some shit for her and I got'cho money," I interrupted.

There was silence for a few moments.

"You got my money?"

Hearing how she calmed at the mention of money pissed me off. She didn't even mention Draya. Gold digging-ass bitch! "Yeah. I got the 800 and some stuff for my baby."

"Yeah. You can come over."

"I'm outside right now. Yo' nigga in there?"

"That's not my nigga. And he ain't here. Just me and the kids. You outside right now?"

"Yeah. I'm gettin' out the car."

By the time I grabbed the bags and got out of the car, Rayna was on the porch with Draya in her arms.

"Look at my baby girl!" I smiled, giving Rayna the bags and taking Draya. She started smiling, laughing, and cooing. And she had gotten bigger since the last time I seen her. Even Rayna's evil ass smiled at the reunion of me and my baby.

"Come in. You don't gotta be a stranger, Drayez."

When I walked in the house, all the kids looked happy to see me, even I'Yanna's little evil ass.

"I got the new Mortal Kombat. Wanna play?" Ja'Shawn asked.

"I'ma catch you another time, li'l man. I just came over to check on Draya."

"You don't gotta leave, Drayez," Rayna said.

"I got some shit to take care of," I lied, going in my pocket to get the money. "Here."

Rayna looked up from checking Draya's bags. When she seen the money, dollar signs shown in her eyes. "Thanks."

I nodded.

"So, um...where you stayin' at?" she fished.

"With Marie for now."

"Oh. You look like you doing good."

"I'm a'ight. You gotta go through somethin' to get to somethin'."

She didn't have a comeback and I didn't give her the time to think of one because it was time for me to go. "Look, I gotta hit it. Let me pick her up tomorrow. I ain't tryna be no deadbeat. I'ma do what I gotta do. I just needed some time to get my shit together."

"Uh, okay. I got some stuff to do tomorrow. Can you get her early?"

"Yeah," I nodded, giving Draya some kisses before handing her to Rayna. Draya started fussing. "What's going on, baby girl?" I asked, grabbing her again. "Daddy gotta go. But I'ma see you tomorrow. I promise."

She looked like she understood me and smiled.

"That's my baby," I said, kissing her one more time before giving her to Rayna.

I turned to leave, but Rayna stopped me.

"Drayez, you don't gotta leave."

I stared into her watery eyes, getting lost for a moment. I seen regret, sorrow, and what looked like love. Then her fucking and sucking that nigga flashed in my head and I became disgusted by the sight of my baby mama.

"Nah, I got some shit to do," I said before turning and leaving. Rayna followed me to the door. Then I thought about something I heard Van say and spun back to Rayna. "You know, real ain't standin' wit' a nigga and celebrating wit' him when he at the top. Real is standing next to a nigga and struggling with him when he at the bottom."

Another stupid look flashed on her face and I walked away before she could say another word.

***

When I left Rayna's house, I got a call from Chantele, Renae's friend. Since I had been on the grind and studying books, I didn't have time for females. But now that I shitted on Rayna and was feeling myself, I decided to have a little fun.

"What's good, shorty?"

"For a minute, I thought you was avoiding me."

"Nah, it ain't like that. I switched hustles and got caught up tryna get back," I explained, stepping into her apartment. It smelled like air freshener and was well kept. Black and white linoleum tile floors, plush blue suede furniture, pictures of her and family members hanging on the walls, and some kind of neo soul music playing from speakers I couldn't see.

"So, you telling me that if I wouldn't have called you, you woulda called me?" she asked, giving me a green-eyed stare.

"Yeah, I woulda called. Eventually."

"Lyin' ass," she laughed. "Sit down. You want something to drink?"

"Yeah. But first I gotta know if them eyes real."

She blinked a couple of times. "Got 'em from my mama."

Definitely a plus. I never fucked a bitch with green eyes and Chantele was looking good, too. She wore a T-shirt with BOSSY on the front, jeans, and white heels. She had a slim body with a nice ass. And she was tall. I couldn't wait to get them long legs on my shoulders.

"That's what's up. What you got to drink?"

"Ciroc. The peach kind. And it's some Tang in there."

"Buss out that Tang, baby. I ain't with that fruity shit."

While she was grabbing the drinks, I looked around to see where the music was coming from. I couldn't find a radio or speakers. Then I heard footsteps coming from the hallway. Desiré walked into the living room wearing a smile, her big-ass titties leading the way.

"Hey, Drayez!"

"Desiré, what's good, baby?" I smiled, taking all of her in. And when I say all of her, I meant ALL of her.

Desiré was a healthy girl - not fat or chubby, but juicy. The boys down south called her big-boned. Her body reminded me of Jill Scott, the R&B singer. Big thighs, wide hips, and her titties... I didn't think I could guess what size they were. Looked like she needed to wear two bras to hold them. She was rocking a cream blouse that showed way too much cleavage and tight blue jeans. Her hair was long and curled like Beyoncé, getting a lot of help from a horse or two. And those lips... Man, I wanted to kiss her.

"You got it. I was wondering when you were going to get your shit together and kick it with us again. Look like you're doing good. Are you back now? Got that green?"

"Nah, I don't fuck with the weed no more. But I got this," I said, pulling a sack from my pocket.

"Damn. Now I don't have a reason to fake call you," she laughed.

"You don't gotta fake call me. We grown."

Her eyes turned to sexy little slits. She was about to say something, but Chantele walked it with bottles of Ciroc, Tanqueray, and three glasses.

"Hell, yeah! I was about to ask you if you had some weed."

"I keep a sack and a wrap."

"Good. Pour some drinks. I'ma be right back."

Desiré poured us some drinks. "Here you go."

"Who is this singing and where the speakers?" I asked.

"The speakers behind the table. And this is India Arie. What you know about her?"

"Nothing. I ain't big into R&B," I admitted, taking a sip of Tang.

"This my girl. She deep, ain't she, Chantele?" Desiré asked.

Chantele plopped down on the couch next to me. "Hell yeah. Sit back and get high with this bitch and she'll take you around the world."

And that's what we did. I never listened to India Arie's music before, but I was starting to like her. An hour later I found it hard to concentrate on the lyrics because Chantele's constant rubbing on my thigh had my dick hard.

"You still fuckin' with that crazy bitch?" she asked, her green eyes low and red.

"What crazy bitch?" I laughed.

"We know about yo' crazy baby mama," Desiré said.

"Nah, that shit been over for a minute. Love ain't real for some people. They only love what you can do for 'em. And as soon as you stop doing it, that shit over," I explained, catching Desiré's eye. She felt me.

"Good. 'Cause I been waiting to do this since I met you," Chantele said, grabbing my face and sticking her tongue down my throat, kissing me aggressively.

Desiré cleared her throat loudly. "Uh-uh!"

We stopped kissing and looked in her direction. She looked embarrassed and uncomfortable.

"Uh, I'm about to leave. Chantele, I'll call you tomorrow."

I don't know why, but I didn't want Desiré to leave. "Wait. Hold on. Don't leave."

"Why? Look like y'all busy," she said, a hint of jealousy in her tone.

"Because I want you to chill."

Something flickered in Desiré's eyes. "And do what?"

"My girl is a prude, Drayez. I love her, but she stuck up." Chantele said, ready to kick her friend out and get it poppin'.

"We can do whatever we wanna do. We grown."

Desiré looked undecided, like her body was telling her one thing and mind saying something else. I knew the weed and liquor had her buzzing good and released inhibitions, so I decided to be bold. I got up from the couch and walked over to kiss her. Desiré's lips were soft, her kiss tender. It felt real. Chantele got up, walked over to us, got on her knees and started pulling down my pants and underwear. When I stepped out of my boxers, the women looked at my package. Desiré was in awe. Chantele looked like she had fallen in love. I went for Desiré's blouse. It came off and her titties was as big as watermelons. The thing she wore for a bra looked like a safety harness. After wrestling the bra off, I took Desiré over to the couch and started sucking them big-ass titties. She moaned and purred like a cat, running her fingers through my fro and rubbing my face.

"I love me a big-ass dick!" Chantele said, getting naked and joining us.

She grabbed my dick and tried to swallow it. I knew Rayna gave good head, but Chantele was ten times better. She gagged, slurped, sucked my balls. When she put 'em in her mouth and started humming, I almost busted a nut. Somehow I got the rest of Desiré's clothes off and started sucking her pink meaty pussy. The noises she made sounded as good as India Arie music. She ran her hands through my hair and grinded on my face until she came. And she was a screamer! When Chantele seen that her friend got hers, she pulled me onto the floor. Before I knew what was happening, she squatted down over me and sat on my face.

"It's my turn now. Suck my pussy, nigga!"

While I sucked her clit, Desiré got between my legs and tried to give me head. After what Chantele just did to my dick, all Desiré could do was keep me hard. Chantele let out a few grunts and came. Instead of getting up, she smashed her pussy on my face. I could feel cum dripping down my face, but she didn't move. A few minutes later, she came again.

"Oh shit! Oh yeah, nigga! Keep suckin'. Keep suckin'!"

I kept at it until she came a third time. When she didn't get up, I pushed her ass off of me so I could catch my breath.

"Damn, girl!" I breathed, wiping my mouth. "You don't play no games."

She looked down at me with lust-glazed eyes. "I'ma get mine."

I was about to get up and fuck Desiré, but Chantele wasn't having that. She grabbed a rubber from her pants and put it on me. Then she impaled herself on my sword. Her pussy was snug, wet, and deep. Desire moved to the couch to sit back and watch.

"Yeah, Drayez! Mmmhhh! I told you I can take all this dick!" Chantele moaned as she rode me. She fucked me hard and fast. I busted my nut, but she hadn't had enough. She changed the rubber and rode me some more. After she came, she got up. I was about to see if I could finally fuck Desiré. She was laying on the couch fingering herself.

"Ah nah, nigga! Come hit it from the back," Chantele said, bending over the couch and spreading her cheeks.

I fucked her from the back, digging her guts out, and she still wanted more. I busted my second nut and somehow she got me hard again and put on another condom. We fucked all over the living room while Desiré looked on in awe. I busted a third nut and this time Chantele couldn't get me back hard.

"Y'all so nasty," Desiré laughed.

"Man, if I woulda knew Chantele got down like that, I woulda popped a Viagra," I breathed.

Chantele was rolling up a blunt, looking at my dick like she couldn't wait for it to get back hard. "Good lookin' niggas with big dicks is hard to find. When I find one, I take advantage. You even got Desiré's prissy ass to join in. I seen you tryna suck that dick, girl!"

Desiré turned a shade darker, blushing. "I can't believe I just had a threesome."

"That wasn't a threesome. When his dick get back hard, I'ma show you a threesome," Chantele promised.

"I'ma have to pass," Desiré said, grabbing her clothes.

I felt cheated. "Hold on. Where you going?"

"I got school in the morning."

"Told you she was prissy," Chantele laughed, lighting the blunt.

"Ain't you too old for school?" I asked, wanting her to stay so I could fuck. I know she had some fiya-ass pussy.

"I'm a teacher," she said, her titties jiggling like crazy as she shimmied into her jeans.

"Keep all them li'l boys lusting after them big titties," Chantele joked.

I watched those big-ass titties as she put on her bra. My dick stirred. Chantele seen it.

"Get outta here school girl. I got my own class to run," Chantele said, licking her lips.

Chapter 9

"I'm tellin' yo' ass, Marie! I ain't takin' this shit no more!"

I opened my eyes and blinked a couple times, listening to Keith and Marie's latest fight. They did this every couple of days. It was a ritual. Like sex.

"I don't know why he keep coming back after she put him out," Tikka said, flopping down on the couch across from me. She looked tired and barely awake. Staying up late to study did that. And to make it worse, her room was next door to Marie's.

"What time is it?" I asked, going for my phone.

"Too early for this shit."

Marie's screams floated into the living room. "You gon' take whatever I tell you to take. You don't run shit. This my house!"

"I can't wait until I turn eighteen," Tikka said. "We should get a house together."

"And how you gon' pay yo' part of the rent?"

"I'ma get a job. Part time when school in, full time during break. Plus, you got some money and can cover me if I fall. Ain't that's what big brothers are for?" she asked, her lips stretching into a smile.

It didn't sound like a bad plan. We both needed a place to live and could kill two birds with one stone. "Tell you what. Get a job, 'cause we gon need to have a legit source of income on the lease. We both gon' be outta here before you turn eighteen."

"I turn eighteen in a couple months."

"I know when yo' birthday is. Just get a job. This argument sound like it's about to get outta hand, so I gotta put my big brother cape on."

The closer I got to Marie's room, the louder their voices became. When I got to the door, Keith was sitting on the bed looking like a man on death row. Marie was pacing the room, talking shit and working herself up. Neither one of them noticed me in the doorway.

"I don't know why I keep puttin' up with yo' funky no-good ass. I shoulda fucked yo' friend, Aaron. He always lookin' at my ass. Least he got a real job."

"Aaron don't want yo' crazy ass. Don't nobody wanna live wit'cho crazy ass but me. Always talkin' 'bout money. You need to get a job."

I couldn't help but laugh. Score one for Keith.

"I'm crazy 'cause you make me crazy," Marie accused.

"Didn't nobody make you crazy. You was born like that," Keith laughed.

Marie stopped pacing and got in his face. "You think something funny, bitch?"

Keith tried to stand up, but Maria slapped him, making him fall on the bed. He got up quicker than I thought he would. Surprised Marie too, because she froze up. Keith picked her up and threw her on the bed. Then he cocked his arm back, about to knock Marie out.

"Don't hit my mama, nigga!" I yelled, stepping into the room.

Keith's arm stopped in midair.

When Marie seen me, she got bold. "Get the fuck off me, nigga!" she screamed, kicking and swinging at him wildly.

"Crazy bitch," Keith mumbled, leaving the room.

"I know you didn't just call me a bitch!" Marie yelled, getting up to chase him.

I grabbed her. Why did I do that?

"Let me go, Drayez!" she screamed, scratching and kicking at me.

Before I knew what I had done, I picked Marie up and slammed her on the floor. Shit! I couldn't believe I just slammed my mama! I stood in shock, watching as she crawled to her knees.

"You bitch-ass muthafucka! Put cho hands on me!" She mugged me, climbing to her feet.

"What'chu do?" Keith asked, appearing at my side and looking like he wanted to fight me.

Being under both their hostile stares made me nervous. For a minute, I thought they might jump me and didn't know what to do, so I snapped. "I'm tired of y'all mu'fuckas always fighting and shit.

Got Tikka n'em all in the middle of y'all bullshit. Y'all act like kids. Fuck wrong wit' ch'all? Keith, grow some nuts, nigga. Quit lettin' Marie talk to you like that. Quit being a bitch-ass nigga. Check her mu'fuckin' ass or quit fuckin' with her." I turned to Marie. "And quit puttin' yo' hands on niggas. If I wasn't here, Keith was gon' beat cho ass. This nigga bussin' his ass for you. Fool-ass nigga love you but you gon' fuck around and run him off. And I'm sorry for slamming you, but you ain't finna be hittin' me. I ain't Keith."

The room got so quiet that I could hear Tikka breathing in the hallway. Keith was looking at me like I was a superhero. Never mind that I called him a bitch. I had checked Marie, something not many people were able to do. And Marie was giving me two different looks. One was proud, like she realized her boy had become a man. I checked her and told the truth. She respected that. The other look was that "mama eye". I had slammed her on the floor and cursed her out, and she was mad about that.

"Yo' muthafuckin' ass ain't finna be comin' in my house and cursing me out and puttin' yo' hands on me!" she snapped.

"My bad, Marie. But you ain't finna be hittin' me."

She stepped closer. "I do what I want. I'm yo' mama! If you don't like the way I act in my house, then you can get the fuck out."

We had a stare down. The proud look for her son look was gone. The dominating woman that put fear in the hearts of niggas was back, and she wasn't backing down. She wanted to win this round, so I let her have it

I left Marie's house and drove around, thinking about what happened. I was changing. Everyone around me could see it. I took to heart the teachings from Supreme's book, searching and challenging myself. And everything that I learned from Van was the icing on the cake.

The ringing of my phone pulled me from my thoughts. It was action.

"Hello?"

"Dray, how you doing, buddy?"

It was Mike, a 40-something-year-old white man that loved to get high. He owned a bar. Every time he called, he spent 500 or better.

"I'm good, Mike. Out and about."

"So good to hear, man. Think you could come see me? I'm at the bar."

"ETA thirty minutes."

"Cool. Thanks, man. Over and out."

I pulled up to Jake's Pub and parked near the front door. The bar might as well have had a "whites only" sign out front because I never seen a black body in the joint.

"Yo, Dray!" Mike called when I walked in.

"'Sup, Mike?"

"Man, I've been wanting to say that since I seen the NWA movie. Great movie. I didn't offend you, did I?"

I laughed. "C'mon, man. I'm not that sensitive. I can take a joke."

"Cool, man. You're cool as shit, brother. We should hang some time. Let's go to my office."

His office was at the back of the bar. After closing the door, he dropped five crispy blue face hundreds on the desk. "You got my regular dose?"

When I pulled the work from my pocket, he looked happier than a dyke in a woman's prison. "Hell yeah, Dray! I needed this so fucking bad. I gotta go kick some people out of one of my houses. Fuckers keep having excuses for not having my rent money. I don't have time for that shit. You wouldn't happen to need a house, do you?"

Talk about perfect timing! "Actually, I do."

He stopped fondling his dope to look up at me. "Seriously?"

"Hell yeah. Me and my little sister. She about to start college. Wanna be a lawyer and Mom's house getting cramped."

He looked relieved. "Shit, when are you ready to move in? I can have those fuckers out in a week."

"In a week."

After having a couple of shots and kicking it with Mike and a drunk white chick, I hopped in the Lumi feeling good as hell. Things were coming together fast. I was making money, looking good, and now I was about to have my own shit. From the bar, I went to my nigga Vic's house. He answered the door looking like he just woke up.

"'Sup with this early shit, nigga?" He yawned.

"Nigga, it's 10 o'clock. Early bird gets the first worm."

"Fuck a worm, nigga. Betta have some weed," he mumbled, locking the door behind me.

"Know I keep that supa dupa," I said, pulling out a blunt as I sat down. "What's up with you, though? What you got going on today?"

"Shit. Just got up. Wondering when this bitch gon' bring her ass back home and cook breakfast."

"I see I'm right on time. A nigga hungry as fuck."

Vic gave me a sideways look. "My bitch don't cook for you, nigga."

I lit the blunt. "This one hitter quitter say she do."

"Since you started gettin' a li'l money, yo' negotiating skills got better. And yo' choice in weed got you a plate."

"When she coming back?" I asked, passing him the blunt.

"I don't know. Her and Desiré made some runs."

Hearing Desiré's name brought back memories of our two-and-a-half-some. "Ole Desiré!" I smiled.

Vic gave me a look. "You fucked Desiré, nigga?"

"Nah. I didn't get the chance. I had somethin' like a threesome with her and Chantele."

Vic's eyes popped. "You bullshitting! You got Desiré's thick ass to have a threesome?"

"Nah, not really. Chantele's dick hungry ass wouldn't let me. I ate the pussy and sucked on them big-ass titties though."

Vic smiled, exhaling smoke from his nose. "This some good-ass weed. But you still a sucka, busta, and hoe trusta. How you gon' eat the pussy but not fuck?"

"I told you. Chantele, nigga."

He grinned like he knew what I was talking about. "That bitch give super head, don't she?"

I was surprised. "You fucked yo' bitch's friend?"

"Yeah. A couple times. We had threesome's and shit. Can't get Desiré to go though. She got some big-ass titties. And I bet that pussy good."

The front door opening made us look up. Renae and Desiré walked in the house carrying bags. When Desiré noticed me, excitement flashed in her eyes.

"'Sup, y'all?" I nodded.

"Hey, Drayez!" the women sang.

Vic faked irritation. "Only person y'all see is Drayez?"

"Quit whining, Vic. Hi," Desiré laughed.

"I see you too much," Renae cracked.

"Yeah, holla at the king of the castle. Now c'mon baby. Let's hit this kitchen and get this stove moving. I'm hungry as fuck!"

Vic handed me the blunt as him and his girl went to the kitchen. Desiré shed her coat and sat next to me. She wore a low-cut blouse that had them big-ass titties showing and she smelled good, like flowers and waterfalls.

"So, what you been up to, Drayez?" she asked, taking my blunt.

"Shit. Just tryna make it. When I was in school, I don't think my teachers smoked weed. And they didn't dress like this," I said, looking at her cleavage.

"You don't know what your teachers did after school. And I don't wear revealing clothes to work. This is how I dress after work. My first grade boys already be ogling me. They li'l bodies would go crazy if I wore this."

"I agree. I'm a grown man and you got my body going crazy."

"Boy, stop!" She laughed, pushing me. "I see you made it out of Chantele's house alive. I was worried about you."

"Yo' girl is a crazy freak. I thought she was gon' kill me."

"That girl is something else." Then she lowered her voice and got serious. "I hope you don't think I'm like that because of what happened."

"What you mean?"

"What we did. I don't get down like that. I think it was the liquor and the weed. And you. Chantele is sexually fluid. She does what makes her feel good and who makes her feel good. I'm not like that. I'm reserved. If I don't got a man, I don't do it."

I stared in Desiré's deep brown eyes, trying to see if she was lying. I had a hard time trusting females. But Desiré kept a straight face, so I played it cool. "Okay. I hear you. I won't judge you by the company you keep or because you was tipsy. I know you think I'm irresistible, so I'ma just hang my hat on that."

She laughed again. "Boy, you is too crazy."

"So, what is it gon' take for us to finish what we started?" I asked, watching as she wrapped those juicy lips around the blunt and inhale. When she moved the blunt away from her lips, a little smoke trail escaped. She opened her mouth, letting out a cloud of smoke before sucking it back in. Watching her smoke weed was sexy.

"I just told you I ain't like Chantele. And why you watching me like that? You got stalker in your DNA?"

"I guess when it comes to you I do. But you still didn't answer my question."

She took another puff of the blunt. I watched her.

"How old are you, Drayez?"

"Twenty-four."

"I'm thirty and past the age of flings."

"Who said it gotta be a fling?"

She gave me a long stare. "Tell me what you want, Drayez."

"Nothing that you don't give willingly. Seem like you got morals and principles. I respect that. You wanna kick it, we can kick it. I got a taste of you and liked it. Now I want more."

"You sound older than you are. Did you go to college?"

"Yep. M.A.T.C."

"Milwaukee or Madison Area Technical College?"

"Neither. I was maintaining at the crib."

She busted out laughing again. "You are so silly!"

The ringing of my phone interrupted our moment. It was action. Party over. Time to get money. "Tell Vic I had to hit it. I'ma call you later."

I had just hopped in the Lumi when my phone rang again. It was Rayna.

"What up?"

"Something wrong with Draya!" she screamed.

The panic in her voice scared the shit out of me. "What you mean? What's wrong with her?"

"I don't know. She having a hard time breathing. Her lips turning blue. I'm about to get in the ambulance right now. We on our way to Children's Hospital."

I hopped in the Lumi and sped two blocks over to Rayna's house only to find the ambulance already gone. I punched the pedal to the floor, ignoring most of the traffic laws as I zoomed through traffic. I caught up to the ambulance and followed them to the hospital. When they stopped at the emergency room entrance, I jumped out the car and ran to the ambulance. They were just pulling the stretcher from the back. Draya was strapped to the bed with a breathing mask on her face.

"What happened?" I asked the paramedic.

"Sir, we need you to move," the woman said.

"That's her daddy," Rayna spoke up.

The other paramedic spoke up. "She's having a hard time breathing. We think it might be a possible allergic reaction. We've given her a shot of Benadryl. The doctor will be able to tell you more."

Seeing my daughter sick was fucking with my head. Her eyes were closed, face swollen, and lips blue. And she looked fragile. Like if the stretcher hit a bump, she would bounce and shatter. I wished I could help her, but there wasn't a damn thing I could do.

When they wheeled the stretcher into the emergency room, a short Asian doctor looked her over while asking us a bunch of questions. I let Rayna do the talking and watched them work. About ten minutes later, the doctor got our attention.

"Sir, ma'am, it looks like your daughter is allergic to peanut butter. We're going to give her some medicine and keep her overnight and run some more tests."

When the doctor walked away, I wanted to bust Rayna in her shit. Bitch almost killed my baby. As I watched the nurses work, Van's words about time and money came to my mind. I understood now. Time was worth more than money. Had Draya been sick and on the verge of death, I would've given every penny that I could make in my life to heal her. Time is more than hours in a day. Time is the currency of life.

We spent the night in the hospital and were allowed to take Draya home the next day. I was happy that my baby recovered so quickly. By mid-day, she was back to being her usual cute laughing self. I was on the floor playing with her when Rayna got my attention.

"I was scared as hell last night."

"Me too," I admitted. "I was willin' to give up every dollar I could make in my whole life to have her get better."

"Me too. Don't none of the other kids got allergies so I didn't know what was going on. I'm glad you came to the hospital."

"I told you I wasn't gon' be a deadbeat."

"I know. And I heard that plenty of times from my other kids' daddies. I'm glad you showing and proving."

"That's what I do. Show and prove. Ain't that right, baby girl?" I said, kissing Draya. She laughed and gave me some baby talk."

"I'm sorry, Drayez."

I looked up at Rayna. "For what?"

"For everything. For not being more patient. For kicking you out and almost stabbing you. And..." She paused, looking away. "For Cartier."

That was his name.

"I don't know what I was thinking doing that. I was mad at you and wanted to hurt you. I wish I could go back and change everything. But I can't. And I'm sorry."

I gave a nod before turning my attention back to Draya.

Rayna got an attitude. "You not gon' say nothing?"

"What you want me to say? That I forgive you? I don't. You sucked a nigga's dick in front of me and tried to kill me over 800 dollars when I spent racks on you and yo' kids. You think sorry supposed to make shit good?"

She looked hurt. "Tell me how to fix it."

"You can't. Do you and I'ma do me."

"That's it? A whole year and it's over?"

"Yeah. You did this. Them lines can't be uncrossed."

She stared at me, eyes pleading for another chance. I turned my attention back to my baby. Rayna got the hint and left the room.

I ended up spending the whole day at Rayna's house with Draya. I lied to my action and told them I was out. My daughter was more important than money.

"You gon' stay for dinner?" Rayna asked later on.

I hated her guts, but I was hungry as fuck. "Yeah. What you making?"

"Pork chops, spaghetti, and corn bread."

"Yeah. Need me to do anything?"

"No. You spending the night, too?"

I searched her face for a sign of something. Hope, strings attached, some kind of expectation or catch. I wasn't sure if she was tryna trick me or just being nice. "Yeah. I'ma take the couch, if that's cool."

After eating, I fell asleep on the couch with Draya in my arms. Sometime during the night, Rayna came and got her. The next morning I was awakened by the kids leaving for school. I had just fallen back to sleep when I felt wetness around my dick. My eyes shot open. Rayna's head was bobbing up and down, her lips wrapped around my pole. I wanted to push her head away, but I couldn't. Shit felt too good. I lay back and closed my eyes. When her mouth stopped sucking, I looked up. She was straddling my lap to ride me. I thought about pushing her ass on the floor, but when I felt the inside of her pussy, I relaxed.

"Oh, yeah Drayez! Mmmhhh!" she moaned, getting into a nice rhythm.

When she bent down to kiss me, images of her sucking Cartier's dick flashed in my head. I wanted to spit and throw up at the same time. I pushed her off me so hard that she flew in the air and landed on the floor. I couldn't shake the image of her and that nigga from my head. It felt like I was reliving it. I wanted to snap. I remembered how she screamed his name while he hit it from the back. Fake screams. I wanted to make her scream for real.

"Get on them knees," I ordered.

She moved slowly. I got behind her, grabbing the back of her neck roughly and forcing her face into the carpet. Then I shoved my dick into her pussy as hard as I could. Felt skin tear, mine and hers.

"Aahhhhh!" she screamed, trying to scoot away.

I grabbed her hips, scooting behind her, humping away.

"Dr-Drayez, stop! Stop! Please, stop!" she screamed.

I didn't even hear her. I was in the zone, trying to go deeper. When she realized she couldn't get away, she fell onto her stomach. I dropped all my weight on top of her and gave her shit the business! She screamed and wiggled until my dick slipped out.

"Stop, Drayez! Get off me!"

I wrapped one of my arms around her neck in a choke hold, using my free hand to put my dick back in. She closed her legs, but I forced them open just enough to get my dick between her legs. When I pushed, Rayna sucked in a deep breath and the cry that came out didn't sound human. I had forced my dick into her ass. Instead of pulling out, I pushed harder and went deeper. I kept forcing until I was all the way in. And then I went ham. Rayna screamed like she was being tortured, but I didn't care. I punished her ass. Then all of a sudden her ass got super wet. My dick slipped in and out easily.

And then my phone rang.

Hearing the sound brought me back to reality. I stopped fucking Rayna and looked down at her. Tears, slob, and snot covered my arm. I was instantly disgusted. I climbed off of her and seen the blood covering my lower half. Rayna got up and ran away, blood and shit dripping down her legs.

What the fuck did I just do? I had snapped, fucked around, and raped my baby mama! A few months ago I would've never done no shit like this. I had changed. But now I wasn't sure if it was for the better.

Chapter 10

Wasn't nothing like having my own shit.

A month had gone by since we moved in the house that Mike owned and I couldn't be happier. I didn't have to listen to Marie and Keith's arguing. It didn't matter what time I came in the house. And most importantly, couldn't nobody put me out. I did the putting out. This was my shit. My name was on the lease. The house was a three bedroom Victorian on the northwest side of Milwaukee. The neighborhood was filled with working class home owners. I didn't have to worry about niggas being posted up or trap house shootings.

"I can't believe you reading a book," Tikka said.

I looked up from reading *The Autobiography of Malcolm X* and seen my little sister standing in my bedroom doorway holding a letter. "You ain't the only one that reads, nerd. What's that?"

"I just got a letter from Tracy. She wants us to put money on our phones so she can call us. I figured since you the man now, you can give me some money to hook our phones up."

"Yeah, I got it. Grab it out of my pants. Damn, I feel bogus. I haven't talked to sis in years."

"You are bogus," Tikka said as she grabbed the money from my pocket. "I'm the only one been keeping up with her. She mad at everybody for not showing her love. She been gone seven years and nobody wrote her but me."

"Yeah, I guess I am bogus. When you write her back, tell her my bad. I don't got time to write, but let her know I'ma keep some money on the phone. Matter fact, grab 200 more and send it to her. I know how that shit feel to be locked up, and that should keep her for a month or two."

"I want to visit her one of these days. You should come with me."

"How you gon' get to Taycheeda and you don't got a car?"

"But you do. And now that we on solid ground, we should show our big sister some love. Let her know that she got family out here that love her."

"Yeah, we gon' have to get up there to see her. Tell her to send us some visiting forms."

"We already on her visiting list."

"Since when? I never filled out a form."

"I did it years ago. For the whole family."

"You know forgery is a crime, right?"

"If showing my sister some love is a crime, lock me up."

I shook my head. "You too smart for yo' own damn good."

"So I've heard." She smiled before walking away.

I sat back and thought about my big sister. Seven years had gone by in the blink of an eye. She was only twenty when she got sent up and hadn't had the chance to experience life. Tracy got thirty years and didn't even pull the trigger. The police killed her nigga and charged her with murder. And not only was she being punished by the system, she was also being punished by her family because we didn't show love. Outta sight, outta mind. I was going to show sis love. For real.

***

"Damo, what's good, nigga?" I smiled, climbing from the Lumi.

Damo was a tall albino nigga that I met at the bar a couple weeks ago. I was buying drinks when he approached to let me know some niggas across the room was whispering about me. Turned out to be a case of mistaken identity and the shit got squashed before it could hit the fan. But Damo showed he was a good nigga by letting me know the move. I bought him a drink and we kicked it. I found out he hustled heroin and the rest was history.

"What up, Yez?"

"You got it, boss. What you doin' on this side of town? I didn't know you got down on the Treys."

"I don't. I'm just tryna catch some paper. This nigga Vel act like he tryna catch so I was gon' cop from you and get my middle man on. But this nigga still ain't rode down yet. If he on some fuck shit, I'ma pop his ass," he said, touching his waist.

I got a little nervous. “You know I ain’t wit’ that drama.”

“This ain’t got shit to do wit’chu, Yez. This on me. You got that work?”

I thought about lying to Damo. All of a sudden I didn’t trust him. But I couldn’t show fear. Street niggas could smell that shit. If he wanted to lose a good plug over ten grams, that was on him.

“You want me to wait with you or get with you later?” I asked, handing him the sack.

“You know I ain’t with that front shit. I know the ten crack commandments. Just post up with me for a minute. If he don’t show, I’ma cop it myself.”

“A’ight. I don’t like fuckin’ wit’ these niggas over here. They shiesty. Glad you got that burner.”

“I don’t leave home without my shit. Carry this bitch like it’s my ID. Rather be judged by 12 than carried by 6.”

“I sold my shit to get back on. I really ain’t with that pistol play anyway.”

Damo looked at me like I disrespected him. “You betta get you anotha one, nigga! Niggas’ll burn yo’ ass for a hunnit dollars. If you gettin’ money, you gotta have that heat. Can’t get caught slippin’ like that, brah.”

He talked about guns and shooting niggas like it wasn’t shit. “You ever pop a nigga?”

He laughed. “Yeah. A couple niggas. I started playin’ wit’ heat when I was a li’l nigga. First time I popped a nigga, I was like fourteen. Went to Lincoln Hills for that shit. Bitch-ass nigga told.”

“Damn, that’s fucked up.” I laughed.

“There that nigga go.”

I looked up as a green Lexus with tinted windows turned onto the block. It parked behind the Lumi and two niggas got out. The driver was a chubby brown-skinned nigga with braids and a thick beard. The passenger was short, skinny, and baldheaded, with gold teeth.

“’Sup, Vel?” Damo greeted him, shaking the chubby nigga’s hand.

"What it do, Damo? You got that work?" Vel asked, looking to me quickly.

"Right here."

Vel took the dope and examined it like a jeweler did diamonds. His passenger didn't seem interested in the transaction, but watched me and Damo.

"This ain't ten grits. And it's brown," Vel complained.

Damo laughed. "Quit playin'."

"C'mon, fam. Knock off a hunnit."

I chuckled, about to speak up, but Damo beat me to it.

"You know the numbers, my nigga. And it's all there. Take it or leave it."

Vel mugged Damo. "I'ma take it," he said, slipping the dope in his pocket and reaching for his waist.

Damo reacted quickly, my nigga's hand becoming a blur. Before Vel could get his gun out, Damo pulled out a big-ass black pistol and shot the jacker twice in the stomach. Vel went down. The other nigga put his hands up, backing away. Damo shot him in the chest. By the time the nigga with the gold teeth hit the ground, I was already jumping in the Lumi.

"Bitch-ass nigga!" Damo cursed, reaching down and taking Vel's pistol and the dope. "Here you go, Yez."

"That's you, my nigga!" I called, speeding away.

Visions of a jail cell flashed in my head. I didn't know if them niggas died and I didn't want to stay around to find out. But the one thing I did know: Damo was a beast! And he was loyal. I gave him the dope as a reward. Niggas like him were hard to find. When I got home, I parked the Lumi in the garage, knowing it was the last time I would drive it.

***

"He put 'em down like that? In broad day?" Van asked, eyes wide with amusement.

"Yeah, my nigga. Looked like some shit outta a western movie. The nigga Vel was already pulling his shit out, but he was too slow.

Damo got down on both them niggas. He tried to give me the work back, but I told him to keep it."

"Damn, that li'l nigga sound savage. I'da let him keep that shit too. You need loyal niggas that a pull that trigger on the team. You might have to get rid of the Lumi though. Fuck with them rentals until you buy something new."

"I was thinkin' the same shit. I need to find somebody to rent one for me."

"'Sup with yo' baby mama, nigga?"

I had to look away. "We ain't on good terms."

"What happened, nigga?"

"Man, Van," I paused, trying to find the right words to explain what happened between me and Rayna. "She fucked me over and I fucked her over."

"What she do, burn you or somethin'?" He laughed.

"You remember when I was fucked up a couple months ago at Vic's crib?"

"Yeah. You was acting like the world was finna blow up and shit. I thought you was finna crawl in a hole and die."

"Yeah, well, seeing her sucking and fucking a nigga in my face had me fucked up. I walked in the house and seen her in action."

His eyes bugged. "You bullshitting!"

"Nah. And they didn't even stop."

Van looked blown away. "Damn, my nigga. Hoes ain't shit. So how you get her back? You fucked her sister or something?"

I rubbed my hands across my face. "Man, I snapped. One night I spent the night and she started fuckin' me while I was asleep. I remembered her fuckin' that nigga and snapped. Threw her on the floor and fucked her in the ass til she was bleeding and shitting all over."

Van just looked at me. He didn't talk for about ten seconds. "You busted open her ass, my nigga?"

"I just snapped. I was in the zone and wanted to hurt that bitch."

Van looked like he couldn't believe what he heard. "Don't ever tell nobody that story. Ever. You snapped, my nigga. You probably fucked her ass up for life," he laughed.

I laughed too.

"But fuck that shit. She got what she got. Work on gettin' that rental. Holla at Mike. He a good dude. I gotta piss. Bust that work down for me. Remember what I told you: 2 to 1 with that lactose. Mix it good."

While Van was in the bathroom, I poured the heroin on a plate and started measuring the lactose.

"What you doing?" Tikka asked, popping into the kitchen.

"What it look like?"

She stood next to me and watched me whip. "What is that?"

"Heroin."

"Can't believe people get high off that stuff. I'm hungry. Can you take me to get something to eat?"

"I can't use my car. Order something or ask Van to take you."

"Ask me what?" Van asked, walking in the kitchen.

"C-can you take me to get something to eat," Tikka stuttered.

I glanced at my little sister. She looked nervous and intimidated. Was she crushing on Van?

"I got you, lil sis. Gotta keep a healthy appetite when you studying. Feed the brain while you feed the mind. Heard you wanna be a lawyer."

"Yeah. I-I wanna help get my big sister out."

"You hear that, Dray? Sis on top of her shit. C'mon, counselor. Let's go put somethin' in that stomach. It's on me."

***

I got up with Mike the next day to grab a rental. I copped a black 2015 Nissan Maxima with tinted windows.

As soon as I pulled off the lot, I got a call from Chantele. She wanted to see me later that night. I agreed without hesitation. I was looking forward to some more top and good pussy.

After hustling the day away, I made it to her house at a little after 11 o'clock that night. When I walked up to her apartment, I could hear music playing. I knocked on the door ready to fuck.

"Who is it?" she called.

"Drayez."

When the door opened, I could tell she was already tipsy and she looked surprised to see me. "What's up, Dray? What you doing over here?"

"You called me earlier and told me to come over. You good?"

She thought for a moment. "Oh, I forgot. Damn. I kinda made other plans."

Shit pissed me off. 0 to 100 real quick! "You already got a nigga in there?"

"C'mon, Drayez. Don't do the jealous thing, baby."

I looked at her like she was stupid. "Jealous? Nigga, is you crazy? I can fuck any bitch I want. I just don't like for mu'fuckas to waste my time. I coulda made other plans."

"Ay, Chantele! Close the door and come back over here!" a nigga called.

"Hold on, Snoop. I'm handling something," she called over her shoulder. "I'm sorry, Dray. I got high and forgot about you. I'ma make it up to you. Don't be mad."

"Don't be mad! Bitch, it's 11 o'clock at night and you got me out here lookin' stupid. Fuck you mean don't be mad?"

She frowned, her green eyes turning dark. "You betta watch that bitch shit, nigga. I ain't no bitch. And I ain't yo' bitch. Jealous-ass nigga, get out yo' feelings. I fuck who I wanna fuck. I pay my own bills and buy my own shit. You don't own me and I don't owe you shit. Just 'cause we fucked don't mean you got rights. You ain't the only nigga I'm fuckin'. I know I suck good dick, and if you mad 'cause I ain't suckin' yours tonight, oh well. You betta go home and jack off."

She slammed the door before I could say another word.

"Punk-ass bitch."

***

"Why do I gotta wear a blindfold?" Tikka asked from the backseat.

"Because it's a surprise," I said. We was in the Maxima. Me, her, and Van.

"You only turn eighteen once, lil sis. You gotta make it special, and me and Dray gon' make sure you remember this for the rest of yo' life," Van said.

I was still surprised that my nigga was out of the house. It was Saturday night and past 10 o'clock and I had never kicked it with him this late. When I pulled into a parking lot and parked, Van helped Tikka from the car and up a flight of stairs. I held the door open.

"Why is the music so loud? And why do I smell smoke? Is this a club?" she asked.

"You gon' see in a few seconds." We led Tikka to our roped off section. "Okay. Take off the blindfold."

She moved slowly.

"Surprise!" we screamed.

Tikka covered her mouth as she looked around, her eyes wide with surprise. We were at a strip club. Marie, Keith, Tina, Manny, Damo, Vic, TC, Van, and me. Half-naked strippers was all around. Money was falling from the ceiling. On the table was a big-ass cake made to look like the Black's Law Dictionary that Tracy sent her.

"Blow out the candles!" Marie yelled.

Tikka removed her hand from her face and blew out the candles. "In a strip club, y'all? For real?"

"Hell yeah!" Tina yelled. "I planned this. Now turn up, bitch!" she said, giving Tikka a shot of Patron from a tray lined with about twenty shots.

Tikka turned to me for help. I smiled and grabbed a shot from the tray. She followed my lead. When I tilted my head back and downed the drink, she copied. Since it was her first time drinking, she gagged and choked.

"There you go!" Vic cheered.

After Tikka stopped choking, we sang happy birthday - the Stevie Wonder version.

"Now c'mon! Let's go to the stage and make it rain on these hoes!" Tina said, grabbing Tikka by the hand and dragging her away.

I went to the bar and got a thousand singles and gave it to the family. Marie tucked the money in her bra so they could have a good time. Keith looked like a kid in a candy store. After we threw money on the dancers, I went back to the table to drink. Tikka and Van joined me a few moments later.

"How you like the party?"

Tikka looked uncomfortable. "It looks like everybody having more fun than me."

"That's 'cause you need to loosen up. Here," Van said, grabbing two shots and giving one to Tikka.

"It's nasty and it burns," she declined.

"You just gotta get used to it. You only need two more and you'll be good. Trust me," Van said, showing his icy smile.

Tikka melted. She took the shot glass and they drank at the same time.

"One more."

"No, Van. It's nasty!" she coughed.

"Just one more time. For me. Please."

Tikka looked like she would do anything Van asked and drank another shot. When the liquor kicked in, it released Tikka's inner wild child. She slapped ass, got lap dances, and partied until she passed out. I made sure to record it all on my phone. She probably wasn't going to remember the night, so I wanted to show her the receipt.

We left the club around 2 in the morning. Tikka was knocked out in the backseat and Van was in the passenger seat as drunk as I had ever seen him. I was fucked up too, but I was able to drive.

"I miss dat shit," Van slurred.

"What's that?"

"The clubs. Makin' it rain. Poppin' bottles. I used to do that shit like er'night. Five G's on drinks. Ten on the strippers. Fuckin' all the bad bitches. Not thots, my nigga. I'm talkin' models. Hoes in magazines and on TV. I miss dat shit."

I never heard Van talk about his past, but I knew he used to be a big deal. “See, that’s the life I want, my nigga. Why you give it up?”

He took his time responding. “Shit almost cost me my family. Almost cost my life. I told my girl I was done with that shit and moved to Wisconsin to get away. But after tasting that shit, I want it back. I wanna go hard.”

“I didn’t know you wasn’t from here. Where you from?”

“Ohio, nigga. Cleveland. The city that Lebron built.”

“What made you leave?”

“I just told you, nigga. But fuck that shit. I’m tired as fuck.” He yawned. “Wake me up when we get to yo’ spot. I gotta call my wife to come get me.”

While Van snoozed in the passenger seat, I thought about the friend I had grown to love like a big brother, but didn’t know shit about. Why didn’t he want to talk about his past? Was he running from something or someone? Or both? I was too drunk to wrap my mind around it, so I let it go. I had to focus on getting us home.

Chapter 11

For the second Saturday in a row, Van was out with me. Tikka's birthday party at the strip club had awakened his inner party animal. Now we was in his blue BMW heading to a local hot spot.

"Don't even pull yo' money out tonight, Dray. Everything on me." Van smiled, pulling out a stack of bills. "Keep stackin' so you can plush the crib and get a new whip. A nice watch wouldn't be bad either."

I glanced at the Rolex on Van's wrist and felt a little envious. Then I looked at the money in his lap. All big bills. "How much is that?"

"10,000. We finna party like bosses, my nigga. I'ma increase you to a hunnit grams, too. That way you can get more money and not be running out so fast."

Thinking about getting more money got me geeked. "Hell yeah! That's what I'm talkin' 'bout!"

"Oh, and before we get up in here and get too drunk and I forget, my daughter's birthday next weekend. She turns five. You should bring Draya. We gonna do a kids' party during the day and a party for the grownups later that night. I want you to meet the fam and some of my wife's friends. Upgrade yo' hoe game, nigga."

"I got hoes, nigga. Fuck you talkin' 'bout?"

"Nah, nigga. Not them hoes that all the niggas in the hood fuckin'."

"That shit don't matter. I just be needing something to fuck on."

"And that's why you need to upgrade, nigga. You a catch, Dray. A young boss. You got money, yo' own pad, own car, and you smart. The females you surround yo'self with should reflect that. You can't be a millionaire and still eating at Old Country Buffet. Boss niggas ain't fuckin' ole girl wit' five kids and five baby daddies. My nigga, you supposed to scroll through yo' phone and every female should be a 9 or better. Managers. Business owners. Models. Bad-ass strippers. Nigga, I was fuckin' the same female as Drake and Lil Wayne and I can't rap and never had a record deal. My face wasn't on TV every day, but they knew I was a boss because of how I kicked it. People gon' judge you by how you carry yo'self. So tonight, I'm finna show you how bosses kick it."

The club we went to was called LIVE. When rappers, ball players, and entertainers came to the city, this is where they partied. This is where the dope boys and money-getting cliques kicked it, the most popular being TBT, also known as Triple Beam Team. They acted like they owned the club.

"We up top, in VIP. Stairs in the back," Van called over the music.

LIVE had two floors. VIP upstairs. Rest of the club on the first floor. I followed Van upstairs, taking in everything. The club was packed. Females were damn near naked. Triple Beam Team was promoting a new rapper, T-Rez, and putting on for the city. They had even hired a fine-ass dime piece from one of those reality shows to host the event.

When we got to the top of the stairs, four big black niggas that looked like they played football stopped us. After showing our VIP badges, they let us pass. I couldn't stop looking around as I followed Van to our seats. Fine-ass bottle girls in tight-ass dresses made sure everybody got what they needed. I seen some athletes, models, and Triple Beam Team members partying it up. I even looked over the balcony and watched the people on lower level watching us.

"We right here," Van said, stopping at a table surrounded by big black chairs.

"Man, this shit is…" I ran out of words to describe how I was feeling.

"This the life!" Van smiled. "Now look for some hoes so we can get 'em up here."

"Y'all want bottle service?"

I looked to my left and seen a dime piece smiling at us. Light skin, long hair, bright eyes, perfect teeth. She was rocking a gray mini skirt so tight that it looked painted on.

"Yeah, we want bottle service," Van spoke up. "Matter of fact, we don't want nobody bringing us drinks but you. What's yo' name?"

She blushed. "Marrissa."

"Marrissa, I'm Van, and this my nigga, Drayez. We gon' start the night with two bottles of Ace of Spades and a bottle of black label," he said, pulling the stack of money from his pocket and giving her a nice chunk. "Keep the change."

She walked away smiling.

"How much you give her?" I asked, watching her ass as she walked away.

"That don't matter. We good. You found some bitches yet?"

"Shit, what up with Marrissa?"

"She bottle service, my nigga. Here to tease. We gon' send her to get the females we want. That's how bosses do it."

I turned back to look over the crowd. There were so many females. All ages, races, sizes, and shapes and easily outnumbered the niggas 2 to 1. I eventually spotted a thick dark-skinned chick with a body like Serena Williams.

"What about her in the orange cat suit?" I pointed.

Van looked at me like I did something wrong. "My nigga, you can pull up to her on any block in any hood. We looking for something like that."

The female Van pointed out looked like she could be on the cover of a high fashion magazine. Fair skin, long curly brown hair, wearing a tight red dress. She stood with three other females that looked like they could be her sisters. They reminded me of the Kardashians.

"Here you go, guys," Marrissa said, setting our drinks on the table. "Need anything else?"

"Yeah. I need you to bring them up here," Van said, pointing to the girls he picked.

She laughed. "I don't think that's part of my job."

Van gave her some more money. "It is now."

Marrissa smiled at us as she put the money in her bra and walked away. She walked downstairs and made her way to the women. After exchanging a couple of words, she pointed to us. They talked a little more before the girls grabbed their purses and drinks and followed Marrissa.

"That's how this shit is, for real?" I asked. I had never seen anything like that. A few months ago, I would've thought they were out of my league. Now all I had to do was sit back and wait for them to come to me.

"We bosses, my nigga. We do what we want. Now start thinking like a boss. Money ain't shit. These hoes ain't shit. We not gon' try to keep they attention. We gon' make them try to keep our attention."

All I could do was smile and take a sip from my expensive ass bottle. A few moments later, the vixens arrived.

"Ay, welcome to VIP. I'm Van and this my nigga, Drayez. Grab some seats. How y'all doin'?"

"Fine!" they sang, sounding like a girl group.

"Does anybody need anything?" Marrissa asked.

I spoke up. "Yeah. Whatever they drinkin, it's on us."

Van gave me a nod and wink while the girls ordered drinks. When Marrissa left, we got to know our company. The one Van spotted was Milena. Her sister was Suelyn. Their friends were Ashley and Daphne. I got drawn in by Suelyn. Mommy was flawless. Long curly dark hair. A perfectly round face. Makeup looked like she had a glam squad. Teeth bright white. Pedicured toes covered by red bottoms. She was short and petite, nothing too big, everything just right. The drinks flowed and so did the conversation. All the girls went to college at the University of Madison. Suelyn was in her third year, studying child psychology.

"So, what do you do, Drayez? Do you play sports?" Suelyn asked, mesmerizing me with her eyes.

"Nah. I own a business. A car service. Kinda like Uber," I lied.

Van gave me a look. I ignored him.

"What is it called?" Suelyn asked.

I hadn't thought past the lie so I said the first thing that came to mind. "Ghetto Pass. It's urban."

"I think I heard of that," Daphne blurted, bailing me out.

"I never heard of it. Maybe because I don't live in the hood," Suelyn laughed. "But business must be good since you can afford thousand dollar bottles of liquor.

"I do okay."

More drinks flowed and we got tipsy while listening to TBT's artist do a few songs. When the club closed, we continued the party in a suite at the Pfister hotel. The room cost almost a thousand dollars a night and had all the boss shit. A Jacuzzi, a steam room, a game room, a living room, a big-ass kitchen, and the bathroom looked as big as my bedroom at home. The shower had three heads and could fit five people. Me, Suelyn, and Daphne had a threesome and I got my dick and balls sucked at the same time. I fell asleep with a big-ass smile on my face. And I knew this was only the beginning.

The next day I was back on the grind. As I drove through the city getting money, last night played in my head. I had kicked it like a boss! Popped bottles in VIP. Slept in a suite and had a threesome with two dimes. Every day, life was showing me that there was so much more to living. A few months ago I was cool living with a female that didn't love me. All I wanted was some pussy and a place to lay my head. Now I wanted more. More money. More cars. More hoes.

The ringing of my phone pulled me from rich nigga thoughts. When I answered, a voice automated system told me I had a call from prison.

"What up, big sis?"

"Hey, Dray. What you up to?"

"Out here on the grind. How you feeling?"

"I'm good. Just wanted to see what you were up to. It's nice to be able to talk to you and Tikka."

"Yeah. Did you get those pictures from her party?"

Tracy laughed. "I laughed so hard when she told me y'all took her to a strip club. And she got a lap dance! That was too funny."

"Yeah. We turned up. You only turn eighteen once so we gave her a party she wouldn't forget."

"Yeah, I bet. But what's up with Tina? Why she not living with y'all?"

"She doin' her own thang. Only thing she concerned about is getting money. She livin' fast."

"That scares me, Dray. I was the same way. Quan had my ass out there doin' all kinds of stupid shit. I don't want Tina to fall victim to the same thing."

"I don't think you gotta worry about that. She not gon' risk her ass for nobody. She don't believe in love. She want money."

"She a hoe?"

"Not like a prostitute. More like a gold digger. Whoever gettin' money, she be around them, tryna get her hands on some of it."

"Damn. I feel sorry for her."

"Don't. She know what she doin'."

"I wish she was more like Tikka, trying to be somebody."

"Tikka is special. I don't know where she got her brains or drive from. She said she gon' get you out and I believe her."

"I know. She so sweet. She said y'all coming to visit."

"Yeah. I can't say when. I'm always on the move. Grinding. But I'ma get my ass on that highway soon. I know I haven't been there for you like I should, but I'ma do what I can when I can. And the phone gon' stay on."

***

"I heard what happened with you and Chantele." Desiré laughed.

We were at Mr. D's, a soul food restaurant. She was sitting across from me looking "regular", as Van would say. Freshly done weave, soft-looking peanut butter complexion, those big soft lips. She wore jeans, a T-shirt, and boots. Even in simple clothes, she looked good. Compared to Suelyn, Desiré was average. But something about her made me prefer the teacher's company over the soon-to-be psychologist.

"She told you about that, huh?"

"Yeah. She said you got jealous and called her a bitch."

"Nah, it wasn't like that. I mean, I did call her a bitch, but not because I was jealous. I was salty that she wasted my time. How she gon' forget that I was coming over? Shit made me feel like a simple nigga. I'm a boss. You don't do that to a boss nigga."

"Whoa, boss nigga!" Desiré laughed. "Don't get all big-headed on me. I like you as Drayez, the cool and laid back guy that's easy to talk to."

And that's why I liked her. She accepted me for me. "And I'ma always be me. But I'm a man that should be respected. What she did was disrespect to a man with dignity and self-respect."

"I don't disagree. I think that having sex with more than one person is a bad idea. If she only had one man in her life and not five, she and you wouldn't have this problem. But that's her life. She's my girl and I love her regardless."

"She fuckin' five niggas?" I asked, unable to let the comment slip by.

Desiré looked like she stuck her hand in a pile of shit. "Oops! Did I say that?"

"Yeah."

"Well, I guess it's four now." She laughed.

Watching her laugh made me laugh and suddenly, Chantele and her niggas didn't matter no more.

"Do you want to fall in love again?" Desiré asked, staring at me with those deep brown eyes that looked like they had so many stories to tell.

"Nah. I'm done with that shit."

"Your ex?"

I nodded. "She played me. I loved her, but she didn't love me back. I should've known better, but I was thinkin' with my li'l head. She got five kids and five baby daddies for a reason."

Desiré looked surprised. "She got five baby daddies?"

"I'm number 5."

"Dang, Drayez. Didn't your mother tell you to stay away from girls like that?"

"Nah. Marie was too busy counting my birthdays til I turned eighteen so she could kick me out."

"Don't do your mother like that!" She laughed, slapping my hand.

"If you knew her, you wouldn't be saying that."

"You are crazy, Drayez. But I don't think you should give up on love just because you had a bad experience. Who hasn't? Love is from God. It makes us feel whole again when we fall apart. It heals us when we feel broken. Cleanses us when we feel dirty. It gives us wings and makes us feel like we can fly."

"What Hallmark card you been reading?"

The light in her eyes dimmed a little. "That wasn't funny. And I haven't been reading cards. That came from my heart. I believe in love. It has power. Sometimes we get hurt by people we love, but it wasn't love that hurt us."

"So, who hurt you?"

She paused. And I swear when she started talking again, her eyes opened up to me.

"I was with him for eight years. I gave him everything he wanted and then some. Then he left me for a skinny white woman."

My eyes popped. "A white girl?"

"Yep. He was white too. I guess the saying about never going back once you have black ain't true because he went back."

My eyes got even bigger. "You was fuckin' wit' a white boy?"

"A white man. Martin. He's a teacher too. I think he loved me in his own way, but not enough to settle down and marry me. He married Ashley, though. And they have kids. I'm not bitter anymore. I just know he allowed me to taste love, but his wasn't the real thing. But it felt good. And I want to feel it again, but for real next time."

Everything she said was real and I felt her. But I couldn't get past one thing. "You was really fuckin' a white nigga?"

"Would you stop saying that? Yes, I did. Now stop it. You don't see me harping over the fact that you got tricked into giving your sperm to a receptacle. Why would you get a woman pregnant that already had kids by four other people?"

That question made me chill. "Okay. I see your point."

She smiled like she won a prize. "I knew you would."

From Mr. D's, we went to a coffee shop that sold all kinds of expensive special brews and coffee beans. After some samples and getting a caffeine high that had me feeling like running down the street ass naked, we went to Desiré's apartment. Her place fit her personality. Thick white carpet, big soft brown couches, glass tables with wood frames, and it smelled like vanilla. What caught my attention was the ceramics with different inspirational quotes on them spread throughout her living room. Most of them were about love. I picked up a heart-shaped one.

"Love is patient. Love is kind; love does not envy; love does not parade itself, is not puffed up; does not behave rudely, does not seek its own, is not provoked, thinks no evil; does not rejoice in iniquity but rejoices in truth; bears all things, believes all things, hopes all things; endures all things. Love never fails."

Desire came and stood next to me. "First Corinthians 13."

I set the heart back on the table. "I don't think I ever had that kind of love."

"Me either. If we did, we wouldn't be standing here now. True love never fails. You want something to drink?"

"What you got?"

"Come to the kitchen with me and find out."

I couldn't keep my eyes off Desiré's gigantic booty as I followed her to the kitchen. It wasn't one of those perfectly-shaped twerking booties, but the kind of ass that you had to look at, even if big asses wasn't your thing. The kind of ass that you built a home around. An ass that you snuggled up behind at night to keep warm. Big, wide, and round. When she opened the fridge and bent over, I slid up behind her, grinding against that big soft booty.

She stood up to face me. "What are you doing? I thought you wanted something to drink?"

"Can't nothing in there stop me from being thirsty."

Her face flushed, breath quickened, and voice got husky. "What do you want?"

I leaned down and kissed her. I wasn't a super kissing-ass nigga, but kissing Desiré felt good. It was slow, her lips soft. Her tongue danced against mine and she let out moans that made my ears tingle. Her hands rubbed my face, neck, chest, arms, and back. I went for her shirt and she went for mine. We threw them to the floor.

"Come to my room."

She took me by the hand and led me. Man, I felt high and we hadn't even smoked yet. Shit was crazy. When we got to her room, we kissed some more and her hands caressed my body like she was trying to remember every muscle. After taking off the rest of our clothes, she lay on the bed and her titties spread out like a chocolate avalanche. I sucked her big-ass nipples and she made beautiful noises while rubbing my face. When I slipped a finger inside the wettest and warmest pussy I ever felt, she made a noise that gave the word pleasure a run for its money. Then she pushed me aside and rolled on top of me. She kissed my lips, down to my neck, collarbone, then my chest, stopping at my nipples. She teased them with her tongue while stroking my dick with her hand. Shit felt good. Then she continued kissing her way down my body until she got to my dick. When she put her mouth on me, it felt good, like what I imagined my customers felt when they used heroin. An instant pleasure shot through my body, tickling my brain. She couldn't give grade-A head like Chantele, but it was enough to almost make me bust. I wasn't ready to get off yet, so I stopped her. When her eyes met mine, I could see lust, fear, and want swirling in them. I lay her back on the bed and climbed between her legs. I didn't have a condom and I didn't care.

"Please don't hurt me," she whispered.

She wasn't talking about sex. Her eyes said more. She wanted more than a fuck. More than I could probably give. But I wanted her too bad to stop and think.

"I won't hurt you."

And then I penetrated. She gasped, arching her back and digging her nails into my shoulders. Shit hurt. But her pussy felt better. I stayed still until her body loosened. She pulled my face to hers and started kissing. I pushed inside her some more. She gasped and moaned, digging her nails deeper. I was halfway there. When her body relaxed some more, I didn't try to go deeper. I wanted to dick her ass down, but I couldn't do her like that. She was special. Rare. Unique. I handled her with care, using all the self-restraint in my being as I got into a slow rhythm.

"Oh my God, Drayez! Oh shit! Oh God!" she screamed, biting me on the jaw. Then she started crying. Shit scared me.

"You good?" I asked, stopping my stroke.

She looked up at me with tear-filled, lust-glazed eyes. "Yes. I'm crying because it feels good. I don't want you to stop. I want more. Please."

So I gave her all that she could take and then some. When I busted my nut, it felt like part of my soul slipped out of me and into her. I fell on top of her, drained and sweaty. She kissed my neck and began running her fingers up and down my spine, from the nape of my neck to the top of my ass.

"How do you feel?" she whispered.

"I don't know."

And that was the truth. I had good pussy before. I had fucked until I didn't want to fuck no more. But I had never experienced what I had with Desiré. It felt like I had known her forever. Like I had touched her body before. Like there wasn't a part of me that she didn't know. Like I belonged next to her. Inside of her.

"I feel…satisfied," she whispered against my neck.

"Is that what it's called?"

She moved my face so that we were looking in each other's eyes. "We made love. It's different than sex. Sex is quick and leaves you wanting more. Making love takes time and it involves emotions. And it satisfies the soul. Are you still thirsty?"

I thought about what I told her in the kitchen. How nothing in her refrigerator could stop me from being thirsty. Turned out I was right.

Chapter 12

Van was right. His wife's friends were dimes!

I was in Van's backyard and his daughter's princess-themed party was in full swing. Van was playing super dad, holding a big-ass princess piñata filled with candy while the kids took swings at it with a plastic whiffle bat. I was off to the side sharing ice cream and cake with Draya.

"When you get that watch?" TC asked. He was sitting next to me eating his third piece of cake.

"Couple days ago. What you think?" I asked, showing off the iced out Movado.

"I think I need to start kickin' it with you and Van. You niggas starting to shine."

"I thought you was cool with being a simple nigga. More money more problems, right?"

"I'm starting to think I might want them problems. Especially if Lexi was looking at me how she looking at you. You know she damn near famous, my nigga?"

Lexi was a semi-famous plus size model. She was tall, healthy, with long legs and the body of a stripper. Big titties, a phat ass, and wide hips. Long blonde hair, green eyes, little thin lips, and a pointy nose. And she was dime piece fine.

"Yeah, Van was tellin' me she just came back from walking a runway in Paris," I said coolly, glancing in her direction. We made eye contact. She smiled. I nodded before turning back to TC. "You wouldn't even know what to do with that, nigga."

"Shit, I would do whatever she wanted me to do." He laughed.

"First thing you gotta do is quit working at McDonald's, nigga. You ain't gon' never catch nothing like that being average. She want a nigga on her level. She don't wanna have to pay for everything. Nigga gotta carry his own weight. Boss up."

"You sound like Van."

"If that's yo' way of saying you agree with me, cool."

TC was about to say something, but stopped. He was looking past me like a starstruck girl meeting Justin Bieber.

"She is so cute! Can I hold her?"

I turned to see Lexi standing over me. Damn, she was tall. Easily six feet. And she smelled good.

"Her hands messy from the cake. Sure you wanna get yo' clothes dirty?"

"I don't care. Give her to me."

She put Draya on her hip and started talking baby talk. I didn't think Draya would take to her, but when she laughed and goo-gooed, I knew it was all good.

TC got up. "I'ma go grab something to drink."

Lexi took his seat. "She is adorable. What's her name?"

"Draya. I think she likes you. You good with kids. Got any?"

"No, no, no. I'm too focused on my career. But I love kids. I used to want to have a litter. Now I just spoil them and give them back to their parents."

"What changed? Why you stop wanting kids?"

She looked at me and smiled. "That's kind of a deep question for our first conversation."

"I'm a deep nigga."

She laughed. "I'm Lexi. Let's start there. You are?"

"Drayez. Van is my boy."

"I know. But I've never seen you before. I've known Van for almost ten years. Back when they lived in Ohio. Were you with ATM?"

"Nah. I just met Van a couple months ago. What the hell is ATM?"

She looked a little nervous. "I don't know if I should say. I think I said too much. I've been known to stick my foot in my mouth. How about we forget Van and talk about who we are? If you're lucky, before the night is over, you might be able to talk me into having kids again."

I chilled at Van's crib for the rest of the day, spending most of the time getting to know Lexi. Turns out she was a freak and wasn't ashamed of it. And neither was I. Party ended around 8 o'clock and most of the parents left with their kids. The grownup party would take place in the basement. I planned on getting fucked up, so Van rolled with me to drop Draya off at home.

"You betta fuck Lexi tonight, nigga," Van said from the passenger seat of the rented Challenger.

"Damn, nigga. You sound like you wanna fuck her."

"I do. She a freak, brah. But I wouldn't even try to pull it. Her and my wife been friends since college. They both would kill me. So you gotta do it for me. Tell me if that pussy good."

"I got you, pervert-ass nigga."

"Yeah, whatever, nigga," he laughed. "Man, Dray, you know I wouldn't be able to do none of the shit I been doing if it wasn't for you, right?"

The seriousness in his voice grabbed my attention. "Fuck you talkin' 'bout, nigga? Shit, I wouldn't be able to do none of the shit I'm doing if it wasn't for you."

"Having a few extra dollars been a blessing. Shit was getting tight for the family. I never was good at budgeting money. Didn't have to budget when you eatin'. But shit was getting too real and me and wifey was fighting all the time. Then you showed up. My wife knows I'm getting extra money, but she don't know where it come from because I be at home all the time. She getting suspicious, though. She don't want me in the streets no more. So just know that that I need you as much as you need me. You my partner. You saved my ass just as much as I saved yours."

I didn't know what to say. I felt forever indebted to this nigga. He took me from sleeping on Vic's couch to having a threesome in a suite with a future doctor. "You know it's all love, brah. One hand washes the other."

Van smiled, the lights on the dashboard reflecting off his grill. "You sound way too much like me."

"If that's yo' way of sayin' you agree with me, cool."

After dropping off Draya, we stopped at the liquor store to grab drinks for the after party. We were walking out when we bumped into a light-skinned nigga with a low haircut and lots of tattoos. When he seen Van, his face lit up like he seen a long lost family member.

"Vincent Van Go!"

I seen recognition flash in Van's eyes, along with something else. Fear.

"Shooter! What it do, nigga?" Van recovered.

"Shit. Just gettin' out. Fuck you doin' in Milwaukee, nigga?"

"This where I landed at. Layin' low and cleaning up my act. What about you?"

"Same shit. How long you been here?"

Van hesitated. "Uh, a couple years. You know they gave me a slap on the wrist since it was the first time I was in trouble."

"Same shit. You still in tune with the rest of them niggas? Larry, Kimo, and Big Fred?"

"Nah. I left all that shit behind me. Focusing on the family. It was good seeing you my nigga, but I gotta get back to the crib," Van said, eager to walk away.

Shooter stopped him. "Chill, nigga. Relax. We put that shit behind us. Gimme yo' number so I can get up with you later."

Van gave him the number.

"Okay, boy. I'ma get with you later. Money time."

"Time is money," Van mumbled before hurrying away.

"What was that about?" I asked after we got in the car.

"Just drive, my nigga. And check them mirrors," Van said, looking out the back window nervously.

His being nervous made me nervous. "You good, nigga? Who was that nigga?" I asked, checking my mirrors.

"Somebody I never wanted to see again."

"What he mean by money time? Who is the niggas he named? Y'all ATM?"

Van stopped checking the windows and looked at me. "How you know about ATM?"

"I don't. Lexi mentioned it earlier and I heard him say money time. That was yo' clique?"

"Listen, Dray. You my nigga and I fuck with you the long way, but I ain't tryna open that door. Just get me to the crib. And circle the block a couple times to make sure ain't nobody following us."

The drive back to Van's house was quiet. My nigga was normally talkative, always laughing. But the nigga in my passenger seat was the exact opposite. He was nervous and scared. I could smell the fear coming from his pores. This nigga had a lot of skeletons in his closet and one just jumped out and scared the shit out of him.

When we got back to Van's house, the basement party was in full swing. Music, liquor, and a few strippers. Van didn't seem to notice none of it. He stayed next to his wife, holding a glass of liquor that he never drank. They whispered back and forth. I didn't know what they were talking about, but it looked like she was trying to console him. Then she looked at me. Gave me a look so evil that the hairs on the back of my neck stood up.

"What the hell is wrong with Van?" Lexi whispered while sucking my ear lobe. She was snuggled up next to me on the couch watching the strippers put on a show with glow in the dark paint.

"I don't know. He been acting funny since we got back. Maybe him and Theresa fighting," I lied, not wanting to tell her about Shooter.

"I don't think so. She's happy. Well, she was. They're depressing me. You want to get out of here and show me if this thing between your legs is real?"

***

Van wasn't answering his phone. I called and texted him for two days and he hadn't answered or returned my calls. I was worried about my nigga. This wasn't like him.

"What are you thinking about?"

I looked up and seen Desiré walking towards me carrying a big-ass plate of food. Cabbage, cornbread, macaroni casserole, and smothered pork chops. "Damn, baby! I didn't know you got down like this."

"I didn't get this thick from eating salads. I know how to cook. And eat. I used to cook for my mother and her church friends every Sunday. Now that I moved out on my own, I don't cook as much. I did this for you. Had you not come over so late, it would've been fresh. I don't like microwave food."

"I'm a busy man. Gotta stay on the grind. I don't think I'ma be able to eat all this," I said between bites.

"It don't matter. As long as you're satisfied."

The way she said satisfied stirred something inside of me. Every time I heard that word, I thought of her. And everything she did satisfied me. The conversations. The food. The sex.

"You like the word satisfied, don't you?"

"I do. Now tell me what you were thinking about that had you lost in thought."

"My nigga going through some crazy shit and now he ain't answering his phone. Its crazy cause I been around this nigga every day for months and it feel like I don't even know him."

"Maybe you don't. Maybe he's running from something or someone and don't want you to get close to his issue. Or maybe he's just being a man and wants to handle his problems on his own. I learned that you all are like that to some extent."

She hit the nail on the head. "You sound like you met him before."

"I just know men. You guys are different in some ways, but the same in others."

I had to hear this. "Like how?"

"Pride, egos, and the need to feel important. That describes all men. And you better not disrespect a man. Have to pay for that. Then there are the little differences. Some want love and happiness. Some want to be a player forever. Some want to grow and build while others want to tear down and destroy. And some don't know what they want until they find it. I think that's you."

I frowned. "What that mean?"

"You tell me. What do you want?"

I stopped eating and thought for a moment. She watched me with those eyes that had become my weakness. Since I had been fucking her, I shared my thoughts freely. I was open and didn't hide anything. So I told her what I wanted. "Money, power, and respect."

"Typical man stuff. But you also want more."

"And how do you know what I want?"

"Because your body tells me. You mouth says one thing, but your eyes and actions say another. You want to be a good father to your daughter. A good brother to your sisters. A good friend to me, maybe more. But you're confused because Rayna took advantage of your love. Now you're scared to give your heart away. None of that is money, power, or respect; but you want it just the same. Maybe even more."

That's why I liked Desiré. She was a thinker, and deep. How could a woman I had only known for a few months know so much about me?

"You scare me," I admitted.

"I know. And you scare me too."

"Why?"

"Because I want you and know that I can't have you. You're being pulled in so many directions. But there is something about you that has drawn me in. I just want you to be honest with me and don't hurt me."

I felt like I should say something but didn't know what. So I let the silence linger until she broke it.

"Turns out you were hungry, huh?"

I looked down at the plate. Most of it was gone. "Compliments to the chef," I said before giving her a kiss.

"Now that you're done, let's go take a bath to wash away the day. I've always wanted to wash your back."

For the first time since I was a shorty, I got bathed by a pair of hands that wasn't mine or Marie's. The bath was erotic. Candles glowed on the sink and music played in the background – "The Truth" by Indie. Arie. When the bubbles fizzed out and the water cooled, we dried off and went to the bedroom. Desire gave me a massage with girly-smelling lotion that had my skin tingling and feeling way too soft. The love we made after the massage could only be described with one word: satisfying.

I woke up the next morning alone. Desiré had to go to work. As I lay in the bed that smelled like her, I found myself wanting to be with her all the time. I wanted to talk to her as much as I could. Fuck her until my dick fell off. Kiss her until my lips hurt. Even now I wanted to call her just to hear her voice and laughter. Damn. I was whipped. Didn't know if I was lost, getting soft, or just falling in love.

The ringing of my phone pulled me from thoughts of Desiré. I didn't recognize the number.

"Hello?"

"What up, nigga?" Van asked.

Relief flooded my body when I heard his voice. "Van, what up, nigga?"

"Shit. On my way to work. I just wanted to holla at you real quick."

"What's going on with you, my nigga? I been tryna catch you, but you didn't get back at me."

"I know. I took a break from everybody and spent some time with the fam. Had to get some shit in order. This my new number. Had to upgrade the line."

"So you good?"

"Yeah, I'm good, nigga. You sound like a worried-ass li'l brother." He laughed.

It was good to hear him laugh. Made me laugh. "That's what's up, my nigga."

"Listen, Dray, I'm pulling up to my job now. Come to the house later on and fuck with me. Plus, I need to know what Lexi pussy taste like, nigga."

I drove over to Van's house later that night. During the drive, I thought about the Dr. Jekyll and Hyde shit Van just pulled. Two days ago he was a scared and nervous wreck. Now he was laughing and joking like everything was normal. Something shitty happened between him and ATM. I looked up the clique and found out ATM stood for About That Money and the clique was a big deal in Ohio. They had seen millions of dollars. Then the Feds came and locked everybody up. I couldn't find that many details on how the bust went down or who told, but somebody always told. In the end, the big boys, Big Fred, Kimo, and Larry got fifty years apiece. A bunch of smaller fish got short state and fed bids. I didn't see nothing about

Van and I couldn't look him up because I didn't know his real name. But the look on his face two days ago would never leave my mind.

After parking behind his BMW, I rang the doorbell. Theresa answered. She was a short and stacked Mexican and black woman. And she was bad. But the mug she wore made her look ugly.

"What do you want?"

I was taken aback by her attitude. "What's wrong with you? Is Van here?"

She continued giving me a cold and angry look. "He's in the basement."

I could feel the heat from her anger and animosity as I walked in the house. I didn't know why she was mad at me, but I didn't like that shit.

"Drayez, what's good, family?" Van smiled when I walked in the basement.

"What's up with Theresa, man?"

"What you mean?"

"She just mugged the shit out of me. Acted like she didn't wanna let me in the house."

"Don't trip on her. I told her I ran into Shooter the other day and now she on one. She think you had something to do with it. But it wasn't nothing you did. She gon' get over it. But fuck that. What up with you and Lexi, nigga?"

I smiled as I thought of her long thick legs. "We good. I hit that shit so good that she wanted me to fly to LA with her. Said some shit about a fashion show and she only had one day in town for yo' daughter's birthday."

"Why didn't you fly to LA with her, nigga? You coulda lived like a boss for a couple days."

"I gotta get this money, nigga. I got shit to do."

"You ever been to LA?"

"Nah."

"You ever been outta Milwaukee?"

"Nah."

"You trippin, li'l brah. That's the city of stars, my nigga. You gotta live and enjoy life. Travel. See and do different shit. You young. When you got the opportunity to do shit like that, do it. This money ain't going nowhere. Shit will be here when you get back. Don't let chasing paper fuck up good opportunities. Money is a tool, my nigga. Not a god. Don't get tied down by shit. Money, hoes, love. None of that shit. Remain unchained so you can do what you wanna do when you wanna do it. Don't let nothing rule yo mind or body but you."

That was the Van I knew.

"I guess I really didn't think about it like that. I was too focused on gettin' money and seeing what was up with you."

"I told you I'm good, nigga."

"So what was up with that shit at the liquor store?"

"Me and Shooter was a part of ATM, About That Money team. They called me Vincent Van Go and we was getting that paper. Theresa tried to make me leave the game, but I was too deep in it. So she left me. Took some money and moved to Milwaukee and bought this house. At the time I didn't care because I was eating. Then I got knocked. First person I called was Theresa. Told her all the shit she wanted to hear and she told me she would only fuck with me on one condition: that I leave the game for good. So I did my time and cut ties with ATM. Seeing Shooter the other day surprised me. I told Theresa and it shook her up too."

The story didn't seem complete. "Why you react like that if y'all was niggas?"

"Because I wanted to get away from them niggas and start new. If he knows I'm here, so will everybody else. I don't wanna put my family through no more pain. Remember what I said about time and money?"

I thought about Draya in the emergency room. "I guess that make sense. Vincent Van Go. You gotta explain that."

"Them vans on the highway, boy. My name is Vincent and I used to make the runs. Shit stuck."

I laughed again. "That shit was too funny."

"I know. But that ain't the reason I called you over. This is," he said, going under the couch and pulling out two black Glocks. "One for you and me. I got 'em from a Mexican nigga at work. They clean."

"What we need these for?"

"'Cause we gettin' money, nigga. Need that heat."

"A'ight. I was thinkin about buying a banger anyway. Good looking."

I kicked it with Van a little longer until my money phone started ringing. I was walking through the house, on my way to the front door, when I ran into Theresa. She mugged me and said something under her breath.

"You say something?"

She mugged the shit out of me. "I said leave Van alone."

"What is you talking about? What did I do? Van is my nigga."

"Just get out of my house. If something happens to my husband, I'll kill you!"

Chapter 13

For the first time in my life, money wasn't a problem. The move to 100 grams allowed me to furnish the crib with black leather sectionals, a 70-inch screen, and all new appliances for the kitchen. I even copped a Sleep Number bed to sleep on. I could change the firmness of the mattress with the push of a button. Shit was glazing. And in the driveway was the newest addition to my boss status: a 2015 Audi A8. Mike got it for me at an auction. I didn't drive it that much because I trapped out of rentals. I was living good. I did what I wanted when I wanted - most of the time. I say most of the time because I didn't want to be in the prison visiting room no more, but I had to ride it out for two more hours.

"Why you keep looking around like that, Drayez?"

I stopped looking around the visiting room and focused on my big sister. Tracy looked good and healthy. Her hair hung all the way to the middle of her back and shined like she used the same products as the women in the commercials. Her beach sand complexion glowed. She had a round face, plump cheeks, dark eyes, and full lips. And the way the prison greens fit her curvy frame had everybody in the visiting room looking in her direction every time she moved.

"I think I'm allergic to prison," I said, scratching my arm.

"How are you going to be allergic to a building?" Tikka laughed.

"I don't know, but I am. My whole body itch. I need some calamine lotion."

"Quit playin', Drayez." Tracy laughed. "So when you gon send me some pictures of my niece? I'm still waiting."

"Damn, I keep forgetting." I turned to Tikka. "Send her some pictures of Draya. I keep on forgetting. My mind be on so much other shit."

"I'm not your secretary. Just slow down and use your phone to send them through Freeprints."

"See, that's why you should do it. You already know how. Don't do yo' big sister like that," I said, playing a guilt trip.

Tikka looked like she wanted to hit me. "I hate you."

"If by hate you mean love, then I hate you too."

"Thanks, Tikka. You know Drayez living fast. Only time he slow down is to fuck one of them fast girls."

A light went on in Tikka's eyes. "Ohh! Ask him about Desiré."

"Who is Desiré, Drayez?"

I laughed. "It ain't what Tikka makin' it seem. Desiré is my friend."

"Nuh-uh. She more than a friend. I seen Drayez around the girls he calls his friends. He treats them like whatever. They don't mean nothing. But when Desiré come over, she feeds him and they take baths together. Be kissing all the time. Do that sound like a friend to you, Tracy?"

"Nah. Sound like more than a friend to me. So, you love her, Dray?"

"What? Hell nah. Love is for suckas. I'm a boss. I fuck hoes and get money."

"Whatever, boss. Bet you won't say that when Desiré around," Tikka laughed.

"So, what's up with Marie? How she doing?" Tracy asked.

"Being as crazy as she wanna be. I think she happy that she finally got the house to herself. Her and Keith probably gon' kill each other," I cracked.

"I talked to her yesterday. She good," Tikka said.

"What about Tina?" Tracy asked.

"Your guess is as good as mine on that one. She fast," Tikka said.

"Well, at least y'all good. Thanks for coming to visit and showing love. C'mon, Drayez. Set the chess pieces back up. This time I'ma play you without my queen."

***

When the weekend came, me and Van were out again, this time at a strip club called Satin. We were sitting at our table and strippers flocked to us like pigeons around bird seed. I had already thrown a thousand singles and had another brick sitting on the table. The dancers stayed close, waiting for me to make it rain again. We also had Damo with us. Van seemed to relax in the presence of the quick-triggered albino, so I kept him with me as much as I could.

"Faaaammm, I loovveee kickin' it wit'chu niggas," Damo slurred, leaning on my shoulder.

"C'mon, drunk-ass nigga. Move!" I shrugged him off and Damo lost his balance, falling on the floor.

"Fool-ass nigga!" Van laughed

One of the dancers helped Damo back into his chair. A thick dark chocolate dancer walked over to me wearing only a bra, thong, and heels. Her ass was so big that it looked made for lap dances and her titties looked big enough to smother a nigga. She sat on my lap and began grinding.

"What's yo' name and what time you leaving?" I asked.

"Why you wanna know?" she asked, bending over and grabbing her ankles while twerking.

"Because I want you to spend the night with a boss. See if you can grab them ankles while taking dick."

She spun to face me, straddling my lap. She wasn't fine, but she was sexy as fuck. Platinum haircut low with brushed waves. Stud piercings in both cheeks and her bottom lip. "My name is Mona. And how you know I wanna fuck you?"

"'Cause you damn near doing it now. And you look like the kind of woman that know a good opportunity when you see one. Trust yo'self."

"You think you a good opportunity?"

"You know I am. What time you get off?"

"I leave when I want. My brother owns this club."

"Go put on some clothes. You coming to my house."

She smirked. "You just gon' tell me what to do? You a cocky-ass nigga."

"Nah. When you know what you capable of, that ain't cocky. That's confidence. And that's what makes me a boss."

She gave me a long "I'ma fuck the shit outta you" stare before getting up and walking away.

"'Bout time you let that bitch leave. I know the inside of yo' draws sticky as fuck!" Van laughed.

"Fuck you, nigga. She coming to the crib. Y'all snatch up something to fuck and let's get outta here."

"I'm good. These hoes all regular," Van said, turning to Damo. "And that nigga so drunk that his dick won't get hard."

We left the club in Van's BMW and went back to my house. Damo and Van slept on the couch. I took Mona to my room and made her call on God and speak in tongues while Jeezy's "Smoke and Fuck" played on repeat. When I got up to piss in the middle of the night and noticed Van was gone, I figured Theresa must've got on his ass.

Later that morning, I was awakened by some bomb-ass head from Mona. After she swallowed my kids, I gave her 300 dollars and sent her on her way. I was locking the door behind her when I heard voices in the kitchen. Van and Tikka sat at the table laughing while eating breakfast from Styrofoam trays.

"What's funny?" I asked, snatching a piece of bacon off Tikka's tray.

"Li'l sis is crazy, brah!" Van laughed.

I looked to Tikka. She blushed and put her head down. I turned back to Van. "I thought you hit it this morning?"

He got nervous and jumpy. "What? Hit what?"

"I thought you left. I got up to piss and you was gone."

"Oh. Nah, I didn't leave. I was on the couch. Damo left earlier."

I looked back and forth from Van to Tikka. Something happened. "What the fuck up with y'all?"

"Nothing, brah. What you talkin' about?" Van asked, looking nervous.

Tikka didn't say nothing. She focused on her food. I got pissed.

"You fucked my li'l sister, nigga?"

Van lifted his hands, palms flat. "C'mon, brah. It wasn't like that."

"As many bitches as we fucked and you go and fuck my sister, fam? You bogus. You don't do no shit like that, brah."

"My nigga, I know that shit sounds fucked up, but she grown. And she came on to me."

I looked to Tikka. She was nervous and scared like she knew she did something wrong. Yeah, she was grown, but she was still my little sister. And then something clicked. In that moment I noticed the way her body had filled out. Tikka was fine. Somehow she had passed from being a goofy acne-faced teenager to a pretty young woman. But I still didn't like Van fucking her.

"C'mon, brah. That shit ain't flying. We niggas with principles. You know certain lines ain't supposed to be crossed."

"You right, my nigga. I crossed that line. But Tikka bad and smart. And she not a li'l girl. Niggas finna be at her and she gon' make her own decisions if she will or won't."

"But you married, nigga. And she was a virgin."

Van raised an eyebrow. "She wasn't no virgin."

I looked to Tikka. "You not a virgin?"

"No," she mumbled.

"Since when?"

"Since I was sixteen."

I was stunned. This was too much information for one morning and I could feel a headache coming on. I went to the bathroom to find a pill. I couldn't believe Van fucked Tikka. That nigga was bogus. You don't fuck yo' nigga's sister. After popping two Tylenol, I went back to the kitchen for round 2.

"Where's Van?"

"He left."

I just stared at Tikka. She looked all innocent and shit. I wanted to be mad at her, but couldn't. "I know you grown now, but I still see you as my baby sister. And I don't like you fuckin my friends."

"Friend," she clarified.

"You know what I'm sayin'. Y'all shouldn't a crossed that line."

"If Van and Tina messed around, would you get mad?"

"Tina been doing what she wanna do since she was little."

"But she your sister too. It's not fair that you treat us differently."

"I know, but you different. You special. I wanna see you shine like the star that you is and not get caught up in yo' feelin's and get hurt."

"And I will shine, Drayez. I know what I want to do with my life. Van has my attention, but not my heart. He's cool and I like him, but I don't plan on falling in love with him. He's married. I'm not stupid. I just like his company."

"I don't know. This shit ain't sitting right. You know me and Van players. Why you wanna fuck with a player?"

"How you know I'm not a player?"

I had no comeback for that.

"Sorry you had to find out like this, Dray. I'm not going to flaunt it in your face, but I'm grown now. I will continue doing what I want. I hope you can accept and respect that."

***

It took some time, but I eventually accepted that Van and Tikka slept together from time to time. I didn't like it, but they were grown.

I was leaving my house, about to get in the rented Camaro, when Desiré's midnight blue Impala pulled into my driveway. Every time I seen her, I smiled.

"Why didn't you tell me you was coming over?"

"I can't come see you whenever I want? Sometimes hearing your voice isn't enough."

"When you put it like that, you can do whatever you want."

"I thought you'd see it my way," she smiled, standing on her tippy toes to kiss me. "Were you about to leave?"

"Yeah. I gotta make a run."

"Okay. I need to talk to you about something important. That's why I didn't call. I'll stay here and wait for you to come back. Is Tikka here?"

"Yeah. But what you wanna talk about? My run can wait."

"No, you go do what you need to do. I'll be here when you get back."

I tried to read her to see if I could get a hint of what she wanted to talk about. It had to be important for her not to want to talk about it on the phone. I wondered if she was going to tell me she loved me. Or maybe she was about to propose.

"Okay. I'ma be back in a few minutes. And gimme yo' keys so I can use yo' car since you blocked me in.

It took twenty minutes to drop Damo off some work and get back home. I was parking Desiré's Impala at the curb when my phone rang. It was Van.

"What up family?"

"Where you at?" he called over loud music.

"I'm at the crib. Turn that shit down."

He didn't turn the music down. "I'm around the corner. Come outside."

I hung up the phone and locked the doors on Desiré's car when Van's BMW turned onto the block. A fine mixed female hung out the sunroof. When he pulled to a stop in front of me, I seen two more yellow bones in the back seat smoking a blunt. Everybody had cups of liquor.

"Get in, nigga!" Van screamed over the music.

"Turn it down!" I called.

He couldn't hear me. Plus, he was drunk, high, and feeling himself. "Get in the car!"

My front door opened and Desiré stepped onto the porch. When Van seen her, he frowned and climbed out of the car.

"What the fuck you doin', nigga? I got some bad bitches, loud, and good drank." Then he went in his pocket and pulled out tickets. "And I got tickets with backstage passes to the Brick Boyz concert. Let's go, nigga!"

Brick Boyz was a hot rap group out of New Jersey. Van knew I loved they music. And he had backstage passes. This was a once in a lifetime opportunity. But Desiré wanted to talk. It seemed important. She was more than a friend. She wasn't my girl, but damn close. Even though she never said she loved me, I knew she did. She was probably just waiting for me to say it first. Fuck. I didn't know what to do.

"Let's go, nigga!" Van yelled. "What you waiting for? When you got the opportunity to do shit, do it. You still young, my nigga. Do you."

"I gotta holla at Desiré."

Van laughed. "My nigga, look at these hoes in my car and then back at Desiré's regular ass. Don't be tied down by shit. Money, hoes, love. Don't let nothing rule you. You rule. You a boss."

I looked at the girls in the car again. They were dimes. But Desiré had something they didn't. Substance. But I also didn't want to pass up another opportunity like I did with Lexi.

"Let me give her these keys."

"My nigga!" Van smiled before hopping back in the car.

Ever since I met Van, I always felt like he gave me good advice. This time I didn't feel so good about listening to him. I turned around and made my way to the porch. Desiré looked devastated.

"I gotta make a run."

"You really going to leave me?" she asked, making it sound final, like I was ending our friendship.

"Something came up. I can't turn it down."

"But what about me? You know that I have to talk to you about something important. Fuck the Brick Boyz, them bitches, and Van!"

That was the first time I ever heard her curse when we wasn't fucking. She was pissed off!

"What you want me to do? Why can't you just let me do what I gotta do? I'ma be back."

"Because I need you here right now. You make hard decisions for people you care about. When you love somebody, you put their needs before your own."

There it was. She loved me. It slipped out so easily that she didn't even know she said it.

"Desiré, you know what I do. You know how I live."

"And you told me that you wouldn't hurt me!" she yelled, tears filling her eyes.

"I'm not trying to hurt you."

"But you are," she whined as the tears spilled. "I told you that you were being pulled in too many directions. I thought that if I kept you satisfied, it would be enough. I can't believe I was so stupid."

"Desiré! Don't—"

"Go!"

"Desiré, I just need—"

"Go, Drayez! Run to your bitches and your friend with all the secrets. I hope it was worth it."

She snatched her keys and pushed me out of the way. I knew I had just fucked up and lost something important. In that moment I realized I loved her. But I was too stupid and pride filled to stop her from leaving.

I tried to enjoy the company of Teela, Vanessa, and Janice. I tried to enjoy the euphoria from smoking and drinking. I tried to enjoy rapping along to all the words of the Brick Boyz songs. But nothing could distract from the emptiness I felt growing inside from losing Desiré. She gave me everything: her body, love, and friendship. She stood before me emotionally naked and I walked away.

"This the life, boy!" Van nudged my arm, grinning from ear to ear.

"We bosses!" I yelled back.

When the concert was over, we went backstage to kick it with the rappers. To my surprise, they knew Van.

"Vincent Van Go! What it do, nigga?" Cash, one of the Brick Boyz yelled.

"Cash Rules! What up, nigga?" Van smiled as they hugged.

"You lookin' good, boy. I see you came from under that indictment. I was worried about you niggas."

"It didn't work out like that for everybody. I got blessed. Ay, Drayez, this my nigga, Cash. We go way back."

"What up, Drayez? Any nigga of Van's is my nigga too," Cash said, showing me love.

"Fa'sho, Cash. Same here."

"Yo, you niggas see we got plenty hoes. And you know we got jars and bottles of everything. Y'all fuckin' with us tonight. Everything on the Brick Boyz!"

The rappers turned out to be some of the coolest niggas I ever met. And they knew how to party. From the concert, we hit up a strip club where the Brick Boyz threw 20 G's. After the club, we drove to the Sybaris Hotel in Glendale and rented a suite with a waterfall in it. We popped bottles, pills, and smoked. Shit started getting freaky and I ended up in the middle of a big-ass orgy. I got fucked and sucked until I fell asleep.

"Drayez!"

When I opened my eyes, Van was standing over me. "What up?"

"Get up, nigga. Party over. Let's go."

I looked around as I got up from the floor. Sleeping bodies were all around me. Most of them were naked females. After I found my clothes, we left.

"That shit was lit, my nigga," Van said as we walked across the parking lot.

"I don't hardly remember shit. I'm fucked up."

"You don't remember them hoes passin' yo' dick around like it was a blunt? That shit was funny as hell!" He laughed.

I shook my head. "Nah, I don't remember none of that shit."

"Don't be surprised if yo' ass end up on the internet. That shit might go viral."

We had just passed a row of cars when the door of a green Honda opened. I looked back and seen a tall dark-skinned nigga dressed in black getting out of the passenger side.

"Van Go!"

Van turned around. When he and the tall nigga made eye contact, Van went for his gun. He was too slow. The big nigga lifted a chrome pistol and started shooting. He was only about fifteen feet away from us and didn't miss. He hit Van five or six times. Somehow Van managed to pull his pistol and get off a shot. He hit the big nigga in the throat. They both went down.

"Van! Van!" I yelled, kneeling over my nigga. His shirt was beginning to soak with blood. I tried to stop the bleeding, but there were too many holes in his stomach and chest. He tried to talk, but only managed to spit up blood.

"HELP! HELP! SOMEBODY HELP!" I screamed.

The Honda's engine revved as it sped away. The big nigga wasn't on the ground, but something was. It looked like a phone. When Van's body started shaking, I knew he was about to die. Blood poured from his mouth, nose, chest, and stomach as he struggled to breathe. His eyes was as big as full moons and all I could see was fear in them. He was scared to die. And a few moments later, the fear was gone.

Chapter 14

It didn't seem real.

Two weeks had gone by since Van died. And even though I had been covered in his blood as I held his lifeless body in my arms, it still didn't seem real. Every day that I awoke, for the briefest moment, I hoped that his murder was a dream. But when the pain of his death and the loss of the brother I never had hit me, reality set in and I knew he was gone.

In one night, I had lost the two closest people in my life. Desiré refused to see me, answer my calls, or return a text. I thought about going to her house, showing up at her job, or calling her from somebody else's phone, but I didn't. Her actions made it clear that she didn't want to fuck with me and I had to respect that. I often wondered what would've happened if I would've stayed at home with her instead of going to that concert with Van. Would he still be alive? Would I be waking up next to Desiré instead of alone?

The bathroom door opened, bringing me from my thoughts and back to the hotel suite. Tikka stepped out dressed in a black pants suit and heels. She looked like a widow. "You okay?"

"Nah. I keep feeling like I should've done more. Like I coulda saved him."

Tikka sat on the bed and put her head on my shoulder. "I know. Sometimes I think about that too. But that's like admitting God made a mistake. I don't think we can stop someone from leaving when it's their time to go. We're just using our love for them to be selfish to try to keep them here."

Tikka was right, but I didn't want to admit it. "It just don't feel right. I know it is but I don't want it to be."

"I think you should just hang onto the good times and be glad y'all met. I know I am. You were a bum before you met Van. Now you're all grown up and independent. Van gave me somebody to look up. I will always love him for that."

"Me too. And I wasn't a bum. I just wasn't sure what I wanted to do, who I was, or what I was capable of." I laughed.

"Basically a bum," Tikka teased.

"Fuck you. C'mon, let's go grab TC. The service starts at 9 o'clock."

I used the rented BMW's GPS to navigate through the Cleveland streets. When I pulled up to the church where Van's funeral was being held, I was surprised to find the lot and surrounding streets filled with cars. It was like somebody famous died. I ended up having to park two blocks over and we walked to the church. The building was overflowing with people coming to pay their last respects to Vincent "Van Go" Meagers. Me, Tikka, and TC found seats in the back. I listened as the choir sang, sounding like angels sending my nigga to heaven. A preacher read a Bible verse and prayed before some of Van's family went to the podium to say final words. Then Theresa went to the podium. She read a poem, bawling her eyes out, making the words difficult to hear. But I didn't need to hear the words to understand what she was saying. She loved Van. A part of her was missing, and he would always have a place in her heart. When she finished reading, Lexi and another friend helped her back to her seat.

Next was the viewing of his body. We would go row by row to pay our final respects. Since I was at the back of the church, it took forever for our row to get up front. I had finally rounded the last pew, twenty feet from Van's casket, when I felt someone watching me. I looked towards Theresa and seen her sobbing with her head down. Lexi was next to her, mouthing something that I couldn't understand. Then she started shaking her head no.

"What?" I shrugged.

She pointed towards the back of the church, telling me to leave. Before I could wrap my mind around what she was trying to say, Theresa looked. Eyes landed on me. The pretty woman that I met at the birthday party a few months ago was gone. Now she looked possessed by the devil.

"It's all your fault!" she screamed, jumping up and rushing towards me.

I was stuck, not knowing what to do. Until she slapped me. Shit hurt. She tried to slap me again, but I caught her hand. Family and friends ran over and grabbed her.

"Let me go! Let me go!" she screamed, trying to get loose.

"Calm down, Theresa. Chill," Lexi said.

"He got my husband killed! I'm fucking you up, Drayez! You got my husband killed!"

In all the commotion, I didn't see Theresa pull off her heels. I just seen a black blur flying at my face. I dodged it. Then a couple of Van's family members approached wearing serious faces.

"Ay, brah. I think you should leave."

I looked in the tear-filled eyes of the three hurting men. They wanted to blame somebody for Van's death and Theresa had already put it on me. I didn't feel like being jumped, so I got up out of there, not able to see my nigga one last time.

On the plane ride home, TC filled me in on what Van was running from. When the ATM indictment came, Van was listed as one of the founders along with Kimo, big Fred, and Larry. They were all facing hundreds of years in the feds. Kimo, Larry, and big Fred all plead guilty and got reduced sentences, fifty years apiece. Van didn't want to spend the next fifty years in prison so he cooperated. He walked away with five years state time, did two, and moved to Milwaukee. I suspected Van snitched so the news didn't surprise me. Nor did it matter. Yeah, Van did some grimy shit, but when you love somebody, you overlook and make excuses for the bullshit they do. Van was my nigga. He changed my life. He taught me shit that I would always remember. That's how I would always see Van.

***

I sat on the couch drinking Hennessey out the bottle, smoking a blunt, and staring at the phone in my lap. The nigga that killed Van had dropped it. I had scrolled through the call log many times, stopping at one name: Shooter. I put the pieces of the puzzle together. ATM knew the Brick Boyz. Cash said it backstage when he asked about everybody that got knocked. And Shooter knew Van would probably be at the concert. They followed us and waited in the parking lot. Shooter was probably driving the green Honda. They killed Van for snitching.

"You know I fucked with Van, my nigga, but he was a rat. What you think them niggas was gon' do once they found him?" Damo asked.

"Van was like my brother. I wouldn't have none of this shit if it wasn't for him. Blood gotta get spilled over this. Shooter gotta die."

"I hear you, brah. And I respect that you wanna clap up the nigga that got down on yo' boy. Had Van not been a rat, I woulda been found that nigga, Shooter, and pushed his shit back. But street niggas deal out street justice. I can't ride for Van, brah. That ain't how it go."

"I hear you, Damo. But I can't let it go."

"So what you gon' do? You never shot nobody."

"I know. But I gotta get this nigga."

"Well, the first thing I'ma tell you is to come up with a plan. You can't just get fucked up and go whack a nigga. That's how niggas end up wit' life. You gotta find where Shooter be or lay his head at."

"How I'm s'posed to do that?"

"You got the nigga's number in yo' hand. Download one of them apps that change yo' number and call him."

"And say what?"

"Shooter was fuckin' wit' ATM so you know he hustling. Niggas that was eatin' like that can't stay away. You see Van. Hit that nigga and see what he movin'. Go from there."

I downloaded an app and made the call. Shooter answered on the second ring. "Yeah."

"This Shooter?" I asked.

"Yeah. Who dis?"

I said the first name that came to mind. "Doc. You good?"

"Doc?" he asked. "How you get this number?"

"C'mon, my nigga. Don't do me like that. I ain't Twelve. I just seen you at the Brick Boyz concert. This Doc, nigga."

"I still can't place the name with the face. Tell you what. Meet me on 29th and Cherry in thirty minutes. I wanna see yo' face. Make sure you ain't tryna set a nigga up."

"I'm tryna eat, my nigga. I leave that fuck shit for fuck niggas."

"Fa'sho. Hit me when you close."

"What he say?" Damo asked after I hung up.

"Meet him on 29th and Cherry in thirty minutes."

"For real? This what you wanna do?"

"I don't got no choice. I gotta ride for my nigga."

Damo stared at me for a few moments before letting out a long breath. "Damn, Drayez. I can't let you do this shit by yo'self. You fuck around and get killed. C'mon, nigga. Let's go."

I let Damo drive the rented Dodge Magnum. He parked on 28th and Cherry and we walked to 29th. We both wore black clothes. I had the 9 millimeter Taurus in the front pocket of my hoody. Even though I was drunk and high, I was still nervous.

"Call that nigga so we can see where he at. We gon' dump on the niggas and get back to the rental," Damo instructed.

I pulled out my phone and called Shooter back. "Ay, Shooter, I'm at the light on 27th. It just turned green. Where you at?"

"I'm in the middle of the block. Black and white brick house. Look for the Lac truck."

Even though it was dark outside, the bright red truck wasn't hard to find. Three niggas stood on the porch of the black and white house. I spotted Shooter immediately.

"Is he on the porch?" Damo asked.

"Yeah. Green hat and green shoes."

"Soon as we get to the walkway, it's on."

The walkway was about forty feet away. With every step, my heart beat faster and harder. It felt like my shit was about to pop out my chest and my hands was ice cold. Damo was the exact opposite, like it was just another day in the park for him. When we got to the walkway, he didn't hesitate. He upped his pistol and started shooting. I followed, my adrenaline taking over as I squeezed the trigger. Fire shot out of my cannon in big flashes. Shooter and his niggas tried to run, but we cut them down. They all screamed as they died. I didn't know who I hit, but I emptied the fifteen shot clip. When the gun clicked, I ran.

***

The next couple of weeks went by in a haze. Shooter and all the niggas on the porch died. The news said they got killed by "a hail of bullets". No suspects. No witnesses. Knowing that I killed the nigga that killed Van did the exact opposite of what I thought it would. I didn't feel better and it didn't lessen the pain from losing my nigga. The murders actually made me shrink inside of myself a little more each day. It felt like I had committed a grave sin, like the mark that God put on Cain's head after he killed Abel was on mine. I prayed for forgiveness. And I dreamt about the shooting almost as much as I dreamt about Van dying in my arms. I smoked and drank more to escape the thoughts and dreams. I even stopped going out in public and hustling. Van was my plug so I had no product. I only had about 10 G's in my stash and I didn't know what I was going to do once that ran out. Shit, I didn't even want to hustle no more. There was too much blood on my hands. I wished I could turn into a simple nigga like TC and get a job at McDonald's, but that wasn't me.

"Don't you wanna do something else besides sit in the house?"

I turned my bloodshot eyes from the TV and looked at Mona. She was sitting on the couch next to me looking sexy as fuck in a red catsuit, her dark skin damn near blending in with my couch. She came over a couple times a week. I normally dicked her down, gave her some money, and sent her on her way.

"What?"

"Don't you wanna leave the house? Why don't you come to the club no more? Every time I come around, you just drink, smoke, and sulk."

"'Cause mu'fuckas ain't shit," I slurred.

She looked at me crazy. "That don't even make sense. Fuck happened to the boss nigga I met?"

I laughed. "Fuck you think you is, bitch? You don't know me. Suck a nigga dick or somethin'. That's all you good for. Hoes like you do anything for a dolla."

She stood, neck rolling, eyes popping, and lips smacking. "Nigga, I don't know who the fuck you think you talking to, but I ain't no punk-ass bitch you can talk to any kinda way. You a weak-minded-ass nigga. Fall apart when yo' niggas die. You act like he was yo' daddy or somethin. Or prolly yo' boyfriend. All you niggas be gay nowadays."

I jumped up from the couch so fast that I got a head rush and almost fell. After catching my balance, I reached my arm all the way back to China and slapped the shit out of Mona. She stumbled and fell. I was about to stomp a hole in her ass when Tikka came out of nowhere and grabbed me.

"Drayez, why the fuck you hit her?"

"Bitch don't talk to me like that in my house! I'll kill this punk-ass bitch! Get the fuck out, you nut drinkin'-ass bitch!"

Mona wiped blood from her mouth as she stood. "You gon' get yours, nigga! I promise you that. I'ma be the last bitch you ever hit."

"Bitch, shut the fuck up and get out my house before I beat cho ass!" I yelled, flinching like I was about to hit her again.

She jumped back, grabbed her purse, and left.

"What is going on, Dray?" Tikka asked, searching my face.

"Bitch ain't finna talk to me like that. Talkin' 'bout me and Van gay. Bitch lucky I ain't kill her bitch ass."

"This don't even sound like you. What's going on?"

Hearing Tikka try to tell me who I was pissed me off. "You don't know me! Fuck you think you is? You takin' up for that bitch? You wanna get bitch slapped too? You wanna be like Tina and Rayna and the rest of them hoes and get paid to fuck? Is that why you was fuckin' Van? Did he pay for some pussy?"

When I finished my rant, I was standing over Tikka with my fists clenched. She was staring up at me with fear and tears in her eyes. The look on her face was sobering. My high was gone, my anger vanished, and I felt like a big-ass fool.

"My bad," I mumbled, looking away in shame.

“So that’s how you feel about me?” Tikka whispered. “That’s how you feel about all women? Wanna blame everybody for what Rayna did to you?”

I sat down, unable to look at my sister.

Tikka stood where she was, staring at me as tears rolled down her cheeks. “Whats going on, Drayez? Talk to me. You’re changing. This isn’t who you are.”

“Ain’t nothing making sense no more. I don’t know what to do.”

“I think you should start by not drinking so much. You’re losing control of yourself.”

I didn’t have a response for that. She was right. Tikka came and sat next to me, wrapping me in a hug. We didn’t say nothing, just sat there hugging until my phone rang.

“You going to get that?” she asked.

“Fuck ’em.”

My phone stopped ringing and then started again.

Tikka answered. “Hello? He right here. Drayez, it’s Rayna.”

“Fuck that bitch.”

“He can’t talk right now. You want me to tell him something? Wait, wait, slow down. Where is Draya?”

That got my attention.

“Drayez, something wrong with Draya!”

BOOK III: POLISH THE HUSTLE

BEFORE SUCCESS COMES IN ANYONE'S LIFE, THEY ARE SURE TO BE MET WITH DEFEAT.

BUT DEFEAT IS TEMPORARY TO SOMEONE WITH DRIVE.

DRIVE BACKED BY PREPARATION CAN OVERCOME ANYTHING.

AND WHEN PREPARATION MEETS OPPORTUNITY, IT EQUALS SUCCESS. THE MIGHTY EAGLE SLEEPS IN AN EGG WAITING FOR BIRTH MUCH LIKE THE BEST VERSION OF THE HUSTLER IS SLEEPING IN A COCOON WAITING TO BE BORN AGAIN.

THAT'S HOW YOU POLISH THE HUSTLER.

EVERY LESSON IS A BLESSING IN DISGUISE.

EVERY FAILURE IS AN OPPORTUNITY TO DO BETTER.

SHINE.

IMPROVE.

WHEN YOU BECOME THE PERSON YOU ARE REALLY MEANT TO BE, YOUR TASTES ARE REFINED.

YOU'VE GIVEN UP WHAT YOU DON'T NEED TO KEEP WHAT YOU CAN'T AFFORD TO LOSE.

EVERYTHING YOU TOUCH TURNS TO GOLD.

THE HOOD IS BEHIND YOU.

THE WORLD IS BEFORE YOU.

Chapter 15

Draya had pneumonia and it was serious. It had been a week since I last saw her. Since I had been in a funk, I hadn't been checking on her. Now she was laid up in the hospital with tubes sticking out of her arm and nose. Rayna was sitting in the chair next to Draya's bed looking a mess. Perm thick with new growth, skin ashy and in need of lotion, and her normally watery eyes were dry. She was rocking a purple Adidas track suit and dirty white slippers.

"What the doctors say?"

"She got fluid on her lungs. She been sick for three days." She paused to sniff. "At first I thought it was a regular cold, but then she picked up the bad cough and her fever got worse, I brought her in. They want to keep her til she get better."

Draya was ten months old, getting bigger and prettier every day. She was normally full of life and loved to play. But right now she was in bad shape. Her breathing was raspy and when she coughed, it sounded like she was about to hack up a lung.

"She gon' get better," I said.

"Our baby is a fighter," Rayna said, sniffling again. "All the shit I put you through and you landed on yo' feet. She got the same spirit."

"I just hate to see her like this. You okay? You sick too?"

"Yeah. Just a li'l bug. How you been? Ain't seen much of you lately."

"I'm working through some shit. One of my niggas died and it kinda fucked me up. Now I'm regrouping."

She looked concerned. "It wasn't Vic or TC, was it?"

"Nah. My nigga Van. You never met him."

"That's fucked up. They say the good ones die young?"

I nodded. "True shit."

"You plan on spending the night? I gotta get back to the other kids. School in the morning."

"Yeah. I'ma be here til she get better. I don't got shit else to do."

"Okay. Call me if she get worse. I'ma come back tomorrow after I send the kids to school."

When Rayna left I closed my eyes, listening to the sounds Draya's machines made while thinking about my baby mama. Those were the most words I said to her since I busted her ass open. And she didn't seem bitter about it. Might have something to do with the 500 dollars a month I had been giving her for child support. She was just like all the money hungry bitches in the world. A few dollars would make any wrong all right.

When Draya started coughing, I pushed thoughts of Rayna from my head. The coughs had awakened her and now she was crying her eyes out.

Draya ended up keeping me awake all night with coughing and crying. That combined with the nurses and doctors moving in and out of the room made sleep a luxury I couldn't afford. I caught a few z's here and there. Sometime during the afternoon, I gave her a wash up and put her to sleep before stepping outside to have a much-needed cigarette. When the smoke hit my lungs and I got the nicotine rush, I wanted to moan like I was getting some bomb-ass head. But the lady sitting in the wheelchair next to me made me keep it cool. It looked like she had been in a car accident. She had a black eye, swollen lips, and casts on her left arm and right leg. Her skin was dark brown, hair wrapped in a ponytail. I couldn't tell how old she was or if she was pretty because of the bruising and swelling on her face.

But I knew she was smoking her cigarette like it was the last muthafucka left.

"Take a picture. It'll last longer."

"My bad," I mumbled, not realizing I was staring.

I found something else to look at while I smoked. I started looking over the cars in the parking lot. Noticed there were a lot of foreigns. Doctors made good money.

"Is that your daughter?" she asked.

"Yeah. That's my baby."

"Where's her mother?"

"She got a couple other kids. Had to get them to school."

Confusion lit her hazel brown eyes. "Y'all got kids or she do?"

I chuckled. "She do."

"I think what you're doing is cool. I mean, fathers supposed to be there for their kids but a lot of 'em don't. So kudos to you."

"Thanks. I appreciate it."

Rayna came back about noon and hung out for an hour or so. Since Draya was still in the same condition, all we could do was let the doctors do their job and wait for Draya to get better.

Two days later her fever broke and she showed improvement. The cough wasn't as harsh and she could eat a little bit, but she was still cranky and slept a lot. I used her nap times to go home to shower and change. Or go outside and take a smoke break, like I was now. I had just lit my cancer stick when the chick in the wheelchair rolled out.

"Can I get a light?"

I handed her my cigarette so she could use the cherry to light her own. The swelling in her face had gone down and the blackness around her eyes was getting smaller. Her hazel brown eyes also seemed to have more life in them. If I had to guess her age, I would've said early thirties.

"Thanks. How the baby doing? She getting better yet?"

"Yeah. Fever gone and the cough is getting better. Doctors say she doin' good. Still a li'l fluid on her lungs and they wanna watch that."

"That's good to hear. Pneumonia is serious. Especially for babies and old people. Sound like you have a strong baby. What's her name?"

"Draya."

She cut her eyes at me. "Like the girls on the *Basketball Wives*, or *Hip Hop Honeys*, or whatever show she from?"

"Yeah. Like that."

She frowned. "How you come up with that name?"

"My name Drayez."

She nodded. "OK. Now it makes sense. Drayez and Draya. That's cute."

"Since you know our name, what's yours?"

"Kianna. Not spelled like the around-the-way girls Keyonna either. K-I-A-N-N-A. My mama was a psychologist and my daddy was a dentist."

"Okay, not spelled like the around-the-way girl Kianna whose daddy is a dentist and mama's a psychologist. It's good to meet you."

She laughed. "I'm just playing, man. My mama wasn't a psychologist and my daddy ain't no dentist. Deborah is a seamstress and Randy is a plumber. Except Randy cleaned more than pipes."

I laughed. "You crazy."

"So, what about you? Who are your mother and father?"

I paused, wondering if I should tell this stranger my personal business. She looked up at me expectantly. Waiting.

"Marie is a don't take no shit, boy I will fuck you up, SSI gettin', drama queen. And my pops…I never met him. Heard he doin' life in the joint. They say me and my cousin got the same daddy. Guess Marie fucked her sister's baby daddy and got pregnant. Don't know none of this for sure. This the shit that get brought up at family reunions."

Kianna just stared at me. "Well, damn. I was just trying to be funny and lighten the mood. But your story sound like it should be in a book."

"Or on Jerry Springer," I cracked.

Kianna laughed way too hard. "Nah, Drayez! You wrong!"

"Quit playin'. You know you wanted to laugh all along."

"Okay, I did. But more at your mother being a don't take no shit, I will fuck you up, SSI getting drama queen. That sounds like my sister."

"So what about you? What's your story?"

I saw a flash of something in her eyes that I couldn't describe, like there was more to her than meets the eye. She was a woman with layers. And secrets.

"I'm the kind of woman that will give you the shirt off my back. But let me find out you lying or using me and I'm taking my shit back."

"An Indian giver?"

"If that's what you wanna call it. I call it stayin' warm. Now tell me who you are."

I thought of something clever. "A humble man with the mind of a chameleon and the heart of a lion."

She looked impressed. "Ooh. Got all deep on me."

"That was the best I could come up with on short notice."

"Nah, you did that. You probably practiced it on a hundred other females already, but you did that."

"Practice?" I chuckled. "I don't gotta practice nothing. What you see is what you get. Practice is for athletes, entertainers, and fake niggas tryna be real. I don't play sports. I can't sing, dance, or act. And I damn sho ain't fake."

That thing flashed in her eyes again. Then she repeated my name like it was a song lyric. "Drayez, Drayez, Drayez."

"Why you say my name like that?"

"You remind me of somebody that I used to know."

"I hope that nigga wasn't a dancer," I joked.

She looked up at me and smirked.

***

Two days later, Draya was almost back to being her normal self. She still had a little cough, but she could eat more and we was playing the kissing game again. Rayna popped up for an hour or two every day to check in and talk to the doctors and then hit it. Draya didn't seem to mind her mother not being around and I didn't either. I preferred it being just me and my baby. And watching her face light up when I read a book made me want to get stuck in those moments forever.

"That is the cutest shit I've ever seen in my life," Kianna said as she rolled the wheelchair into the room. The swelling had gone down completely, her black eyes were almost gone, and her hair was combed and flowing past her shoulders. She seemed to be getting finer every day.

"What's up, Indian giver?"

"Watching you in here winning a dad of the year award," she said before turning to Draya. "Hi, princess!"

Draya just stared.

"She gotta warm up to you."

"She is too cute. Let me hold her."

Kianna rolled her chair next to me and I sat Draya on her lap. Kianna made funny faces and Draya laughed.

"You should put her in baby commercials. I swear she is the cutest little girl in the world."

"Hollywood ain't ready for my baby. She would take over the town. Have li'l boys stalking her. I ain't doing no time for beating up baby stalkers."

"You are too crazy." She laughed. "But she make me wanna have a baby."

"Why you don't got kids? You seem like a natural."

"I'm thirty-eight and past the age of trying to raise babies. Plus, my life is too fast for kids."

"You sound like me. Tell me about the fast life you lived."

That something shown in her eyes. "Let's just say that I found out the hard way that everything that glitters ain't gold."

"Amen," I agreed.

"So, what do you do? I noticed you been in the hospital for a week and either you don't have a job or you have a really understanding boss. But the clothes say you got style. And since you ain't a singer, dancer, or actor, that only leaves a couple things."

I was surprised the way her mind put all that shit together. Told me she was sharp and paid attention to detail. "Let me find out you the police," I cracked.

"If I was the police, I woulda had a gun and shot the muthafuckas that did this to me. Nope, I ain't the Feds."

"I thought you was in a car accident or something. Who did this to you?"

She gave me a look that told she wasn't going into details. "Don't worry about it. Let's just say that I learn lessons the hard way. Pain will teach you what pride won't let you learn."

Since I knew she didn't want to talk about her injuries, I cracked another joke to lighten the mood. "I know you practiced that shit!"

"Forget you," she smiled. "It's in me, not on me."

I was about to throw another jab when Rayna walked in the room. When she saw Kianna holding Draya, I could almost see her body temperature rise.

"Uh oh!" Kianna mumbled, handing Draya back to me.

"What the fuck is this, Drayez?" Rayna snapped, pausing to wipe her nose. "Why is this bitch holding my baby?"

"Chill out, man. This Kianna. She in the room a couple doors down."

Rayna mugged Kianna, snatching Draya from my arms. "I don't appreciate you having yo' friends around my daughter. I don't know her. And since you just met her in the hospital, you don't know her either."

I mugged the shit out of Rayna. "You finna go there, for real? You got niggas in yo' house all around Draya and I don't say shit. I give you enough money to pay yo' rent every month. Them niggas don't. Fuck out my face with this shit about her holding Draya."

"Uh, I'll talk to you later, Drayez," Kianna said, wheeling herself towards the door.

I grabbed the wheelchair to stop her. "Nah. You ain't gotta leave. She the one that ain't been here. I been talkin' to these nurses and doctors and takin' care of Draya. I been waking up in the middle of the night when she coughing and crying. If I wanna bring my friends in this mu'fuckin' room, I can."

"That don't mean she gotta be holding my daughter," Rayna said before sniffling.

"Man, you worried about the wrong shit. You need to be tryna see when she get out the hospital instead of worrying about who holding her."

The argument paused when the door opened and Doctor Kavich stuck his head in the room. "How's everybody doing?" He smiled. When he noticed the looks on our faces and felt animosity in the air, he stopped smiling. "Is everything okay? Should I come back later?"

"Nah, you good, Doc," I spoke up. "You a busy man. What's up?"

"You are too kind, Mr. Alexander. I just wanted to pop in to check on Draya's progress," the doctor said, looking Draya over. "The nurses told me she was doing better. If this keeps up, a couple more days and you guys should be able to take her home."

"That's good to hear, Doc."

"I have a few more rounds to make. I'll check in later. Have a nice day."

The room grew quiet after the doctor left.

"I'm going to have a smoke," Kianna said, rolling out of the room.

Since I didn't want to be in the room with Rayna, I followed Kianna outside.

"Why you do yo' baby mama like that?" Kianna laughed.

I took a long pull on my Newport. "If only you knew all the shit she put me through."

"I can only imagine. Y'all don't even seem like each other's type. She seems ratchet and you seem…a couple levels above her pay grade."

"That was a good metaphor," I chuckled. "But there was a time when I was below her pay grade. I met her when I first got out the joint. Beggars can't be choosy."

"And so you fucked her without a rubber. How many kids she got? Wait, let me guess. Four?"

"Close. Five."

Her eyes got big. "How many baby daddies? Don't say five."

I laughed.

Her eyes got bigger. "She got five baby daddies!? Oh my! What number are you? You better not say number five."

I took another puff of my cigarette.

Kianna burst out laughing like she was watching stand-up comedy. "You're number five? Damn, Drayez!"

"I was a beggar. I couldn't be choosy."

Kianna kept laughing, slapping her leg and wiping tears from her eyes. “I’m sorry for laughing, but that was too funny. I wasn’t expecting all that.”

“It’s all good,” I managed, feeling some type of way about her laughs at my expense.

“So how long has she been treating her nose?”

That shit got my attention. “What?”

Kianna looked surprised. “You don’t know?”

“Know what?”

She looked uncomfortable. “I don’t know if I should say. I thought you knew.”

I got mad. “What the fuck is you talkin’ about? Quit bullshitting.”

Kianna searched my face. “Your baby mama is a powder head.”

I looked at her like she was crazy. “Fuck is you talkin’ about?”

“That’s why she keeps sniffing. She’s not sick. Her nose is running.”

Rayna had the sniffles for a week. She said it was a cold, but it didn’t seem to be getting better. In that same time, Draya had almost gotten over pneumonia.

“I’ma kill this bitch!”

When I got to the room, Rayna was sitting on the bed with Draya watching a Disney movie. I stood in front of the TV, searching her face for a sign of drug use.

“What the fuck you doin’, Drayez? Move!”

“You fuckin’ wit’ that shit?”

Fear shown in her eyes. “What shit?”

“You know what the fuck I’m talkin’ ’bout. Fuck you doin’ all this sniffing for? Why yo’ cold ain’t gone? It’s been damn near a week.”

“I-I don’t know. I don’t be taking medicine.”

“Bitch, stop lyin’ to me! I ain’t stupid. Fuck you puttin’ up yo’ nose?”

She looked away. “I just do a li’l bit of powder every now and then.”

"What the fuck, Rayna? When the fuck you start doin' this punk ass shit?"

She got quiet.

I shook my head as I looked at her pathetic ass. Fucked up hair, dry eyes, runny nose. Kianna was right. We wasn't each other's types. Never was. I was a fool for settling for someone I had no business sticking my dick in.

"I'm through giving you money for child support and I'm takin' Draya."

She got loud. "No the fuck you ain't! You ain't taking my baby!"

"Bitch, that's my baby. The doctors see that I'm the only one that's been here. I'll take yo' ass to court if I got to. And I got money to buy a real lawyer. Get'cho ass drug tested. You gon' lose all yo' kids and food stamps. I want my baby."

Rayna looked like she wanted to fight me, but knew better. The Drayez she knew was gone. She didn't know or understand the man that stood before her today. I would do anything and everything to make sure my daughter was safe. Even if it meant fucking up Rayna's entire life.

She must've recognized the seriousness in my eyes because she got up and walked out of the room.

Chapter 16

I didn't see how Rayna and other females with multiple kids did it. Being a parent to a ten month old twenty-four hours a day was a job. Everywhere I went, I had to take Draya. Everything I did, she did too. I couldn't go to sleep until she went to sleep. When she woke up, I had to wake up. And she was expensive. My back room had been something like a guest room/storage room, but now it was Draya's. I spent almost five G's getting everything she needed: dresser, bed, TV, clothes, high chair, strollers, bottles, toys, papers…Everything. I didn't bother getting nothing from Rayna's house. She could have all that shit. I just wanted my baby.

"Never in a million years," Tikka said as she walked into the living room.

I was sitting on the floor in the living room with Draya on my lap watching *Frozen* for what seemed like the fiftieth time. "Beat it with the jokes."

"I think I'ma write Ellen and tell her how you went from being a drug dealer to a responsible parent." She laughed. "She'll probably give you a house or car."

"Funny shit. Betta hope that when you have kids, you find a nigga as good as me."

"You're right about that. You've definitely set the bar high for my future husband. But for real, brother, I'm proud of you. She don't need to be around Rayna's dope fiend ass."

"I know. But this shit is hard. A real fuckin' job. I ain't having no more kids."

"You're going to leave Draya lonely? No brothers or sisters?"

"That's what daycare and school is for. I ain't doin' this shit no more."

Tikka sat down next to me and wrapped an arm around my shoulder. "I hear you, brother. So, how are you doing? Seems like you're back to being normal. I noticed you haven't been drinking your life away lately."

"I can't. I gotta take care of her. That was just a phase. I was fucked up. I lost my nigga and…"

"Desiré?"

"Fuck you talkin' 'bout?"

"I know you, Dray. She meant a lot to you. Losing her hurt just as much as losing Van."

I gave up the front. "Yeah, I fucked that up."

"She was a good one. I liked her. And she loved you. She was the one you let get away. You try to call her?"

"Not in a while. She never got back to me, so I'ma respect that."

"I don't know much about love, but I think that if you really love somebody, you should do everything you can to get them back. You shouldn't give up."

"I didn't. She did. If she loved me, why didn't she get back at me? I left plenty messages and texts."

"Because you hurt her. You chose Van, the concert, and those girls over her. You have to sacrifice for the people you love, like you do for Draya. That's how you show love. It's an action word."

When my phone rang, a part of me hoped it was Desiré. "Hello?"

"Hey, Mr. Mom."

Hearing her voice made me smile. "What's up, Indian giver?"

"Nothing. Bored. Thought I'd called you and see what you were up to."

"Chilling with my baby and watching *Frozen*. She won't let me leave from in front of the TV."

"I never got the chance to see that. I think it won a bunch of awards and made a lot of money."

"Yeah, it's not bad. The snowman is a trip. I got it on DVD. You can pull up next to me and Draya if you want."

"I just might take you up on that offer. My SSI getting-ass sister and her kids are annoying the shit out of me. These Parklawn project apartments are way too small. I'm not used to this."

I laughed. "Yo' bourgeois ass can't handle them projects, huh?"

"It's not the projects; it's the kids. They noise bounces off the walls. And all my sister do is scream at them all day. That shit giving me a headache. I need a break."

"My house is quiet. Just me, Draya, and my li'l sister. C'mon through."

"Where do you live?"

"Over on Grantosa."

"Damn, Drayez. What the fuck you doing over there? Why don't you live in the hood?"

"'Cause I wanna live. Shit. I stay away from all the bullshit."

"I don't got no way to get over there. I'm on hard times, man."

"Don't trip. Catch a cab. I got you."

"You sure?"

"Yeah, you good. I liked yo' company at the hospital. Plus, Draya likes you and my baby got an eye for good people."

An hour later, I heard a car's horn blowing outside. When I walked outside, Kianna was getting out of a cab. She still wore casts on her arm and leg, so she used crutches. And she looked good. Not dime piece fine, but an easy 8. The swelling and bruising was gone and her skin glowed. She had thick hair that flowed past her shoulders. I had only seen her in a hospital gown so I didn't know she had a body. The yellow jeans showed off her slim hourglass figure and the cream halter top showed nice titties. And she was tall. 5'10". When she turned to speak to the driver, I checked out her ass. It was nice and poked out just right. It fit her frame perfectly.

"You taller than I thought," I commented, handing the driver a 20.

"Played forward in high school. Baby Lebron!"

I reached out to help her onto the sidewalk, but she ignored my assistance and gave me a look that said she was a woman with pride that handled her own business.

"I got it. Thanks."

I kept my hands to myself and led the way into the house.

"Damn, Drayez. This is nice. I wasn't expecting this," she commented, looking around the living room.

"Fuck you thought, I was living in a trap house?"

"Not a trap, but definitely not this," she said, flopping down on the couch. "Hi, Draya!"

Draya laughed and crawled over to her.

"Told you my baby got good taste."

Tikka walked in the living room. "Hi, Kianna."

"Hi. You must be Tikka. Heard a lot about you."

"That's me. What did Drayez tell you? If it's anything bad, he's lying."

Kianna laughed. "No, everything was good. Said you were going to school to be a lawyer. Do the damn thang, gurl! Need more black people in the courtrooms."

Tikka smiled at Kianna before turning to me. "I like her. Don't let her get away. I'm going out. I need some money."

"Don't you got a job?"

"Yeah, but I don't get paid til next Friday. I need a loan."

"Stop calling it a loan because you ain't gon' pay me back," I said, fishing a bill out of my pocket. It turned out to be a fifty. I was about to put it back, but Tikka snatched it.

"This will do. Pay you back after law school, when I become your attorney. Love you!"

And she was gone. I just stared at the door. Kianna started laughing.

"What's funny?"

"You. You're only twenty-four and taking care of your sister and daughter. What the fuck planet are you from?"

"How is calling me an alien a compliment?"

"It's not. And what did she mean by let *don't me get away?"*

I thought about Desiré. "Long story. Is you ready for F*rozen*? I'm tellin' you right now, Olaf is a fool."

After watching *Frozen* for the fourth time that day, I needed something to eat. "You hungry?" I asked Kianna.

She raised an eyebrow. "You better not say you can cook too. I swear to God if you know how to cook, we gettin' married tomorrow."

"Nah, I don't cook. I'm a sammich nigga. A sammich, chips, and one of Draya's cakes'll do me good. Unless you wanna order something."

"Tell you what. How about you let me cook for you and Draya? It's the least I can do for your hospitality. Got anything to make a meal?"

I shrugged. "Tikka do the shopping. I just eat. But we can find out together."

I tried to help her up from the couch, but she gave me that look again. Instead of helping her, I grabbed Draya and went to the kitchen. I ended up finding some real food. Kianna put together meatloaf, mashed potatoes, gravy, and biscuits.

"So, when do the casts come off?"

"I'm taking this thing off my leg tomorrow. I have a hairline fracture in my ankle. The one on my arm will be another couple weeks. Broke my ulna."

"You still haven't told me what happened."

"Yes, I did. Lesson learned, the hard way."

The more I was around Kianna, the more I wanted to know about her. She was cool and easy to talk to. But she had secrets. And there was a look in her eyes that told me she had been through some shit. I wanted to know what the shit was.

"People that build walls are hiding from something," I said.

"Or we're just waiting for the right person to show how much they care and climb over it. Can't cast your pearls amongst swine."

"You callin' me a pig?"

"You know what I'm saying. I'm not an open book. Think of me as a diary. When you find the key, everything will reveal itself."

"How can I find the key if you don't tell me where to look?"

"And that, Drayez, is the 64,000 dollar question. Come taste this and tell me what you think."

She was cooking a red paste in a small pot. When I walked over, she scooped some onto a spoon. "What is it?"

"My special meatloaf sauce. Tell me what you think."

I tasted it. The sauce was sweet, spicy, and smoky. "That shit is fiya!"

After dinner, we sat around watching movies, kicking it about everything. Draya went to sleep around 8 o'clock and I broke out the Hennessey. When I got buzzed up, I wanted to get touchy, but

Kianna gave no signs that she wanted to give up the pussy and I didn't press. We ended up talking until we fell asleep. I woke up a little later and covered Kianna with a blanket before going to bed.

I woke up the next morning to Draya rubbing my face. She was hungry. I got up and set out some towels and a toothbrush for Kianna before making breakfast. I was sitting at the table feeding Draya when Kianna came out of the bathroom looking refreshed.

"I hope you don't ever change."

I looked up from my bacon and saw Kianna staring at me like I was a prize on *Wheel of Fortune*. "What you mean?"

"Stay like this: humble, kind, and respectful. A family man. The world is so fucked up, but meeting you gives me hope that there are still good black men out there. We need more like you. Don't change. I knew somebody like you once. A long time ago."

"Who was he? What happened?"

"My ex. He was a good nigga until he started getting money. Got big-headed. The saying is true: 'more money, more problems'. For my ex, money became his god. Money is a tool and not to be worshipped."

"My nigga Van used to say that shit. It kept me humble."

"I knew you were a hustler."

"I used to fuck with that boy. Now that my nigga dead, I kinda left that shit alone. He was my plug. But I gotta figure out something because shit gettin' tight."

"Why not get a job? You're smarter than the average nigga?"

"That job shit ain't for me. I got the spirit of a hustla. The only thing a job would do is dull my skills and make me waste away. I need that fast money. 500 dollars every two weeks ain't the life for me."

"Money is not everything. It destroyed my relationship. It made him big-headed. It changed him."

"Yo' nigga's problem was he stopped making money and let it make him. I got money and made a way for my people. Took care of my responsibilities. Most niggas get money and give that shit away. I gave some away, but I mostly gave to my family. I'm raisin' my daughter and keeping a roof over my sister's head so she can focus on college. Also taking care of my big sister up north. I can't do this making 500 dollars every two weeks. I hustle because my responsibilities demand it."

Kianna nodded in agreement. "When you put it like that, I feel you. I don't even think 500 dollars would cover your rent. I get it. Just be careful. The game ain't the same. Niggas changed."

"What you know about the game?"

That look shone in her eyes again. "I seen some things."

"From yo' ex, huh? Who is he? Is he major? My money running out and I need a plug."

"I'll tell you about him one day. How about you hook a sistah up with some of that bacon? And if you don't mind, I need a ride to my sister's house."

After dropping Kianna off at her sister's and agreeing to get up with her later, I got up with Damo. I was ready to get back on the grind.

"Where you at, nigga?"

"I'm in traffic. What's good, nigga? You shook that depressed shit?"

"I did. I gotta get this paper. I need a plug. What you got?"

"Man, Yez, I need what you had. I'm fuckin wit' a li'l somethin', but it ain't shit."

"It don't matter. Just put me in. I gotta start makin' some money. I'm damn near broke."

"A'ight. I'ma holla at this nigga and hit you back. The nigga only movin' li'l shit. Nothing major."

"That's cool. Just get at me."

I hung up the phone feeling better than I had in a long time. Mike had been on my ass about getting some work and I was ready to get the trap back poppin'.

I ended up waiting all day for Damo to hit me back. Kianna hit me up about 5 o'clock and I went to pick her up. We chilled at my crib and watched movies, but I wasn't really into it because I kept thinking about Damo.

"What's up, Drayez? Where you at? Why you all dull?"

I turned my head to look at Kianna. She was rockin' a red blazer, white T-shirt, jeans, and heels. She had gotten the cast taken off her leg and was looking classy and sexy at the same time.

"I'm watching the movie."

"No you ain't. You're looking at the TV, but you're not here. What's up?"

"A'ight, you got me. I'm thinkin' 'bout this money. Shit gettin' real. My nigga was supposed to hit me up earlier, but I ain't heard from him. I can't stop thinkin' 'bout that shit. I need a plug. I got shit to do."

"Nothing you can do but wait. Worrying won't change anything."

"Easier said than done."

"You want to do something to keep your mind off the hustle?" she asked, biting her bottom lip.

I looked to Draya sleeping on the floor. Tikka was gone. "Hell yeah! What you got in mind?"

She motioned for me to come closer with her index finger. I leaned in. Her lips were soft and the kiss was sexy and aggressive. I went for her blazer. It came off right along with her T-shirt. She wasn't wearing a bra. Her titties were perfect handfuls. I lowered my head, flicking my tongue across her nipple. She shuddered and moaned. I went back and forth from the left one to the right one until they were hard enough to cut glass.

And then my phone rang. I reached for it, but she grabbed my hand.

"I gotta get this. It might be my nigga."

Disappointment flashed in her eyes, but she let me go.

The call was from Damo. "What up, nigga? Tell me something good."

"I'm wit' the nigga right now. All he got is ten. He want 700. You want it?"

"I'm on my way. Where y'all at?"

By the time I finished the call, Kianna already had her clothes on.

"I gotta make a run."

"Go ahead. I'll watch Draya."

"You sure?"

"I know how the game goes, Drayez. Go do what you have to do. I'll be here when you get back."

She didn't have to tell me a third time. I met up with Damo and he introduced me to a nigga named Big Dawg. Big, black, fat-ass nigga that breathed like he just ran a mile. We made the exchange and I was back to the crib. I walked in the house feeling good.

Kianna greeted me with a smile. "You good?"

"Hell yeah!" I said, heading for the kitchen. I dumped the dope on the counter to inspect it. It was browner than I would've liked, but I didn't have a plug, so I couldn't complain. It had fentynal in it, so I looked for the lactose to cut it.

"What are you looking for?" Kianna asked.

"Something to cut this shit with. I can't find my lactose."

"How much is it?"

"Ten grams."

"How much you pay?"

I stopped searching the cabinets to look at her. "Why you asking all these questions?"

"Because I wanna know if it's worth it."

"I paid 700. I'ma try to double that. Maybe triple."

She looked satisfied so I went back to my search. I ended up searching the whole kitchen, but still didn't find the lactose.

"You okay?" Kianna asked.

"Hell nah. It got fentanyl on it and I need to cut it, but I can't find my shit."

"I might have something in my purse that can help. Let me check."

I started putting my dope back in the bag. "Fuck is you talkin' 'bout? You ain't finna play in my shit."

She gave me a look before leaving the kitchen. She came back a few moments later with a bottle of pills.

"What's that?"

"Benzodiazepine. Doctors gave it to me for the pain, but I don't like pills. You can cut heroin with it. Let me see your work."

I reluctantly gave her the work and watched as she crushed the pills with a spoon and mixed it with the dog food. The way she moved told me she had done this before. When done, she stepped back, wearing a smirk.

"Who the fuck is you? And don't bullshit me this time? You know more about dope than I do, don't you?"

She let me squirm a few seconds before telling me. "You heard of the Triple Beam Team?"

"Yeah. Er'body heard of TBT."

"I helped start it."

I bust out laughing. I laughed for a good minute too. Kianna just watched me. When I seen she was serious, I stopped laughing.

"You serious?"

"Yes. Carl is the founder. His real name is Carlile White. That's my ex."

My eyes damn near popped out of my head and my jaw dropped like cartoon characters when they seen a fine girl. Carlile White was a millionaire and I couldn't believe his ex was in my kitchen mixing my dope.

"You used to fuck with Carl, for real?"

"Until a couple of weeks ago, yes."

"What the fuck happened? You was living in mansions and shit. The nigga got Bentleys. How you end up in the hospital and not able to take care of yo'self?"

A faraway look shown in her brown eyes. "He got big-headed. I was with Carl for six years, before he was big time. I knew him when he was nothing. I helped him bag up ounces and stuffed dope in my pussy when we got pulled over. Then we started getting real money. Thousands turned to hundred thousands. Condominiums, cars, jewelry, shopping sprees. I was Cookie and he was Lucious, the real life *Empire*. Carl used to be a humble nigga, but the money changed him. Couldn't tell him nothing. Not even me. I knew he cheated on me, but I ignored it as long as he didn't flaunt it in my face. And then he started disrespecting me by bringing his other bitches around. Said he was a god, and gods did what they wanted. I didn't want to lose my man, so I compromised and let him bring other bitches in our house. In our bed. But he didn't stop there. He had females all over America. I got jealous. I started finding them and threatening them. I even fucked some of them over. Carl got mad and we fought. He beat my ass and left me on the side of the street like I was trash."

I watched Kianna's face as she told the story. I seen love, pain, hurt, betrayal, and sadness. When she finished, I said the only thing that fit the moment.

"Damn!"

"But fuck Carl. What we had is over. I see your potential, Drayez. And just like you, I'm not a 9 to 5 bitch. I'm used to living a certain way. Having certain things. I'm not used to people taking care of me. I get my own and play my part. I'm a real life boss bitch. And the first thing I will tell you is to throw that dope away."

"What? You crazy?"

"No, I'm not. That shit is garbage. You are going to fuck around and kill somebody with that shit. I know everything that it takes to make it to the top. I been there. I want to get back and take you with me. I can upgrade you Drayez. I'm not playing. I want to be your boss bitch. I choose you."

I had never been chosen before so I mumbled, "A'ight."

"I choose you, Drayez," she repeated.

"Okay. Shit, what I'm supposed to say?"

She laughed. "Anything but that."

"You chose wisely," I tried.

She laughed harder. "Whatever. Now the first thing we're going to do is get rid of this," she said, grabbing a paper towel and going for my dope.

"Hold on, Kianna! Wait!"

It was too late. She pushed my dope in the sink and cut on the water. My heart went down the drain with the work.

"Trust me, Drayez. I did you a favor."

"Sho' don't feel like it," I sulked.

"You will thank me later. I'm going to take care of everything tomorrow. And now that that's taken care of, how about we finish what we started on the couch. My body ain't been touched in weeks and I need to see if you can handle a boss bitch!"

Chapter 17

The gloves were off!

Kianna was my bitch and we was about to consummate our relationship like husbands and wives after marriage: by fucking! And since she was my bitch, I was going to fuck her like she was my bitch. No taking it easy. It was time for the smackdown!

I left Draya on the floor in the living room and took Kianna to my room. We stripped our way to the bed, leaving a trail of clothes on the floor. Our tongues explored each other's mouths while my hands squeezed her phatty. It was jiggly and soft. I grabbed a Magnum from the drawer, checking out her body as I slid on the protection. Nice titties. Flat stomach. Shaved pussy. A little gap between her thighs.

"I hope you know how to use that," she sang as I climbed between her thighs. "Fuck me good."

Hearing those words and seeing her body got me geeked. I shoved my dick inside her, pushing all the way in until our pelvises were touching.

"Ahh shit, Drayez!" she yelled, making a noise like she was drowning, wrapping her arms tightly around my neck.

I stayed still until she relaxed. Her walls were tight, hot, and wet. When I felt her grip loosen on my neck, I started drilling that pussy.

"Wait, Drayez! Slow down," she begged, trying to get away.

I didn't let up or slow down. I long-stroked her pussy fast and hard.

"Wait! You too deep. It hurts. Oh God!"

That shit was music to my ears. I had a boss bitch running from the D. She couldn't take it. Had me on 10! I was so geeked that I couldn't hold back my nut. Only took about two minutes before I was skeeting. When my dick stopped spasming, I rolled over, searching for my pants. I needed a Newport.

"You got some good-ass pussy," I mumbled, lighting the square.

When she didn't respond, I looked over. She was sitting up, her back against the headboard, a confused look on her face. I had never seen a female react like that.

"You good?"

Disappointment and anger flashed in her eyes. "What the fuck was that, Drayez?"

"What you mean? I fucked you like a boss."

She looked even more confused. "That's what you call that?"

I was starting to feel self-conscious. "What you talking about?"

Her face scrunched like she was trying to think of the right words to say. "That was whack."

I felt like I got slapped. "What? I put it down. Had yo' ass runnin' from my shit."

"'Cause that shit hurt. I wanted you to make me feel good, not bring me pain. You can't just stick your woman and make her scream. That's not what sex is about."

I felt embarrassed and didn't know how to respond. "When I fuck, the screams turn me on."

"That's all wrong, Drayez. You got a big dick, but you don't know how to use it," she said, straddling my lap and grabbing my piece. "This is not a battering ram. Just because you can go deep don't mean we like it. You didn't fuck the shit out of me, nigga, you tried to hurt me. What makes you think I liked that shit? You wouldn't like it if I sucked your dick and kept scraping you with my teeth. You would make noise, but I bet that shit wouldn't feel good."

It felt like she was shitting on me and I didn't wanna hear no more. I tried to get up, but she squeezed my dick.

"You want to get up? That's it?"

"What you want me to do? I ain't finna just sit here and listen to you shit on me."

"I'm not shitting on you, Drayez. I'm criticizing you. I'm a boss bitch. I speak my mind. If I see you slipping, I'm supposed to say something so you can fix that shit. I'm telling you that I don't want to be hurt when we fuck. Now what are you going to do about it?"

I stared in her eyes for a moment. She wanted me to fix it. "What do you want me to do? What do you like?"

She smiled. "That's right. When you don't know something, ask. Don't drive us off a cliff because you too much of a man to ask for directions. And what I want is to feel good. Yeah, a little pain is okay when mixed with pleasure. You start off slow. Ease your way in and pay attention to my body. Don't be in a rush. When I want more, I'll open myself up to you. Please me, and I'll please you back. Just because I make noise don't mean I like it. Feel me. Listen to the kinds of noises I make. You'll know what I want because I'll ask for more or try to take it. I can take dick, but I can't take you trying to bust my cervix. Now, I know you probably need a little time before you get back hard, so I think the best way to make up for trying to hurt me is to make me feel good. Let me show you how to eat pussy."

***

I woke up the next morning with Kianna standing over me holding Draya.

"What up? What time is it?"

"Time for you to get up. Let's go get this money."

"What you talkin' 'bout?"

"Get up so you can find out. I already fed Draya. Your food is in the kitchen. We need to drop her off with Rayna and make a couple of moves. Now are you going to lay there and stare at me or get your ass up?"

I hit the bathroom to get fresh before going to the kitchen. Kianna fixed me a plate of pancakes, eggs, and sausages. She was on the phone the entire time I ate, sounding like she was making plans to start a Fortune 500 company. About the time I finished eating, she hung up the phone and gave me mine.

"Call Rayna. Tell her to babysit."

"It ain't even 9 o'clock. What the fuck is you on?"

"We gotta get this money. We can't take Draya. Call Rayna."

"How we gettin' the money?"

"We gotta take it."

Visions of my night with L-Dog flashed in my head. "What you mean, take it?"

She sighed like I was getting on her nerves. "We need a lot of money to start with. We're not doing that ten gram shit like you had last night. I'm talking about real money. Call your baby mama."

"How much is real money?"

"At least 50 thousand. Maybe a hundred. Trust me, Drayez. Call Rayna."

She said it coolly, like fifty thousand dollars was going to drop out of the sky. But I was eager to ball, so I stopped asking questions and called Rayna.

"What, Drayez?" she answered with a big-ass attitude.

"I need you to watch Draya."

"Oh, now you want me to have her. I thought—"

"I don't got time for this shit, Rayna. I'm finna drop off Draya and give you some money."

She was quiet for a moment. "Okay."

After I got dressed, I dropped Draya off and gave the powder head a hundred dollars. From there, Kianna directed me to an auto salvage. I parked the A8 in the lot and we walked in through a side door. The auto garage was big, filled with cars and car parts. Along the wall was a makeshift front desk. Behind it was an office. A short, buff, dark-skinned nigga walked out wearing a du-rag and an extra small tank top. Nigga had so much muscle that I was positive he took steroids. It looked like he worked out in his sleep. When he saw us walking towards the counter, he sized me up before looking at Kianna. Recognition shone in his eyes.

"Kianna! Is that you, bitch?" he squealed in a high-pitched voice.

"Fantasia, get yo' ass over here, girl!" Kianna screamed.

He ran around the counter and locked Kianna in a hug, picking her up and spinning around in a circle. Both of them let out high-pitched screams. I stood there in awe, surprised that the buff-ass nigga was gay.

"When you get out, Fantasia?"

"I been out for almost a couple months. If yo' ass woulda got out that condo a li'l more, you would know. What you doing in our neck of the woods?"

"I need to see Trav."

A deep voice spoke up. "Who lookin' for me?"

I looked towards the office and seen a skinny dark-skinned nigga standing in the doorway. He was about my height with a shiny bald head. He wore a dingy gray T-shirt and holey black jeans. He chewed on a toothpick.

"What's up, Trav?" Kianna smiled

Surprise lit his eyes when he recognized her. "Hell nawl! If it ain't the woman that broke my heart and took a piece of it with her."

Kianna blushed. "Stop it, Trav."

Trav looked at me and we had a stare-off. "Who's the Boy Scout?"

Fantasia looked at me too, but he wasn't sizing me up no more. Nigga was checking me out like he wanted to holla. I mugged the shit out of his ass. He mugged me back, flexing his chest. I turned my aggression down a notch. I had made my point.

"Chill, Fantasia," Kianna intervened. "This is my nigga, Drayez."

"Nigga as in nigga? Or nigga as in friend?" Trav asked.

"Nigga as in nigga," Kianna cleared up.

Trav smirked.

Fantasia looked disappointed. Bitch-ass nigga.

"So what can I do for you?" Trav asked, resting his elbows on the counter. He was looking at Kianna like he wanted to fuck while twirling the toothpick with his tongue.

"I need some hardware."

"Ain't this 'bout a bitch!" He laughed, sounding like an evil villain. "Look how the tables turn. I needed yo' help with Carl, but you turned me down. Why should I help you?"

"C'mon, Trav. You know I couldn't get between you and Carl. Y'all had to work that out on y'all own. You my friend and that was my nigga. I couldn't pick sides."

He eyed her for a moment before smirking. "What's up with Carl's ole bitch ass anyway? Since you got a new nigga, shit must've got rough at the condo, huh?"

"He put me in the hospital. Kicked me out on my ass like a dog."

"Told you that nigga wasn't shit," Trav spat. "You was s'posed to be my bottom bitch. I knew that pretty boy was gon' fuck you over. I neva trust a nigga that think he look better than his bitch."

"What you want me to say? That you right? That I was stupid and in love?"

"You said it." He grinned, twirling the toothpick.

"So will you help me?"

Trav looked her over again. "Yeah, I'ma help you out. I still love yo' crazy ass. What chu need?"

"Two Glocks with silencers."

Trav licked his lips. "What's in it for me?"

Kianna leaned forward, poking her ass out as she rested her elbows on the counter. Their faces were close enough to kiss. "You know I built TBT. Carl wouldn't be shit without me. And I'm about to do it again. I'ma take you outta this junkyard and put you in a mansion. I'm building a team and I want you on it. You wanna play with the big boys again?" she asked, using her teeth to take the toothpick from his mouth.

Trav looked hypnotized, like he was caught under her spell. And then he smiled. "You sexy muthafucka, you! I'll follow yo' ass to hell with gasoline draws on!"

Kianna kissed his lips and put the toothpick back in his mouth. "I love you too, baby."

"Fantasia, go get them boxes," Trav ordered. "What you need the heat for? Who finna have a funeral?"

"Nobody. Yet. I just need some capital."

"From where?"

"You already know."

Trav laughed. "You's a cold-ass bitch!"

"I need a car too."

Trav lifted his arms in the air. "Pick one."

***

"Fuck that shit was about?" I asked as I whipped the black Chrysler van through traffic.

"Trav and Carl used to be friends. Fantasia is Trav's little brother."

"What they fall out for? You?"

"Nah. Trav did security for TBT. Started asking for more money because he took more risks. Carl said no. Trav walked."

"He really love you?"

"I don't know. Maybe. We messed around one night when Carl was out of town. I was drunk. I didn't fuck him, but he ate my pussy. After that, he started sayin' he loved me. He wanted me to leave Carl and be with him. But Trav is crazy. For real. Certified loony bin crazy. He probably got bodies buried all over that salvage yard. I can't fuck with nobody like that."

I chewed on what she said for a moment. A certified homicidal maniac was in love with my bitch. Something was wrong with that picture.

"So, what we doing? I'm talkin' about me and you. You told him I was yo' nigga. This serious?"

"The one thing I know about a man is he's going to do him, regardless of what his woman tries to do for him. She can give him everything in the world: the best pussy, the best head, all her love. But a man is still going to want to fuck who he wants to fuck. And a man with money is worse. He wants to do *him* and doesn't want to be tied down. That's how y'all built. Do what you wanna do, fuck who you wanna fuck. Don't wanna answer to nobody. I didn't understand that until I was laying in that hospital. Fuck love, Drayez. It's all about loyalty. I didn't understand that and that was my downfall. I got in my feelings and got jealous. Never again. I don't need a bunch of dicks like y'all need pussy. I just need one. I will always be there for you because I choose to be loyal to you. You are a good man and I like you. But I won't fall in love with you. And I don't want you to fall in love with me. I want us to be partners in this. One hand washes the other. Hold me down and I will hold you down. No matter the situation, I got your back."

I took my eyes off the road for a second. Those hazel brown eyes was staring at me intently.

"Where yo' boss ass been all my life?" I smiled.

"Everything happens when it's supposed to happen." She laughed. "Now pay attention. This is the plan."

We sat in the van for hours watching the white house. And as soon as the sun went down, we made our move. We crept around outside the house, checking the windows. All the rooms were empty, except the bathroom. Kianna used a key to let us in the front door. The floor was carpeted, so we didn't have to worry about making noise. The living room was simple. White furniture, gold lamps, and expensive fish tanks. A tray of food was on the table in front of a big-ass TV. Kianna led the way towards the bathroom, keeping our silenced pistols ready. The toilet flushed and the door opened.

"Oh shit!" the nigga yelped when he seen us.

He was my height, stocky build, brown skin, with a dying gray front tooth.

"Hey, Donovan. Bet you not happy to see me," Kianna taunted.

"K-Kianna, I'm-I'm sorry. Carl said that—"

Clap!

The silenced pistol barely made a sound.

"Ahh!" Donovan screamed, grabbing his nuts and falling on the floor.

"Kianna what you doing? I thought we wasn't shooting nobody?" I said.

"He helped Carl beat me up, didn't you, Donovan?" She didn't give him a chance to respond before she shot him in the stomach.

"Ahh! Please, Kianna! I was just doing what Carl told me to do."

"And now you about to pay for it."

Clap!

Donovan stopped screaming as the hole in his forehead trickled blood. A red pool began forming on the floor behind his head.

"What the fuck, Kianna!" I yelled. "You said we wasn't shooting nobody."

"I said you didn't have to shoot nobody. He put me in the hospital, and now his ass dead. Let's go get this money."

When she walked away, I looked down at the dead man. His eyes were still open, wide with fear. *What the fuck Kianna got me in?* I questioned myself, following her down a flight of stairs and into the basement. We removed a couple parts from a small boiler until a small bag was revealed. After tucking the bag, we got up out of there.

"I thought we was partners," I said after we were back in the van.

She tried to look innocent. "We are, Drayez."

"Why didn't you tell me you was killing him? You knew that shit before we went in the house. You said Carl put you in the hospital, not Donovan."

"What do you want me to say? I told you I'm a diary. Donovan's ass is dead and I'm not sorry. He shouldn't have put his hands on me."

"But that don't mean you lie to me. You s'posed to be my bitch. We building this shit based on loyalty and trust. If you trusted me, why didn't you tell me everything? If you wanted to kill the nigga, I woulda understood."

"Would you?" she asked, challenging me. "Have you ever killed anybody?"

"Yeah."

She studied my face and saw I was telling the truth. "I'm sorry. I didn't know you got down like that. I thought you would try to talk me out of it."

"You think I'm a soft-ass nigga?"

"No, it's not like that. But I didn't think you pulled a trigger before."

"Well, now that we got that out of the way, is there anything else that you not telling me? Put that shit on the wood because I don't want that shit popping up later."

"I don't got no more secrets, Drayez. That's my word."

I took my eyes off the road to give her a stare. "A'ight, cool. Now that we got this money, where do we cop from?"

"We have to go to a club to meet your new connection. I got us the money. The rest is on you."

We went back to my house to get dressed. I threw on a black Armani suit while Kianna raided Tikka's closet and found a sexy black dress. Then we were off to a club called LAVA. I could hear Reggaeton music pumping from the club's speakers as we approached the club. The inside was packed with all shades of the Latin race. Some were as dark as Africans in Nigeria, others as white as Europeans in Europe. And the women looked exotic. Van would've loved this spot. Kianna grabbed my hand and led me to the bar.

"What can I get you?" the curly-haired, brown-skinned bartender asked.

"Two double shots of Patron XO and two Coronas," I ordered.

She dipped away to get the drinks.

"Look all the way in the back," Kianna said in my ear. "Silver shirt and sunglasses."

I turned my head slowly. At the back of the club were tables. It wasn't a VIP section, but it was obvious that those seats weren't for everybody. About ten Latinos of all shades sat at the table. The one wearing the silver shirt and sunglasses sat in the middle. He was big and burly, light-skinned, bushy eyebrows, and long wavy hair pulled into a ponytail.

"Here you go, papi," the bartender said as she served our drinks.

I gave her a twenty.

"How you wanna play this?" Kianna asked.

I downed the double shot. "You said Diego knows you, right?"

"We've met, but Carl did the talking."

"Okay. I lead. You follow."

After Kianna downed her shot, we grabbed our beers and I led the way to the back. I stayed in Diego's line of sight, stopping when I was a few feet from the table. I couldn't see his eyes behind the glasses, but I knew he saw me. I nodded. He didn't nod back, and everybody at the table looked hostile.

"Can we talk?" I called over the music.

Diego took the glasses off and looked at me from head to toe. Then he looked to Kianna. His eyes were about to come back to me, but they went back to Kianna. Then he smiled. "Where ya boy toy?" he asked, his accent heavy.

"I left the boys alone."

He smiled again and waved us closer. "Who you?"

"I'm Drayez."

"You know Carlito?"

"Nah. Never met him."

"Why you come here then?"

"I want to talk."

"About Carlito?"

"Nah. About me."

"Then why you got Carlito's chica?"

"She's my chick now."

Diego smiled again. "Come sit down. Tell me how Carlito's chica becomes you chica."

Chairs came from out of nowhere and slid behind me and Kianna. All eyes were on us as we sat down.

"Talk."

"I met her at the hospital. Carl beat her up. I helped her out. Now she's with me."

He nodded, eyeing Kianna for a moment then looking back to me. "One man's trash anotha man's treasure. What do you want?"

"To do business."

"I don't know you. Me and Carl have good business. Why should I ruin that for you? Why should I trust you?"

"Because I want to make you rich. I'm better than Carl on every level. She knows that and that's why she is with me. I got big plans and I want to be great. If I become great, that will make you greater. I just need the opportunity to prove it. The thing that separates me from Carl is, I believe in love. Not love as in romance, but L-O-V-E."

A question shown in his eyes. "Explain."

"Loyalty over everything. If I'm down with you, I'm all the way down with you. My contracts get written in blood. I mean what I say and say what I mean. Death before dishonor. Principles before pleasure."

Diego stared into my eyes, evaluating my words and assessing my worth. This was do or die. I didn't have a plan B. I needed this.

"You have very big cojones, Drayez. And your words are, how do you say? Impressive. I kill strangers who come to me for business. But since you have Carlito's chica, I let it go. Me and Carlito have been doing business for many years, but I am loyal to my product and money. And maybe a little competition might not be a bad thing. I will give you an opportunity. Maybe we will become great. For now, let us drink and be merry. But first, you must eat the worm. Miguel! Go get the snake."

One of his boys got up from the table wearing a big-ass smile. Something was up. I looked at Diego and saw that he was smiling too. I turned to Kianna. "What this shit about?"

She looked sick. "You have to eat the worm in the bottle of tequila after you drink the liquor."

Miguel came back a few moments later with a fifth of tequila. The worm that floated inside looked as big as a garden snake. I knew I was about to be sick.

Chapter 18

Six months later...

If it wasn't for Kianna, I would have drowned in the ocean while trying to swim with the big fish. But she kept me afloat and held my hand until I could swim on my own. The first deal I made with Diego was a buy/front. We took 100 G's from Donovan, enough to buy two and a half kilos of heroin. I watched like a kid in science class as Kianna turned those two and a half bricks into four. It took us two months to get the work off. The next time I saw Diego, I learned that Carl had broken their contract and found another plug. This was great news for me because I now had Diego to myself. From that meeting, I walked away with four kilos. Kianna turned four into six and the rest is history.

Six months later, I was having real money, so much that I could wipe my ass with hundred dollar bills, set 'em on fire, and not even care. No bullshit. I actually did it. Out of my partnership with Diego, we - me and Kianna - birthed GMT: Get Money Team. The product we moved was so good that we were slowly taking over the north side of Milwaukee. Everybody had GMT's name in their mouths. We even had a few low level beefs with TBT. I was putting a dent in their pockets. The way I was moving up the ladder, it was only a matter of time before GMT and TBT were in an all-out war. And I was ready for that.

Trav handled GMT security and the nigga was a beast. He had a military background. Special Forces type shit. I had a real life Rambo on my team that had connections to get rocket launchers, 50 caliber machine guns, and grenades. Anything we needed. And he kept a team of killas ready to move when I gave the word. I couldn't believe Carl let him get away.

I never imagined that I could build an empire. But I did. A million dollars passed through my hands every month, and I gave most of it away. Had to keep my teams fed. And the team seemed to be getting bigger every day. But I made sure to keep the inner circle small: Kianna, Damo, Vic, and TC. Me and Kianna made the plans and passed them down to Damo, our second in command, and he made them come to life. Vic and TC were really around to collect and oversee. I knew they wouldn't bust a grape in a food fight, and I didn't expect them to. I just needed them to do my bidding whenever it needed to be done and be my extra set of eyes and ears. They excelled in those responsibilities.

"Get mon-ney! Get mon-ney! Get mon-ney!"

Hearing the Get Money Team's chant pulled me from my thoughts. I was sitting at a table surrounded by my GMT family. Damo, TC, and a few niggas from the hit squad stood around making it rain. The stripper on Vic's lap was Mona, my old jump-off. The look on my nigga's face told me he was enjoying her hard work. When I started getting money, Kianna told me to invest. I put 100,000 dollars into Satin, the club owned by Mona's brother. He used the money to open up a Satin in Atlanta. Now Mona worked for me. Boss shit.

"Hey, Drayez!" a female sang behind me as hands rubbed my shoulders. Moments later, Selena and Mya, my newest additions to Satin in Atlanta, were standing in front of me. I handpicked both of them out of LAVA during one of my meetings with Diego. Selena was a short and stacked Puerto Rican mamacita that was as pretty as she was thick. Long curly black hair, soft brown skin, big-ass double D titties, and an ass that I could set a glass on. Her counterpart, Mya, was Columbian. Light skin, long brown hair, green eyes, and full lips that loved sucking my dick. She was tall, fit, and slim like a volleyball player.

"What's up, ladies?"

"Why you sitting all by yourself?" Selena asked, sitting on one of my legs and running her fingers over my platinum GMT charm. 20 G's on my neck.

"I was just enjoying the view. Mona know how to put on a show."

"So, you don't want our company?" Mya asked, sitting on my other leg.

"Now, why you gotta put words in my mouth?"

"Good. I haven't seen you in a while and I miss you."

"So did I," Selena echoed. "I was hoping that you were staying for a couple days. I like waking up next to you."

"I only got one night in town. Vic getting married tomorrow and then I gotta get back to the Midwest."

"Aww!" they whined.

"But don't trip, babies. You know it's enough Drayez to go around. We partying at the Hilton. Bad bitches only."

"Hey! Bad bitches only!" Selena sang, snapping her fingers and grinding on my lap.

"Drayez? Look at this fool-ass nigga!" Damo called.

I looked to see what he was talking about. Mona was lying on the floor, on her back, legs open like the letter V, toes pointed to the ceiling. Vic was between her legs dry humping the shit out of her.

"Fool-ass nigga!" I laughed.

GMT left Satin a couple hours later in two party busses filled with strippers. Every time we stopped at a red light, the girls got out and shook they asses in the middle of the street. Cars honked their horns and niggas screamed and threw money out the window. Before I knew it, we had about twenty cars following us around the city. When we pulled up to the Hilton, we left all them niggas in the parking lot and GMT rode the elevators up to the Presidential suite. Inside, the drinking, smoking, and partying continued.

"Fuck Kianna at?" TC asked.

I pulled my attention away from the sexy show Mona and Selena was putting on. They had gone from dancing to touching and touching to kissing. Shit was about to get sexual. I hadn't thought about Kianna until TC brought her up.

"I don't know. She was supposed to meet us at the club but never showed. She might be in the other suite asleep."

"You should call her, my nigga. You know she gon' wanna see this."

Kianna loved watching females fuck, especially bad bitches. I think she had a porn addiction because her phone was filled with lesbian porn. And she loved getting her pussy ate by a female. She said bitches knew what they were doing. I didn't judge. I loved that shit. Threesomes was a regular thing for us. And since Selena and

Mona was super bad, I was about to try to get a foursome. I called Kianna, but she didn't answer, so I sent a text.

When Selena and Mona's clothes came off, they lay on the floor grinding their pussies against each other. The show was erotic as hell, but I wasn't fully paying attention. My thoughts stayed on Kianna. She had changed my life, turned me from a fake boss into a real one. I used to think the money I got with Van was something, but in real life, I was just a worker. Me and Kianna had created a brand. A movement. I had my own 750 Benz and lived in a mini mansion. I did what I wanted when I wanted. I embodied Kanye's lyrics: "you can't tell me nothing!" And it was all because of Kianna. She meant a lot to me, but when I tried to tell her, she checked me. She told me not to get on no emotional shit. That was three months ago. Since then, my feelings had grown. There wasn't a doubt in my mind that I loved her, but she wouldn't let me show it. To her, we were friends, business partners, and fuck buddies. How she separated the emotions from our relationship was a mystery to me.

Movement from Mya pulled me from my thoughts. "C'mon, baby." Then she looked at the stripper next to me. "You too."

Mya and the thick brown-skinned chick led me to the master bedroom. I set my pistol on the dresser as they undressed me. When I lay in bed, they tag teamed my dick with their lips. I noticed the brown-skinned chick had the same complexion as Kianna. Then I began to wonder why Kianna didn't text me back.

"You good, Drayez?" Mya asked.

I looked down to see what she was talking about. They were looking at my limp dick like it was a worm.

"Yeah. I think I'm a li'l tired. Y'all go ahead. I'ma jump in in a few minutes."

I watched half-heartedly as they went at it. They put on a good show, but I wasn't that interested. I kept thinking about Kianna. Why didn't she come to the club? Why didn't she call to let me know she wasn't coming? Why didn't she text me back? The next thing I knew, I was fully dressed, tucking the pistol in my waist as I left the room. I barely noticed the orgy taking place on the floor as

I left the Presidential suite. I took the elevator one floor down to the suite me and Kianna were staying in. Kianna was there, and she wasn't alone. Sitting on the couch next to her was a nigga I would never forget. Light skin, bald head, trimmed goatee, iced-out TBT chain. I could feel the rage building.

"What the fuck is this, Kianna?"

She looked scared, eyes wide like a deer caught in the headlights. "Wait, Drayez! This not what you think," she said, shooting to her feet.

The nigga looked bothered, like I was interrupting something.

"What the fuck is this, then? Let me hear this shit."

"We was just catching up. I didn't even know he was in town until I ran into him on my way to the club. We came here to talk."

"Ay, don't I know you, nigga?" he asked, peering at me as he stood.

I mugged him from head to toe. "Nah, you don't know me, nigga. But I'm *Get Money Team.* We takin' over Milwaukee," I barked, pointing to my GMT chain.

He looked at Kianna. "He Get Money Team?"

I spoke for her. "We Get Money Team."

He looked at me and laughed. "Yo' soft ass is Get Money Team? I remember you now, Dray. You got a baby by that ratchet-ass bitch with the big booty. Rayna. She sucked my dick in yo' face, nigga!" He laughed again.

Kianna gave me an "is he for real?" look.

"That weak-ass bitch wasn't shit, nigga. Weak-ass niggas fuck weak-ass bitches."

"Ah nah, nigga. Quit cappin'. She told me 'bout cho bum ass. Neva thought you would be the one giving us competition."

He turned to Kianna. "You really fuckin' this nigga?"

"You betta watch that slick shit, nigga," I warned, ready to off his ass.

"Or what, nigga?" He flexed.

Kianna stepped between us. "Don't do this, Cartier! I'ma talk to you later. Just leave."

"Well check yo' man then, shorty. Nigga over there lettin' out a lot of hot air!"

"I'll bury yo' bitch ass next to Donovan!" I mugged, itching for a reason to pull my pistol.

I watched my words register in Cartier's eyes. "You killed Donovan?" he accused, going for his waist.

I went for my gun at the same time.

When Kianna realized Cartier was pulling a pistol, she grabbed his arm. He pushed her out of the way but by the time he got his gun out, mine was already in his face.

Pow!

The 40 caliber bullet went through his right eye and he fell to the ground like Deonta Wilder had hit him with an uppercut.

"Bitch-ass nigga!" I cursed, spitting in his face.

"Drayez, what the fuck did you do?" Kianna screamed, kneeling beside him.

"Fuck you mean? You saw him reach. Nigga got what he had comin'."

Kianna started crying. "No, Drayez. Damn. Why did you bring up Donovan? Why didn't you let him leave?"

"Fuck is you cryin' for? You heard that nigga disrespecting me. I'm a boss! Fuck that bitch-ass nigga."

"He was like family, Drayez. This is Carl's brother."

Shit! This was her ex's brother. She had love for this nigga. But she was my bitch and I couldn't go soft. Fuck that nigga.

"You shoulda thought about that before you brought the nigga in our room. How you gon' bring competition where I lay my head at? What, you plotting against me?"

She stood up to face me, tears rolling down her face. First time I ever saw her cry.

"I told you we were just talking. He said Carl been looking for me. Cartier was like my brother. After everything me and you been through, you think I would betray you like that? We built this. Why would I set you up for something that is mine as much as it is yours?"

I couldn't answer that.

"How I'm supposed to know what you will or won't do when you having secret meetings? You didn't come to the club. You didn't answer my calls. And then I find you in the room with the enemy. What I'm supposed to think?"

"I would never do anything to hurt you. You my nigga. I told you I'm loyal to you. Loyalty over everything."

She hit me with my own words. Damn. I regretted making her feel pain, but not for killing Cartier. "I'ma get rid of the body. You clean that blood up. Where them big-ass Louis Vuitton suitcases?"

"In the room?"

I went to grab the luggage and call Damo.

"What up?" He answered, sounding out of breath.

"I just offed a nigga. Come to my room."

"What? Right now?"

"It's an emergency, nigga! Come help me get this nigga outta here."

By the time I emptied the clothes from the suitcase and took it to the main room, Damo was knocking on the door.

"Who is this nigga?" he asked, helping me fold the body into the suitcase.

"TBT nigga name Cartier. Carl's brother."

His eyes got big. "Fuck he doin' in y'all room?"

I glanced at Kianna. "He like her brother. Kianna used to fuck with Carl."

"Damn, my nigga. You know they got cameras all through this bitch."

"That's why we gotta make sure they never find the body."

We took the suitcase to an abandoned warehouse. There was a big empty oil drum inside like the ones homeless people lit fires in to keep warm. We put in the suitcase with a car tire and poured on gasoline. Human flesh and burning rubber was the worst smell I ever smelled in my life. But it burned the body to ashes.

Cremated that nigga hood style.

"You sure you can trust Kianna?" Damo asked as I drove back to the hotel.

"I saw her put in work before. She a down-ass bitch."

"That ain't what I asked. The nigga was like family. She watched him die and cried over it. Her feelings got hurt. Bitches are emotional and deal in feelings. You sure you can trust her?"

Damo made valid points, but she was my bitch. "Yeah. She all the way down with me. I can trust her."

"Why was the nigga in y'all room? This why she didn't come to the club?"

"Yeah. They was catching up. Said Carl looking for her."

Damo didn't look convinced. "I don't know, fam. Shit don't sit right with me. She tried to hide that nigga from you. If you wouldn't have went back to that room, ain't no telling what woulda happened. And now Carl looking for her. Why? Do he wanna kill her or get her back? You sure you can trust her?"

I wasn't sure any more.

Chapter 19

I felt no remorse for killing Cartier. Not a drop of guilt. No tingling in my conscience. Nothing. He got what he had coming and deserved to die. I had changed. I didn't know when or have the words to describe the process, but in the year since I left Rayna, I had done a 180° turn. The first time I was a part of a shooting, with Twan and L-Dog, I was terrified. I was so scared that I left most of the money with a nigga that didn't lift a finger to take it. Then there was Van's murder. That shit haunted me for months. I could still smell his blood and see his empty eyes. I lost myself in the depression that followed. Then I got my hands dirty and killed Shooter. I felt remorse for that, like I had done a great evil. When Kianna killed Donovan, I didn't feel a thing. At that point, killing was becoming normal. And now that I had spilled more blood, I realized that killing was easy. It didn't take much to pull a trigger and take a life. I had done it twice. And I knew, without a shadow of a doubt, that I would do it again.

"We have to do something about the money."

Kianna's voice pulled me from my thoughts. We were in the office in Trav's auto salvage. Just me and her surrounded by boxes of money. The money machine chattered as it counted a stack of bills. Kianna wrote the number down in the notebook. I grabbed the stack of bills from the machine, wrapped a rubber band around it, and put it in a box to my left. I grabbed another stack of bills from a box to my right and loaded it in the machine. The machine chattered again as it counted the bills. We did this once a week. 400,000 to 600,000 was our weekly average, depending on how much work TC and Vic gave out.

"I know. I been tryna find shit to invest in, but people don't wanna fuck with this dirty money. I'ma have to get out a lil more."

"We need to find somebody to clean it for us. We can't keep looking for businesses to invest in. We have to put too much trust in too many people," Kianna said before writing in the book again.

I changed the money. "What you got in mind?"

"Lace."

"What the fuck is that?"

"Not what. Who."

"Who the fuck is that?"

"A hedge fund manager. She can take our dirty money and make it clean."

"Shit, why you ain't been called her?"

"If I could, I would."

I gave an impatient look. "You ain't making no sense. Why can't you call her?"

"Let's just say we don't see eye to eye."

"Here you go with this mysterious shit again."

"I'm not being mysterious. Me and Lace can't be in the same room. You have to get in touch with her and convince her to help you. She can't know about me."

"A'ight. Gimme the number."

"It's not that simple, Drayez. You can't just tell her to help you clean your drug money."

"Why not just bribe her ass? Them crooked muthafuckas will do anything for the right price."

"We don't know if that will work. But I do know that she will go. She did it for Carl. Why use a bribe when you can use what's between your ears and legs?"

I caught on. "Oh, it's like that?"

"Yeah. Carl don't fuck with her no more. They had some bad blood. I can't approach her because she knows I used to fuck with Carl. This is on you again."

"Okay. So, I gotta fuck her before I approach her with business."

"Yep. But she fucked up."

"Fucked up how?"

"Her face is fucked up. Acid attack. Most of the skin on her face is gone."

"Damn. It just had to be a catch," I laughed. "So the bitch look like Freddie Kruger, huh?"

"Yeah. Something like that. But we need her, so you'll have to put her looks aside. If we get her on the team, we won't have to worry about finding businesses to buy into."

I nodded. "Shit sound good to me. Tell me more about her so I can come up with a plan."

"I will. But first we have to deal with this," she said, studying the notebooks. "The money is short. I thought I made a mistake last week, so I checked with Vic and TC. They said it was all there, but it's not. Last week it was short twenty-five thousand. This week it's 40."

"You serious?" I asked, grabbing the notebook from her hand. There were rows of numbers. Accounting shit. But I saw the numbers circled in red. My body temperature rose with my anger. I called Damo.

"What up, Yez?"

"Call Vic and TC. Tell them niggas to get all the hood captains and meet us in the garage. It's an emergency."

***

"We got a thief amongst us," I said calmly, letting my words linger in the air.

We were in Trav's garage. A big-ass table had been set up in the middle. I was at the head. Seated around the table were my fifteen hood captains. They were mostly my clientele from when I first started hustling. Once the kilos started rolling in, I told them my plans to start GMT. They all signed on, putting their personal ambitions aside to focus on a greater goal. Now they moved my product in the streets and controlled entire blocks. Also in the garage were Trav, Fantasia, TC, Damo, Vic, and Kianna. They watched from the background.

"Last week somebody stole twenty-five thousand. This week, forty. Y'all know I show plenty love. I make sure everybody eats. I can't allow this to slide. I need somebody to stand up and be accountable. This is the opportunity to come forward. Since we family, I give you my word that no harm will come to you or your loved ones. This is the only chance you will get to stand up."

I let my eyes roam over my team, looking for a sign of guilt. A twitch. A scratch. Somebody to stand up and be accountable. But nobody moved. Everybody met my eyes, holding their heads up like they were telling the truth. But somebody was lying. I needed to change my tactic to find out who.

"Seven," I spoke, addressing the tall skinny nigga with shoulder-length dreads and gold teeth.

He startled at the sound of my voice. "What up?"

"Talk to me. Who stealing from me?"

"I don't know, Dray. I can only speak for myself and my shit come back good every week."

I gave him a long stare before moving on. My eyes fell upon a boyish-looking female dressed in jeans and a T-shirt. "Star. Tell me something, baby girl. Who biting the hand that feeds 'em?"

"This don't got nothing to do with me, Drayez. My shit one hunnit. Gon' stay one hunnit."

I believed the bitch. But my problem still wasn't solved. I pulled a .357 Magnum from my waist, setting it on the table. Somebody cringed. A dark-skinned weasel-faced nigga looked spooked.

"Talk to me, Drew. What you know?"

"I-I don't know nothing, Dray."

I gave Fantasia a nod. He walked quietly over to Drew and stood behind the chair. The musclebound homosexual intimidated everybody, wearing his classic way too small tank top.

"You know who behind you?"

Drew snuck a peek.

Fantasia mugged him, flexing his muscles.

"C'mon, Dray. I-I didn't take no money. I didn't."

"But you know who did, don't you?"

He looked away.

I was tired of playing games. I picked up the gun and cocked the hammer, pointing it at his chest. "Who took my shit, nigga?"

"C-C'mon, Dray! It wasn't me. P-please!"

I nodded to Fantasia. He moved fast, grabbing Drew's arm, holding it straight out and smashing it over his knee. Bones cracked and crunched as the arm broke in half.

"Aaaah!" Drew screamed, falling to the floor.

I walked over and pointed the .357 in his face. "Last chance, nigga. Who took my shit?"

He closed his eyes and whispered, "Tree."

My eyes found him immediately.

The 6'9" hoopster turned trap star looked terrified as he stood. "P-please, Dray. It-it wasn't like that."

I pointed the tramp at his chest. "Sit cho ass back down!"

He did.

I walked over and put the pistol to his temple. "You stealing from me, nigga? You of all people should understand teamwork. That's why yo' ass didn't make it to the league, huh? 'Cause you ain't no team player."

"I-I didn't mean to—"

"Shut the fuck up, nigga!"

He cried silently.

I looked to the rest of my team. "Let this be a lesson to anybody that steals from the team. Trav! Bring me that blow torch!"

"C-C'mon, Dray. Please don't kill me," Tree whined.

I slapped him with the pistol, making him fall on the floor. "Didn't I tell you to shut the fuck up, nigga!?"

Trav came back with the blow torch and striker, blood lust in his eyes. "Let me do it, my nigga."

I tucked the pistol and grabbed the torch and striker. "I got this one. You got the next one. Damo, come help Fantasia and Trav hold him down."

Tree screamed like he was dying as they held him on the ground. After lighting the torch, I brought the blue flame to Tree's wrist. His skin and blood bubbled and burned as the fire cut through flesh and bone. Shit stank and reminded me of Cartier's body burning inside the drum. Tree's screams were eardrum-shattering. When I finished, his hand was laying apart from his wrist. I went for the other arm.

"C'mon, Dray. Chill," TC spoke up.

I was caught up in the moment and wanted to cause the thief more pain. "This don't got nothing to do with you. Niggas steal, they lose they hands before they lose they life."

"You doin' too much, brah. You going too far."

I pulled the .357 from my waist so fast that it was pointed at TC before he could blink. "Don't tell me what the fuck is too far, nigga! You stole from me too? You wanna lose a muthafuckin' hand?"

TC was so scared that he couldn't speak.

"Chill, Dray!" Vic yelled.

I pointed my gun at him, cocking the hammer. "You want some too, nigga? You muthafuckas work for me. Don't question shit I do. Say another word and I'ma put cho shit on the floor!"

"Drayez, stop!"

I turned to Kianna. She was looking at me with anger, pity, and disappointment.

"What are you doing, baby? This is the team. We are family. You are losing yourself."

I looked at the gun in my hand and then at TC and Vic. They were as scared as I had ever seen them. Damn. I wiled out on my day 1's. Threatened to kill them because they tried to stop me from going over the edge. I lowered the gun, looking away in shame. My eyes landed on Tree. He wasn't screaming anymore, but he was in pain. I pointed the .357 in his face and squeezed the trigger.

Pow!

***

I was driving my silver Mercedes Benz 750 through traffic, loving the way the big luxury car floated down the street. It felt like I was riding on air. I had the windows down and music turned all the way up, the foreign car's sound system bringing out the dynamics in the bass booming beat as I listened to Rich Homie Quan's "Never Fold". This was my shit. It got me geeked every time I heard it. I grooved in the seat as I pulled up to the stoplight. I was about to start the song over when something caught my eye. There were two cars ahead of me, a black Lincoln and a white Intrepid. Two people dressed in black jumped out of the Intrepid and ran to the Lincoln. One of them pulled the driver from the car and slapped him with a pistol. The other one went for the back door and pulled out a short blonde-haired white woman. When he threw her to the ground, I jumped out of the car.

"Ay! What the hell y'all doing?"

They ignored me and hopped in the Lincoln. I ran after the car, not realizing that somebody got out of the Intrepid behind me. Something hit me in the back of the head and I went down. When I looked up, my 750, the Intrepid, and Lincoln were all speeding away.

"Are you okay, Mister?

I turned to the sound of the voice. It didn't match the face.

"Yeah. Somebody jumped me from behind. You okay?" I asked, getting to my feet and keeping my eyes locked onto her icy blue ones.

"Yes. Just shaken up a bit. Can you help me with my driver?" she asked, kneeling over a big white man laid out in the street. "Paul, wake up!"

When she slapped him, he sprang to life. "Where is that son of a bitch!" he grumbled, trying to get up.

"They're gone. You have a bump on your head."

"I'm calling the police," I said, pulling out my phone and dialing 911. I explained everything as best as I could. "The police are on the way. I think we should get him to the sidewalk and out of the street."

"Thank you for helping us," the woman said as we moved Paul to the sidewalk.

"It was nothing. I would've wanted someone to help me. I'm more worried about this bump on my head than the car. How are you? Did they hurt you?" I asked, keeping my eyes focused on those pretty blues.

"No. I'm a tough cookie. I've been through a lot. I'm mad that I left my purse in the back seat. My phone and keys are in it."

While she spoke, I tried not to focus on her face, but I couldn't help it. Her shit was fucked up. She looked like Skeletor, the villain from He-Man. The top layer of skin had been burned off, leaving behind a shiny, unnatural looking mask. White scar tissue formed across pink and purple skin. Green and blue veins were mixed in, spreading across her face like spider webs. Her nose was gone too. It was really just a hole in her face. But she did have pretty eyes. I tried to stay focused on them.

"They probably just some young punks that will throw out all our personal shit. Or maybe drug addicts looking for a quick couple dollars."

"I hope you're right," she said before turning to Paul. "That bump looks nasty. I think you need to go to the hospital."

"No, I'm not leaving you. I'll be fine."

"It's okay, Paul," I spoke up. "I hear the police. I can make sure she gets home safely. By the way, my name is Dray."

She shook my hand. "I'm Lace. Sorry we had to meet like this."

I spoke to the police for about thirty minutes, giving two statements about the carjacking. After the questioning, they offered rides. I took the backseat next to Lace while Paul went to the hospital. During the ride, I got her number. Everything was going according to plan.

***

Two days had passed since the carjacking. I was in the auto salvage with Trav, Fantasia, and Kianna discussing ways to color coordinate the money bags of the hood captains to prevent another Tree and Drew situation.

"How is the back of that head, Dray?" Fantasia laughed.

"That shit ain't funny. I shoulda popped yo' big ass. See if you bulletproof like the Incredible Hulk."

The muscle bound homosexual turned out to be pretty cool. And he was 'bout that action. If work needed to be put in, he didn't hesitate to be on the front line.

"I had to make it look real. And I barely tapped yo' ass. You need to work out a li'l more. Matter of fact, you should open a gym. Be a good way to stay in shape and make money."

"That ain't a bad idea. But for now, how about you keep yo' hands to yo'self. Damn near knocked me out."

Trav's deep voice cut in. "Punk hit hard, don't he?"

"Sound like you know firsthand," Kianna laughed.

"I do. Told that fag he ever hit me again, I'ma kill him. Don't care if he my brotha."

"Nigga, what I tell you 'bout callin me a fag?" Fantasia mugged.

"But you is a fag. How come I can't call a fag a fag? A dog is a dog. A man is a man. A fag is a fag."

Fantasia's muscles seemed to grow bigger. "I told you to watch yo' muthafuckin' mouth!"

"Ay, y'all chill that shit!" I raised my voice. "We family. Ain't no need for violence."

"But he a fag," Trav mumbled.

Kianna slapped his arm. "C'mon, Trav! Stop."

"I got cho fag!" Fantasia mumbled, storming away.

My phone rang, pulling me away from the action. I didn't recognize the number. "Hello?"

"Can I speak with Drayez Alexander?" a white man asked.

"This is me. Who's calling?"

"Detective Quaid. I'm calling because we found your car."

"That's good. Is it still in once piece?"

"That's why I'm calling. We got an anonymous tip this morning and found your car as well as Miss Martenalli's, in an abandoned garage. Cars were ransacked. Everything of value is gone, but the cars are still in one piece."

"Long as the car is still in one piece. When can I pick it up?"

"Within the hour. I'm just waiting for them to finish dusting for prints."

"Do you know who the jackers are?"

"No leads yet. My guess is some punks trying to get a couple bucks to get high. They were amateurs. Those cars were worth a lot to the right people."

Kianna was staring at me when I hung up. "Who was that?"

"Police. They found our cars."

"Call Lace."

"I'm already on it," I said, searching my phone for her number and making the call.

"Hi, Dray! I was just thinking about calling you," Lace answered.

"I just got off the phone with the detective. They found our cars."

"I got the same call. They were in an abandoned garage. Said pretty much what you said. Some guys looking for some money to get high."

"Yeah. Most criminals are not smart. So, how you been? I wanted to call, but I didn't want to invade your life."

"It wouldn't have been an invasion. We were victims of the same people. We have to stick together. You can call any time."

"Guess I over thought that." I chuckled. "You sound well. Are you?"

"Yeah. A carjacking isn't the worst thing I've been through. How is your head?"

"Good. An ice pack, aspirin, and rest did the trick. How's Paul?"

"He's okay. Has a concussion. I gave him the week off. He swears he wants to come back to work to protect me. How brave."

I seen an opening. "So, who's going to drive you around? Is the job open?"

"I know a guy in a hundred thousand dollar car isn't asking me for a job?" She laughed.

"If it allows me to see you again, then yes. I need a job."

She was quiet.

"Hello? You still there?"

"Yes. You want to see me? Why?"

"Because victims have to stick together."

Chapter 20

Opera wasn't that bad.

When the final act of *Romeo and Juliet* ended, I stood with the crowd and clapped as the actors bowed. After leaving the theater, I settled into the back seat of the town car with Lace. This was our third time seeing each other. Even though her face was all kinds of fucked up, I liked Lace. She was thirty-three years old, humble, down to earth, and had a fun personality. She also had a nice body from hitting the gym five days a week. The little black dress showed off her hard work and dedication. Another thing I liked was her mind. She was smart, traveled, and knew a little bit about everything. I had never met a female like her. She was a different caliber than I was used to. I wish I knew her before she lost her face.

"So, what did you think?"

"It wasn't that bad. When you first mentioned the opera and Shakespeare, I was like, nah. But I'm glad I came. It was different."

She hit me with those blue eyes. "See. What did I tell you? It's good to get out and experience different things and different cultures. The world is so big and there's so much out there. We hurt our growth by limiting ourselves to what we're used to. Think of people like water. Still water goes stagnant. Moving water stays fresh."

"I like the way you put that. Who would've thought a near tragedy would bring two people from different walks of life together as friends."

She grabbed my hand, entwining our fingers. "I'm so happy we met. You make me feel things I haven't felt in a long time. Thank you for seeing past what I look like. I get judged so much by people that don't know me. They see me and think I'm a monster because of my…" She stopped talking, looking like she was about to cry.

I pulled her close, wrapping her in my arms. "It's okay. I know what it feels like to be misjudged, walked over, and used. We are kindred. Everything happens for a reason. Maybe God allowed us to meet so we could help each other."

She sighed like a child whose father had taken away their fears. "You're so sweet. Tell me more about you. I just want to hear you talk."

"I don't know where to start."

"What do you do? You know so much about me. I feel like I hardly know you."

When I kicked it with Lace, I made sure to keep our conversations focused on her. I wanted her to feel comfortable, un-judged, and in control. Now that she wanted to know about me, I wasn't sure what to tell her. I didn't know if she could handle the truth. She had an innocent soul, appearing to be above the life of crime and violence. Plus, she had never mentioned Carl and I didn't want to bring him up.

"I'm self-made," I managed.

She tickled my ribs and laughed. "What does that mean?"

"It means I picked myself up from the bottom by my own boot straps. Made my own way."

She lifted her pretty blues and tried to read my face. "I know what it means, but why are you being so mysterious? You don't trust me?"

I searched her eyes for judgment or disappointment. Nothing showed but genuine interest. "I'm a drug dealer. I created a team that controls most of the drug trade on the north side."

She gave a knowing look. "I figured as much. When I used to date, most guys couldn't wait to talk about what they did for a living or how much money they make. I noticed your reluctance to talk about yourself, which is rare for a successful man – except for those with something to hide. I knew someone like you. In some ways, you remind me of him. But you seem realer. More authentic."

I acted surprised. "You dated a drug dealer!?"

"You don't think this Ivy League girl has a past?"

"Not in a million years. So, who was he?"

She lay her head on my chest. "His name is Carl. We dated for a little while. He founded Triple Beam Team. I had never known anybody powerful in the life of crime and I was drawn to the danger. Things were going well until I found out he had a girlfriend. She left nasty messages on my phone and stalked me. I told Carl about it, but he convinced me she was old news and he only wanted me. I believed him. Then one day she attacked me and threw acid in my face. Carl drifted away after the attack and eventually stopped coming around."

Damn. Kianna was scandalous.

"She took my beauty, Drayez," Lace cried. "I was gorgeous. I could've been a model or actress. But I wanted to make a way with my brains, so I chose to work in finances. But now I wish…"

I kissed the top of her head. "It's okay. The acid didn't take away your beauty. It made you shine. Showed what you're really made of. Made you stronger. Beauty is more than skin deep. It doesn't matter that your face was injured. You're still a beautiful person."

She looked up at me like a thirsty woman that had been teased by the taste of sweet water. She wanted more.

I palmed her face in both my hands, using my thumbs to wipe away her tears. "If we only appreciate and value the people that look perfect, we will miss blessings. Nobody is perfect. Not one. The Bible says so. And love isn't about finding the perfect person. It's about loving an imperfect person perfectly."

Shit, I might as well had been Moses parting the Red Sea for his people to cross over to escape the chasing army. Lace grabbed my wrists, looking at me like I was her savior. Her black Moses.

"I said I would never get involved with another drug dealer, Drayez. But there is something different about you. I knew it from the moment we met. The way you risked your own safety to help me. And now you have made me feel safe and desired again. Thank you."

When her lips moved towards mine, I didn't hesitate. This was bigger than burnt flesh and an ugly face. The future of GMT depended on this moment. I closed my eyes, thinking of Kianna's pretty mouth and started kissing Lace like I loved her. When we came up for air, her breathing was heavy, skin flushed. I could see the need in her eyes.

"I-I don't know how to say this, Drayez."

"Say what you need to say, baby."

"Will you stay with me tonight?"

"What took you so long to ask?"

***

Most of the time my life was one big-ass party. Night clubs, strip clubs, hotel suites. Party, party, party! I was rich. I made it. I did what I wanted when I wanted. Today was no different, except today was my birthday. July 21st. The Day the earth spawned the Get Money Team founder. Kianna planned a twenty-four hour bash that had me in awe. Last night me, my inner circle, and a few niggas from the hit squad flew a private jet to Florida. Stretch Hummers drove us from the airport to a packed club. WET was the hottest thing in Miami. In the VIP we popped bottles with rappers, celebrities, and bitches so bad that Van would've jumped out of his grave to fuck. When the club closed, we hit a strip club. I lost count of how much money I threw. We didn't leave the strip club until noon. From there, we hit up a water park. I popped molly like multivitamins so I didn't get tired. Later that night we were back at club WET. I was on the dance floor spraying bottles of Aces on females like that shit was water. A hot rapper from the dirty south named AK-47 put on a concert and shouted out my name like I was Big Meech. I felt like a superstar. I had it all: money, power, and respect. But I still wanted more. I wanted it all. Everything this life had to offer. And I wouldn't stop until I got it.

"You enjoying yourself?" Kianna asked.

I took my eyes off the sex scene between two groupies that unfolded on the floor of the stretch Hummer. "This shit feels like a dream, baby."

"That's good, baby. Happy birthday, you boss-ass nigga!"

Kianna turned back to the lesbian action, but I couldn't take my eyes off her. My bitch was bad. Soft milk chocolate skin. Sexy-ass hazel brown eyes that glowed when I made her cum. Thick healthy hair that she never "disrespected" by putting a weave in. A bad-ass body that I loved getting wrapped up in at night. And she was headstrong with a will made of iron that kept her disciplined and focused. I had lost control many times during our journey to riches, but she remained focused and put me back in my place. I wanted more of her. All of her. Her entire heart.

But she wouldn't let me have it because of Carl.

"Why are you staring at me like that?" she asked, turning to face me.

"Because I lo—"

"Oh shit! Damn!" Vic yelled.

I heard the scream and looked to the floor and saw clear liquid gushing from one of the groupie's pussies.

Kianna was in awe. "Ohhh! A gusher!"

Any other time a cum spray would've been the shit. But I was too caught up in my boss bitch to give it much attention. Kianna felt me watching her and got serious.

"Don't do this," she whispered. "Love is not for bosses. It makes us soft and weak."

"But I can't help it."

"Yes, you can. You have to. I'm not in love with you, Drayez. And I won't fall. You my nigga and I fucks with you. That's it. Fuck love."

Her eyes showed the hurt love dealt. I had to look away because I couldn't stand seeing the pain. I turned my attention back to the floor. Fuck love.

When the Hummer pulled up to the strip club, we continued the party inside. Off the jump, somebody caught my eye. Baddest bitch I ever seen in my life. Red bone. Short. Thick. Long hair. All she wore was sparkly pasties on her big-ass titties, a black thong, and heels. When I seen that ass, I knew I had to fuck. It was easily the fattest and best-looking natural ass I ever saw. Muthafucka didn't have a wrinkle, blemish, or pimple. And she was pretty. She looked Asian and black, like something in a nigga's wet dream.

"Damn, that bitch bad!" TC said.

"It's my birthday, nigga! I got first dibs."

Her name was Summer and it fit her perfectly because she was hot enough to burn a nigga. She danced for me most of the night and my dick ached from the touch of her soft skin.

"I want a private show," I whispered in her ear.

She ran her hands over my chest, staring in my eyes. "I don't do private shows for just anybody."

"Good thing I'm not just anybody. You know who I am. GMT going worldwide."

She gave a sexy smile before turning around and bending over. Her ass shook like a tsunami. Shit was sexy as fuck. After twisting around, she bent over like she was doing a crab walk, pussy in my face. Then she flipped onto a handstand like a gymnast, doing the splits in the air. From the handstand, she did the splits on the ground and started twerking. Then she was back on my lap grinding. It was so impressive that I wanted to stand up and clap. Instead, I said, "I want my private dance."

"Ask and you shall receive."

"Happy birthday, baby!" Kianna called.

Summer led me to the back of the club and down a hallway filled with private rooms. From behind those doors I heard whispers, moans, cries, and screams. We went to the last door in the hall, right next to the exit. Inside was a couch, table with a radio on it, and a small bathroom with the door closed. There were also mirrors on the walls and ceiling.

"Sit down," she said, looking a little nervous.

"You good?"

She glanced towards the bathroom door. "Yeah. I told you I don't do this for anybody. What you want?"

I sat a stack on the table. "Don't think about it. Just do it."

She turned on the radio and Beyoncé's "Dance for You" began playing. Then she was on my lap, her soft skin making my dick hard as steel.

"You want me to do something about that?" she asked.

"Hell yeah."

She slithered down my body like a snake, getting on her knees and unbuttoning my pants. I watched her pull my dick out and put it in her mouth. Shit felt too good. I closed my eyes and let her go to work.

"Suck dick good, can't she?"

I knew that voice anywhere. My dick went soft and a chill went up my spine as his last threat played in my head. I opened my eyes and saw him standing in the bathroom doorway holding a big-ass gun. Summer stopped giving me head and stood up.

"Nah, nah, keep suckin', bitch. Prolly da last nut dis nigga gon' buss."

She moved towards me, but I slipped my shit back in my pants.

"When I heard you and my bitch-ass li'l cousin was gettin money, I couldn't believe dat shit. Da streets sayin y'all li'l bitch asses got the city on lock. Den y'all bitch asses got da nerve to show up in my neck of da woods. I told you I was gon' get cho ass, didn't I?"

"Fuck you want, L-Dog?" I mugged.

"Oh! And you tough now?" he taunted. "Wish yo' bitch ass had dis same heart back den. My nigga Twan'd still be alive. What'chu thank 'bout my new patna? Bitch bad, ain't she? Keep trick-ass niggas like you gettin' me paid."

I looked at Summer. Coldness shone in those slanted eyes. Punk-ass bitch.

"How long we finna do this, nigga? What the fuck you want?"

"I'ma start wit' dat watch, nigga. Take it off."

I set my Presidential Rolex on the table, racking my brain for a way out of this. I knew one false move could get me killed.

"Then I'ma need you to let my bitch put dese cuffs on you so I can get cho ass out that back do'. When we get to my spot, I'ma need you to have yo' team bring me 250 G's. Dat's for gettin' my nigga whacked."

"Just let me go and I'ma give you the money."

He laughed. "You thank I'm stupid, nigga? Yo' dumb ass the one dat put my bitch-ass cousin on yo' team. Nigga can't hold water. Goin' live on da Book led me right to y'all ass. Put dese cuffs on him, baby."

While Summer cuffed me, I thought about TC setting me up. That shit sent a fire through my bones. "TC set me up?"

"Nah. Bitch-ass nigga ain't got dat much heart. Da problem wit'chu fake-ass street niggas is y'all put er'thang on da Gram or da Book. You niggas want the whole world knowin' y'all finna do dis and dat. I'm surprised the Feds ain't been booked you stupid-ass niggas."

A noise at the door made Summer and L-Dog freeze.

"Open the door, Drayez! You ain't finna keep her all to yo'self," Kianna called from the hallway.

L-Dog stayed cool, looking at me and whispering, "Don't say shit or I'ma kill yo' bitch ass." Then he turned to Summer, pointing his gun at the door. "Open it."

This was my moment. L-Dog was focused on the door, not paying attention to me because I was cuffed. I waited until Summer unlocked the door. I raised both my feet and kicked the table as hard as I could. It slid across the floor and into L-Dog's knees. The gun went off.

Pow!

Somebody screamed.

L-Dog stumbled and lost his balance. Before he got right, I rushed his ass, banging into him and trying to get him to the ground. But the li'l chubby nigga was strong and didn't go down. We started wrestling and he tried to shoot me but I grabbed the gun, pointing it away as he squeezed the trigger.

Pow, pow, pow!

"Let my shit go, nigga!" he yelled, punching me in the jaw.

The nigga hit hard, but I didn't let the gun go. If I did, he would kill me. But that meant I couldn't stop him from hitting me. I just hoped Kianna and the shooting had alerted my team.

"Let him go!" Summer screamed.

A second later, I felt the worst pain I ever felt. A fire spread between my legs and a white light flashed in my brain. I didn't want to let go of the gun, but my nuts hurt too bad. L-Dog snatched the pistol from my hand as I fell to the floor. This was it. Fuck. I got tricked by a punk-ass bitch and now I was about to die. I looked up at L-Dog as he pointed the pistol at me. I could see his finger applying pressure to the trigger. Then his eyes looked towards the door. I glanced over just in time to see Fantasia running into the room with reckless abandonment. L-Dog raised the gun too little too late. Fantasia jumped in the air like he could fly, his arms outstretched like he was Superman. He crashed into L-Dog, tackling him to the floor, and started going to work. Fantasia snatched the gun away and started beating the shit out of L-Dog.

I was getting to my feet when I heard another loud smack.

"Punk-ass bitch!" Kianna screamed.

Summer fell to the floor next to her nigga.

"You good?" Trav asked, popping into the room with the rest of GMT.

"Yeah. Somebody get these handcuffs off me," I said.

"What the fuck happened?" a security guard asked, running into the room too little too late.

"Fuck it look like, nigga? This bitch set me up!" I snapped.

A tall skinny nigga that looked like he could be Snoop Dogg's twin stepped in the room and took in everything quickly. "Fuck is this?"

"Is that L-Dog?" TC asked, finally noticing his cousin knocked out on the floor.

"Who the fuck is L-Dog?" the skinny nigga asked.

"Bitch-ass nigga used her to set me up. This the kinda shit you let go on in yo' club, Slinky?" I accused.

He looked disrespected. "Fuck you, nigga! I don't know that nigga and I don't get down with that jack shit. I get money. I don't need to steal shit."

I pointed to Summer. "Well, what the fuck is this?"

"Shit, you tell me. Bitch is a dancer. This shit never happened in here before. How the fuck you know this nigga, L-Dog, anyway?"

"We got history. Ay, somebody get me out these muthafuckin hand cuffs!"

"Looks like y'all history just showed up in my present. It's a back door right here. I need y'all to get all this shit outta my club before the police come."

"We need that security tape," Trav spoke up.

I saw dollar signs flash in Slinky's eyes. "How much is it worth?"

Trav put a gun in his face. "Yo' life, nigga!"

Slinky didn't look fazed.

"Chill, Trav," Kianna spoke up. "10 G's for the tape and we get to keep them," she said gesturing towards L-Dog and Summer.

Slinky looked at Trav like he wanted to say something but held his tongue. "Clean this shit up. Send somebody with me for the tape.

***

L-Dog didn't wake up until we pulled out of the parking lot. His face was swollen and bloody as he looked around the stretch Hummer to me, Kianna, Damo, TC, and Trav. "Damn, Dray. Turns out you ain't da bitch ass nigga I thought you was."

Nobody said a word in response.

"You still a bitch though, li'l cuz. You gon' let dis nigga kill yo' own flesh and blood?"

TC looked away.

"You always gon' be a bitch," L-Dog mugged before turning back to me. "Do it, Drayez. Let's get dis shit over wit'."

When I didn't talk, he got the hint. The Hummer stopped about five minutes later.

"Get the fuck out." I told him and Summer.

"Fuck I look like?" L-Dog snapped. "I ain't finna make dis shit easy, bitch-ass nigga. You gon kill me, den do it."

As soon as he finished talking, the door opened and Fantasia snatched him out like a rag doll. I grabbed Summer and we all got out. It was late and we were at a deserted part of the beach. Nobody around to hear the judgments. There were big-ass rocks about a hundred feet ahead and I could hear the surf slapping into them with the force that only trillions of gallons of water could bring. We led my enemies to the edge of the rocks.

"Can you swim?"

"Fuck you, bitch-ass nigga. You still a bitch. Dis buff-ass nigga a bitch. And TC, you a bitch for lettin' dese bitch-ass niggas fuck me up!" L-Dog snapped.

"If you wanna live, this yo only shot. Jump."

Summer looked out over the water. It was dark and hard to see what was out there. It was probably a twenty or thirty foot fall. Might be more rocks below. And the way the surf was beating, those rocks told of a sure death.

"Please, Drayez. I didn't know it would come to this. I don't—
—"

"Shut the fuck up, bitch!" I said, pointing my pistol in her face. "If you don't jump before I get to 3, you dead. 1. 2…"

She jumped. There was a loud smack and then the waves came. Everyone knew she died. I turned to L-Dog. When he mugged me, I knew he wasn't going to jump. I offered my gun to TC.

"Kill him."

TC's eyes got wide. "What?"

"You the reason I'm going through this. He said you told him we was in Florida. Did you?"

"I didn't know he was in Miami, Dray. You like my brother. I didn't mean for this to happen."

"But it did. And you gotta fix it."

TC studied my face, searching my eyes, pleading. I didn't blink or waver. He reluctantly took the gun and pointed it at his cousin. Tears rolled down his face.

"I can't do it, Dray."

"Gimme a gun, Trav." When he did, I clicked off the safety and put it to TC's head. "His life or yours."

"C'mon, Dray. Don't do this, bro."

"You did this. You gotta clean it up. Him or you."

"I ain't no killa. And he my cousin."

"Do you think he would hesitate to kill you? He don't give a fuck that y'all share the same blood."

TC cried harder. I tried to will him to kill L-Dog. I needed to know that he was all in with me and GMT, that he would do anything to protect the team. This was his test, and there was only one way he could pass. I couldn't go back on my word that I would kill him. I would do whatever necessary to protect the team. To protect me. I needed TC to do the same thing.

"I can't do it," he sobbed, lowering the gun.

I gave Fantasia a nod and he pushed L-Dog off the rocks. He didn't scream as he splashed into the water.

I kept my eyes on TC as he wept openly. I felt his pain. I knew this nigga when I wasn't shit. When I didn't have, he gave without thinking twice. He had seen me at my worst and my best. He was a loyal friend. My nigga without a doubt. But the stakes were bigger now. It was about more than friendships, and old times, and memories. It was about loyalty and trust. He had seen too much and not killing L-Dog made me question his loyalty.

Fire barked from the pistol when I squeezed the trigger. TC fell like his legs had been snatched from under him. I could feel the darkness taking over my soul as I walked away.

Chapter 21

By the end of the year, GMT was rolling in the money. Not only did I have the streets on lock, but thanks to Lace, I was a legit businessman. I owned stocks and bonds. I had a portfolio worth two million dollars. In a few years, I could go legit. I had gone from street hustler to entrepreneur. I was bigger than I could've ever imagined. And I made sure the whole fam was taken care of. I bought the house on Grantosa for Tikka and Tina. I bought Marie a house too. I set up a college fund and trust fund for Draya. I got Tracy the best appeal attorney money could buy. He thought she had a strong case and said he could have her out in a year or two. Me, Kianna, and Draya lived in a plush mansion in Brookfield. My whole team was eating good and I didn't have a care in the world. Until I opened my front door and seen the look on Vic's face.

"Damn, nigga. Why you looking like the world finna end? Don't tell me Renae put you out?" I cracked, reversing the joke they teased me with when Rayna used to put me out.

He didn't find the joke funny. "I need to holla at you, bro."

We settled in my living room. My shit was decked out, too. Thick-ass royal blue carpet that hugged my feet every time I took a step. My couches were imported from Italy. Marble tables. And instead of a TV, I watched movies on a projection screen that covered my entire wall.

"What's good, my nigga? Why you lookin' like somebody died?"

Vic breathed deep, getting emotional. "I want out, Dray."

I stared at him for a moment. Vic's dreads had grown to the middle of his back and he had gained a little weight. That told he was eating good. He no longer had to talk his baby mamas out of money. He was the provider. And he drove an Infiniti truck, wore designer clothes, had jewelry. He had bought a house. Now he wanted to give it all up.

"You want out of GMT?"

He nodded.

"Why?"

"This shit starting to be too much. All the shit I seen. Losing TC. The drama. I just feel like I need to get out before it's too late."

When he mentioned TC, I saw something in his eyes that told me he hadn't forgiven me for killing our boy. "You know I had to do that, right?"

"No, you didn't, Dray. That was our nigga. He fucked up, but he didn't deserve to die for it. That shit happened eight months ago and I still think about it every day. That was our nigga."

"But I couldn't trust him. I wasn't sure about his loyalty."

Vic got mad. "That's bullshit! You know TC was loyal. He was like our brother. You tried to force him to kill L-Dog. He wasn't no killa. You the one that changed. You not the same nigga we knew, but he stayed the same. He was still a simple nigga. And you killed him. How do I know you won't kill me?"

"C'mon, Vic. You trippin'. You know I'm not gon' kill you. We day 1's. We like brothers."

"So was TC."

"But that was different. He fucked up and needed to fix it. If he woulda killed L-Dog, he would still be here. TC almost got me killed. I couldn't let that go."

"But it was an accident. Yeah, he fucked up, but that don't mean he deserved to die."

"And that's where we differ. This is about more than us. This about a movement. A team. Niggas gotta put in work and carry they weight. I loved that nigga. He was family. But lines gotta get drawn."

"So, if I fuck up, you gon 'kill me too?"

My eyes didn't lie.

When Vic saw the answer, he pulled the GMT chain from his pocket and set it on the table. "You my brother, Dray. And I know if it came down to it, you would do me like you did TC. I'm not a killa, my nigga. I just wanted to get some money and fuck some bitches. I did that. I don't want to get in too deep or lose myself in this shit. I'm not ready to die. I wanna walk away while I still got the chance."

I couldn't decide if he was making a well thought out move or being a coward. I knew he was a simple nigga when I met him. He wasn't a killa, nor did he have dope boy dreams. And now that shit was getting real, he wanted to get out before shit hit the fan.

"Uncle Vissy!" Draya laughed, running to Vic.

When he picked her up in his arms, the grim look faded from his face for a moment. "Hey, princess!"

Draya was getting bigger every day. She was two years old and I swear my baby was the prettiest thing in the world. Cute and smart with a personality as big as the city. Her hair was twisted into eight pigtails that hung past her shoulders and she wore one of her many princess dresses.

"I'm going to Granny Marie's house. Can you come too?"

"Sorry, baby girl. I got a few things I need to take care of. Can I take a rain check?"

She looked cute in her confusion. "What is that?"

"It means I'll meet you over there some other time."

"Aw, man," she frowned.

Watching Draya and Vic made me realize he would always be what he was. He charmed females. He had even charmed my daughter. He was still the same nigga. I changed. And I realized that he wasn't scared of me. He was scared to become me. He wanted to remain him. A simple nigga. The same thing TC wanted until I took that away.

"C'mere, Draya."

She hopped off Vic's lap and bounced over to me. "What, Daddy?"

"Can you go find Kianna? I need some time with Uncle Vic."

She bounced away smiling. "Okay, Daddy."

When I stood, Vic stood with me. "I love you, my nigga. And I'm sorry for what happened to TC. If this shit ain't for you, get out. I get it. I changed and you wanna stay you. No matter what, you gon' always be my nigga."

After a hug, Vic walked out the front door. I knew that would be the last time I seen my nigga.

***

"Is that Kanye?" Manny asked, pointing to the other side of the catwalk.

I looked. Sure enough, it was Yeezy. But I refused to look like a starstruck groupie just because I shared the room with a superstar.

"Yeah, that's that nigga," I said nonchalantly, looking down the runway towards the curtains. I was ready for the show to start.

The show I was talking about was the Yves Saint Laurent Fashion Show in LA. Everybody who was somebody wanted to be here, but only a few got the privilege. Me and some of my GMT niggas had front row seats. Since Manny, Tina's boyfriend, was the newest GMT member, I brought him along to show him how GMT moved. I had been invited by Lexi, the plus-size model I saw from time to time. This was her biggest gig to date and she wanted me to be a part of it.

"Ay, that's Kevin Hart!" Manny pointed.

I spun to face him. "My nigga, you with a money gettin' team now. We not groupies; we bosses. We don't get excited by famous people. They get excited by us. Stay composed. We GMT."

"My bad, Dray. I'm from the hood. All this shit still new to me."

The fashion show was a hit. I saw a bunch of bullshit I wouldn't be caught dead wearing, but a few pieces caught my eye. The main event for me was watching Lexi strut down the runway. She smiled and blew kisses at me when she walked by. I got hating looks from a few stars and I loved the envy. I had something they didn't. From the fashion show, we took a helicopter back to the Trump Towers. We had just stepped off the elevator when we bumped into the Brick Boyz. Before I could stop him, Manny got his super fan on.

"On shit! Brick Boyz. Lemme get a picture!"

I mugged the shit out of Manny before extending my hand to the rap group. "Brick Boyz, what's good?"

"Yeah, yeah. What up, fam?" Trapster mumbled, ignoring my hand as he walked onto the elevator.

I felt disrespected. "What the fuck was that, nigga? I said what up?"

He looked at me like I was a piece of shit. "Fuck is you, nigga?"

My niggas sized up the Brick Boyz. There were four of them and six of us.

"We GMT, nigga! You know who we is. Get Money Team!" Damo mugged him.

"Don't nobody give a fuck about that locals shit. We platinum," Snowman said.

"Fuck platinum. We in the streets, nigga!" Trav said, reaching for his waist.

"Hold on! Hold on!" Cash stepped in, lifting his arms. "Ay, don't I know you?"

"Yeah. I kicked it with y'all when y'all came to Milwaukee. Me and my nigga Van."

Recognition shone in Cash's eyes. "Oh yeah. You the nigga that was gettin' his dick passed around like a blunt."

My niggas looked at me funny.

"We was fucked up that night," I explained.

Cash reached for my hand and we shook. "Yo, what's good with you, family? I see you looking good."

"GMT, baby. We all over the Midwest. About to be worldwide."

"Yeah, I heard AK-47 rappin' about you niggas. That's you, huh?"

"Yeah. We comin' up."

"And that was fucked up what happened to Van Go," he said sadly.

"He was too much for this cold world. He in a better place."

"That nigga was the Jakes, yo," Snowman said.

I wanted to beat his ass. When Cash saw the look on my face, he spoke up.

"Okay, money. We gotta hit this radio station. We throwing a concert tonight. Come fuck with us."

I nodded. "I wouldn't miss it for the world!"

***

The concert was packed. Fans jumped around, held up phones, and rapped the lyrics as the Brick Boyz performed on stage. Me, Damo, Trav, and Manny mobbed through the crowd wearing serious looks. We were on a mission. The backpacks me and Trav carried were our tools. He would cause the distraction and I would show the world who GMT was.

The crowd was separated from the stage by a gate. Security guards stood posted in the middle. I nodded to Trav when we got near the gate and he disappeared into the crowd. A moment later, there was a lot of pushing, shoving, and screaming. Money was being thrown in the air and the crowd was trying to grab as much as they could. When security seen the commotion, they went to investigate. Me, Manny, and Damo used the distraction to jump the gate and rush the stage. When the Brick Boyz saw us running towards them, they got spooked.

"What ch'all doin'?" Snowman asked.

I snatched his mic and faced the crowd. "These niggas ain't no Brick Boyz! We the real Brick Boyz! Get Money Team takin' over. G-M-T! G-M-T! G-M-T!" I chanted as we pulled money from my backpack and started throwing it in the crowd.

The concert goers went wild! I was so geeked that I ran and jumped in the crowd and crowd surfed. Security tried to chase us, but we got away. GMT!

***

I was awakened the next day by my phone. I untangled myself from Lexi and Kendra, another model from the fashion show, and reached for the phone. It was Kianna.

"What up, baby?"

"Are you fuckin' serious, Drayez!? You threw money at a Brick Boyz concert?"

"How you find out about that?"

"It's all over social media and TMZ. What the fuck, Drayez? Why you do that shit?"

"Chill, baby. Fuck you got yo' thong all up yo ass for? You know I be jackin' and stuntin'. That's what I do."

"That shit was hot, Dray. They said you threw a couple hundred thousand dollars. The Feds are going to see this. You went too far this time."

"It was only a hunnit. And what the fuck the Feds got to so with this? You being paranoid."

"I'm being paranoid, huh? Well, Bertrand is here."

That got my attention. "Bertrand? Diego's man?"

"Yeah. He looking for you."

"How the fuck he know where we live?"

"I don't know. But that's not important."

"Well shit, if that ain't important, what is?"

"The Feds got Diego. Bertrand got away. He came to warn us."

It got hard for me to breathe. "Diego got knocked? You serious?"

"Why the fuck would I play about something like this? Yes, I'm serious. While you're out there trying to become number one on the Fed's list, real shit is happening. You need to come home."

***

We caught the first thing smoking out of LAX. During the entire flight, I hoped that everything was a mistake. Diego couldn't have gotten knocked. Without him, there was no GMT. I didn't have a plan B. I also didn't know what the Feds knew. Did they have pictures? Was my phone tapped? Was GMT about to get caught up in a sweep?

As soon as I walked through the front door, I was greeted by Draya. "Hi, Daddy!"

"Hey, baby," I said, blowing off my princess and going to find Kianna. "Where is Bertrand?"

"He left a couple hours ago. He was spooked and probably on his way out the country."

"What did he say? Do the Feds know us?"

"He don't know. His ass can barely speak English, but he told me they were set up during a buy. Had a big shootout."

I flopped down on the couch like I had been shot. Diego had a shootout with the Feds. Wasn't no way out of that. It was over for my big homie. I closed my eyes as visions of my empire, my organization, and my team crumbled in my mind.

Chapter 22

A week had passed since Diego got knocked. Shit was all over World News.

"Drug Lord arrested after shootout with Federal Agents! Three agents murdered! 5 drug dealers killed! Edwardo 'Diego' Bermudez captured!"

He had been on the Feds' watch list for five years and had ties to a Columbian Mafia. Police in different countries were locking up his associates. Since the Feds hadn't kicked in my door, I figured I was safe. For now. But all GMT operations were on hold until this shit blew over. And then I would have to find another plug. Get Money Team moved twenty kilos of heroin a week. Millions of dollars in cash every month. And somehow I had to find another supplier.

I considered closing shop and leaving the game. Kianna and Lace planted those thoughts. But if I left the game, what would I do? What would happen to GMT? We had only been around a year and hadn't grown past the Midwest. Besides my stunt at the Brick Boyz concert, most people didn't know who we were and I wasn't satisfied with that. I wanted GMT to be national. I couldn't let my baby die before it grew up. It wasn't even as big as TBT yet, and I would be damned if I let a nigga named Carlile be bigger than me. It was a GMT world.

"Penny for your thoughts," Kianna said from the passenger seat of my 750.

We were heading to a spa. I didn't care for massages and facials, but Kianna swore by it. She said it would help me relax.

"I'm just thinking about the team."

"Stressing won't help. Nothing we can do for them. We all have to wait it out. Hopefully they saved some of their money. We gave everybody enough to eat with."

"Yeah, I know. I want what's best for everybody. But at the same time, I want GMT to be legendary. Bigger than all the money-gettin' cliques out there. I want us to go down in history."

"You realize that the bigger we get, the more chance we have of getting caught?"

I mugged her. "Why you tryna shit on my vision? Don't you want the same thing?

"I'm not shitting on your vision, Drayez. And I don't care how big and famous we get. I just want to live good like I'm accustomed to. I don't care about the fame and infamy. I think we'll last longer if we don't chase the fame. I care about longevity. Why do you think TBT has been around for so long? Why do you think Carl is still free? At the beginning, before he got too big-headed, he wanted money, not the fame. We agreed on that."

I hated when she brought Carl up. Sometimes she talked about that nigga like he was a God and that shit pissed me off. "You know I ain't Carl, right?"

"I didn't mean it like that. You know that. Don't go there. I was just trying to make a point. Sometimes money is more important than fame. Fame is fleeting."

"So is money."

"I know. That's why I wanted to make sure we got Lace so we wouldn't have to worry about our money fleeting. Our money is making money. Carl - I mean, I - knew we needed her."

I didn't care about money and fame no more. I was tired of this bitch constantly talking about Carl. "Listen, if you love and miss the nigga so much, why the fuck you still livin' in my house?"

She sucked in a sharp breath. "Your house? That's my house too, nigga. You wouldn't have none of this shit if it wasn't for me. Nigga, I made you!"

I smashed the brakes and pulled the car over. "That's what you think? That you made me? Nigga, I'm self-made! I'm a boss! You didn't make shit. You should be thankin' me for saving you. When yo' ass didn't have a dime in yo' pocket and couldn't even pay cab fare, I paid that shit. You was sleeping on my couch. You didn't get the plug from Diego. I did. When niggas think of GMT, they think of me. I got you living good again. I saved yo' ass."

"This is what I'm talking about: your emotional ass. You're just jealous of Carl because I loved him and I won't fall in love with yo' ass."

Her words cut deep. My hand moved out of instinct and slapped the shit out of Kianna. As soon as my hand left her face, I realized I fucked up. Kianna wasn't just any female. She was a boss bitch down to ride or die. And most importantly, she was a killa. I had watched her off the last nigga that hit her, and she turned that same rage on me. Murder flashed in those hazel eyes and her manicured nails became knives.

"Muthafucka!" she screamed, scratching my face and clawing at my eyes.

"Bitch, quit!" I yelled, grabbing her wrists.

She bit my hand, trying to take a chunk out of a nigga. When I let her go, she was at me again, using her nails like Freddie Kruger claws. I took my foot off the brake, pushed her into the passenger seat, and dove on top of her ass. I could feel the car moving, but I was more concerned with getting Kianna under control.

When I was on top of her, I pinned her arms between us so she couldn't scratch me again. Then I reached my right hand up and started choking her ass. She jerked beneath me, struggling to breathe as thick veins bulged out her forehead and side of her neck. Her eyes bugged out like Kermit the Frog's and her face began turning purple. I thought about killing her ass. I was close.

A loud-ass horn made me look up. The Benz had drifted into oncoming traffic and we were about to go head to head with a semi-truck. I let go of her neck and yanked the steering wheel. The Benz whipped back into the right lane, barely missing the truck and spinning around in a half circle. I got thrown up against the door, but I didn't stay long. I jumped back in the seat and mashed the brake. When I looked up, the car was facing the wrong direction. I pulled to the side of the road to gather myself. Kianna was in the passenger seat, holding her throat, struggling to breathe.

"Drayez," she said hoarsely. "You ever put yo' hands on me again, I'ma kill you."

I had never been worried about her hurting me until that moment. I reached out to her, "Kianna, I'm—"

"Don't touch me!" she screamed.

When she reached for the door handle, I didn't stop her. The trickle of blood down my face made me look in the mirror. It looked like I had a fight with a cat and some of the scratches were bleeding. I had fucked up. Damn. I was stressed and needed a drink.

I pulled away from the curb and found the nearest liquor store. People inside gave me crazy looks, but I didn't give a fuck. I grabbed a fifth of Hennessy, threw a 50 dollar bill on the counter, and walked out. I drank and drove as a mixture of emotions filled my body: anger, rage, sadness, hurt. And then the liquor kicked in.

I don't remember driving there, but somehow I ended up at a familiar apartment complex. I left the keys in the ignition and stumbled into the building. After falling against the door, I put my finger against the doorbell and kept it there. The chime went crazy as I lifted the bottle to my lips again.

"Wait! Stop! Who is it?"

I continued to lay against the door and press the doorbell. Locks clicked and when the door opened, gravity took over. I fell to the floor like a dead body. If it wasn't for the thick-ass carpet, I would've busted my head open.

"Drayez! What happened?"

When I got my focus, she was standing over me. Those eyes with those stories. And those lips. I immediately felt at peace. The cold-ass world didn't seem so cold anymore. I could finally close my eyes and rest.

***

"Kill him."

"W-what?"

"You the reason I'm going through this shit. He said you told him we was in Florida. Did you?"

"I didn't know he was in Miami, Dray. You like my brother. I didn't mean for this to happen."

"But it did and you gotta fix it."

"I can't do it, Dray."

"Gimme a gun, Trav." I put the gun to TC's head. "His life or yours."

"C'mon, Dray. Don't do this, bro. Please."

"You did this. You gotta clean it up. Him or you."

"I can't do it," TC cried, lowering the gun.

I squeezed the trigger, but nothing happened. TC spun and lifted the gun to my face. His tears turned to blood and red flames burned in his eyes. I tried to shoot him again, but the gun didn't work. Then he laughed. It was evil. It made my skin crawl and body grow cold.

"You gon' pay for what you did to me, Drayez!"

White light exploded behind my eyes when he pulled the trigger.

"Shit!" I screamed, waking up. Cold sweat covered my body and all around me was dark. Was I dead? Was this hell?

And that's when I recognized her smell. When my eyes adjusted to the dark, I immediately knew where I was. But how did I get here? When I sat up, the headache kicked in. It felt like a little person was inside my head throwing a temper tantrum and my throat hurt like I swallowed a box of thumb tax.

I looked around, my eyes landing on the baby wipes on the dresser. A framed picture of Desiré and a baby made my eyes pop. Damn, she had a baby!

She had moved on and found that healing love she was talking about. So why the fuck was I still in her bed?

I moved faster than I should've and almost passed out. When my head stopped spinning, I stumbled towards the door. I heard music when I stepped into the hallway. "Good Man" by India Arie. The music brought back memories. Then I got the sudden urge to piss. I stopped in the bathroom to drain the snake and noticed two toothbrushes in the holder. Desiré and her nigga's. I thought about how to react as I washed my hands. Should I go stunt on her, or leave without saying a word? I chose the first option. I was going to let her get a taste of the GMT founder!

When I walked into the living room, Desiré was sitting on the couch shuffling a stack of papers. She looked even better then I remembered. Hair was rich, thick, and had grown past her shoulders. Those deep eyes looked even deeper. Her peanut butter complexion was glowing. And those lips… She was wearing a snug white T-shirt that showed off them big-ass titties. The blue pajama bottoms did nothing to hide her figure, a figure that looked a little slimmer than the last time I saw her.

"You making me nervous." She giggled.

All that GMT boss shit went right out the window when I heard her laugh.

"Oh, my bad. You look…different."

She looked me up and down. I was rocking Balmain from head to toe with my iced-out GMT chain. "So do you. You can sit down if you want."

I sat opposite her, noticing two cups of coffee on the table. One must've been her niggas.

"That's for you," she said, reading my thoughts. "I poured it when I heard you in the bathroom. I figured you might need it. That Henny ain't no joke." She laughed, glancing at the almost empty bottle on the table.

"You right about that," I agreed, reaching for the mug. It was a special brew. It tasted like cinnamon and vanilla.

"I put your keys in your pocket. Nice car."

"Thanks. Sorry for just popping up on you like this. I was drunk and didn't know what I was doing."

"No, you're not. Otherwise you wouldn't have done it. But it's okay. You looked like you needed help. I did what I could for your face. What happened?"

For some reason, I didn't want to tell Desiré about Kianna. "I had a fight with a cat."

"Looks bigger than a cat. Maybe a lion or panther."

"Yeah. A lion."

Silence followed. But not for long.

"Do you love her?"

The question was unexpected and I wasn't sure how to answer. If anybody else asked me the question, the answer would've been yes. But in Desiré's presence, I wasn't sure. When I compared my feelings for both women, even though I hadn't seen her in over a year, Desiré won by a landslide.

"She won't let me."

I don't know how she did it, but I swear Desiré smirked with her eyes. "She won't or you won't?"

I took another sip of coffee, using the pause to gather my thoughts. "She won't. She's my business partner, with benefits. I think we clicked because we both got hurt by people we loved. We agreed not to grow feelings but somewhere along the way, the lines got blurred."

"Is that what happened to your face?"

"We had an argument because she compared me to her ex."

She laughed. "And you didn't like that, huh? You don't have to answer that. I know you didn't."

Silence again. This time I broke it.

"Enough about me. How you been? You had a baby?"

She got defensive. "Who told you about Junior?"

"Nobody. I saw the pictures in yo' room."

She relaxed. "Oh. Yes, Junior is my world. Having him makes my life complete. He gives me so much love, joy, and laughter. I never knew I could love another human being as much as I love my baby."

I thought about Draya.

"How is Draya?" she asked, reading my mind again.

"How do you do that shit?"

"What?"

"It's like you know what I be thinking. How you do that?"

"You're not a good poker player, Drayez. What's in your head is written on your face."

I made a mental note to work on my poker face. "Draya is good. Getting big. She's two. So, where yo' man at? Who is Junior's daddy?"

Desire stared at me, searching my face. My chest burned as I waited for an answer. I could feel jealousy and envy swirling in my core.

"Vic didn't tell you?"

Damn. Vic finally fucked. "Nah, he didn't tell me."

She looked away. "I wanted to call you back so many times. I just wished you would've fought for me a little harder, like they do in the movies. Send flowers to my job. I wanted to come home and see my house overflowing with bears and balloons. But you stopped calling after a couple of days. You knew where I lived and worked, but you never came. So I moved on with my life."

"So you gon' fuck Vic and have a baby by him?"

She looked offended. "What? No! Are you crazy?"

"You mentioned Vic and I thought—"

"He's your son, Drayez."

My heart stopped beating. No shit. It felt like my heart stopped and I had to catch my breath. "I got a son?"

She laughed. "Yes. Drayez Junior. I'm surprised Vic never told you. I told Renae not to tell him, but I know she did. And I wanted to tell you the last time I saw you but…you know."

I chose the concert, Van, and the girls over her.

"I'm sorry about that." I knew I fucked up but my pride… Then I thought about my son again. "But shit, I got a son!"

"Yes. He's almost one."

I went over and wrapped her in a big-ass bear hug. She was soft, warm, and smelled good.

"Okay, Drayez!" she wheezed.

"Shit. My bad," I loosened my grip. "So where the li'l nigga at? Let me see him."

"He's with my mother. He was here when you first came, but I told her to come pick him up. I wanted to talk to you before you met him."

"About what? Let's go get him. I want to see my boy."

"You will. I promise. But it's late and they're asleep."

I checked my watch. It was past midnight. Meeting my boy would have to wait a few hours. I didn't know what else to do or say, so I just stared at her. She looked so good. And she gave me a son. In that moment, my feelings for Desiré grew even stronger.

"What?" She blushed.

I looked from her eyes to her lips. They looked so soft. When I leaned forward, to my surprise and relief, Desiré met me halfway. Our tongues grooved like they never separated, not missing a beat. She kissed with longing. Love returned home. We paused long enough to take our shirts off. She wasn't wearing a bra. I caressed and rubbed those big-ass titties before sucking her nipples in my mouth. She made beautiful noises, giving India Arie's voice a run for her money. Her hands did those things they did; rubbing my face, neck, chest, arms, and back.

From her breasts, I kissed my way to her stomach, tugging at her pajama bottoms. She lifted up just enough for me to pull them off. No panties underneath. I kissed my way to her pelvis and wiggled my tongue on a spot at the top of her thigh. She gasped and bucked, grabbing my shoulders. I moved lower, spreading her legs and kissing my way to her shaved pussy. It smelled like everything good, heat pulsing from it in waves like a vent. Instead of digging in, I kissed and licked her inner thigh.

"Ssss! Mmmm, Drayez!" she moaned.

I moved to her pussy, sliding my tongue around the lips.

"Oh, my God!" she moaned as a shiver ran through her body.

I went to her clit and licked and sucked until she came. When I stood to take off my clothes, Desiré looked up at me in a daze. Her cheeks glistened from the tears. When I climbed between her legs and stuck my dick inside her walls, the only thing I could say was, "Damn!" No words could describe how good her pussy felt. After she adjusted to me being back inside, I used every ounce of discipline and skill I learned from Kianna to bring her pleasure. She cried and screamed my name until she lost her voice.

Chapter 23

Lying in bed with Desiré in my arms felt right, like how my life was supposed to be. She was a good woman. Smart, fine, funny, non-judging, independent. And now that I knew she hadn't fucked a nigga since the last time I hit it, over a year, I added faithful and loyal to the list of everything that made her a good woman. Being around her made me feel good in all kinds of ways. Kianna who? Right now it was all about Desiré, and I wanted to keep it that way.

"You gotta let me get y'all up out this apartment. This ain't no place to raise a baby. You need a house with a backyard. Junior needs his own room."

"What's wrong with my apartment? I've lived here for five years."

"Well, for starters, you only got one bedroom. He gon eventually need his own space. And you ain't got no backyard."

"I don't know if I'm ready for a house yet. I talked to my mom about it and I know I'll need one eventually. But I've always pictured my house being a home like the Luther Vandross song. I don't want to be in a whole house with just me and Junior."

"I'ma be there."

"Will you be in and out, or there to stay?"

Truth be told, I wasn't ready to give up my lifestyle. I did what I wanted, when I wanted, and I loved the freedom. She read the look on my face.

"Do you love me, Drayez?"

I took my time answering. "Yeah, I do."

"But not enough to settle down with me?"

"I don't know. You know how I am. I didn't want to be in love or have kids. I always wanted to do my thing. Do what I wanted when I wanted. In less than twenty-four hours, you changed everything. I don't know what to think."

"What do you want?"

"To be there and take care of you and my li'l nigga."

"You know that I don't need you to take care of us, right? I've done fine on my own. I know you're his father and you love me and want to take care of us, but I don't want you part time. And he doesn't need a part-time daddy."

Her words cut me. "You giving me an ultimatum? You sayin' all or nothing?"

She sat up to look at me. "That's not what I'm saying. You can come see your son any time you want. You can take him out and spend time with him. I'm not going to stop you from being his father. But I don't want you buying me houses and making love to me if I can't have you for good. I want a home, not a house. I want a man, not a baby daddy."

Shit was too heavy. I grabbed my cigarettes and lit a stick. "C'mon, Desiré. Think about this a li'l more."

"I thought about it for over a year. I know what I want. You're the one that doesn't know what you want."

I raised my voice. "I just told you what I want! I want to be there for you and my son."

"That's not it. You want to have your cake and eat it too. But you can't this time. A year ago you wanted money, power, and respect. From what I've heard, you got that and some. But you aren't satisfied with that and still want more. How come you're not satisfied if you got what you always wanted?"

I never thought about it like that. I did have everything that I wanted. And I still wanted more. Why? "I think I'm addicted to it. I went from being a bum-ass nigga to on top of my shit. I don't want to let it go."

"But you have to. What you're doing won't last forever. It can't. I heard about Van and TC. That was sad. Vic said he walked away because he didn't want to die or end up in a cell for the rest of his life. That's the only place your lifestyle will lead. I don't want you to die, baby. And I don't want to bring our son to see you in a prison visiting room. I want you with me, raising our son and Draya. I don't want our kids looking up to a drug dealer. I don't want our son to grow up to be like you if this is what you're going to be."

I heard those words hundreds of time, but leave it up to Desiré to make me feel them. Shit was real. I didn't have a comeback, nor could I deny the truth in her words.

"What will it take for you to be satisfied, Drayez?"

"I don't know. I've been chasing this fame lately. I know it ain't worth a cell or grave, but I still want it."

"I don't think you want fame. Maybe infamy. You don't want to be famous for fame's sake or riches. You want to be famous for being a killer or drug dealer."

"A killa?" I asked, raising an eyebrow. If Vic told her I killed TC, I was killing his ass.

"Vic didn't tell me anything. I guessed it. He said you changed and I can feel it. You're different. Darker. Especially your eyes. You've done some dark things and Vic is scared of you. He never said it but I saw it in his eyes when I ask about you. But what you've done doesn't matter to me. I love you unconditionally. I just want you because...you satisfy me."

***

"Where you been and why haven't you been answering your phone?" Kianna asked when I walked in the house.

"I ran into somebody that I used to know," I mumbled as I walked to the bedroom.

"That's it? That's all I get?" Kianna asked, following me to the room. "I called hospitals and jails looking for your ass and all I get is some shit about somebody that you used to know?"

I went to the closet and began undressing. I had the same clothes on for two days. Even though they were clean - Desiré made sure of that during our baths - being in the same clothes made me feel dirty. "What you want me to say? I told you where I was. You want me to go into detail?"

There was a hint of something in her eyes, but it disappeared before I could figure out what it was.

"No, you don't gotta go into details. It's been two days. For some reason, I expected you to come home...different."

"You expected me to apologize?"

She got mad. "No!" Then she softened. "I mean, yes. Look, Drayez, I just want things to be the way they were. I don't wanna fight. You my nigga. But I'm not sorry about what I did. You put your hands on me and I meant what I said. Don't put your hands on me no more. But at the end of the day, we're partners. I want what's best for us."

As I looked in Kianna's face, I couldn't help but compare her to Desiré. Kianna was a bad-ass boss bitch. Desire was a woman. Kianna wanted the finer things. Desiré wanted love and happiness. Kianna wanted to be my partner. Desiré wanted to be my wife. Kianna wasn't in love with me. Desiré loved me unconditionally. For the first time since I met her, I realized Kianna was replaceable.

"I'm not sorry I slapped you, Kianna. You got outta line and needed to be put in yo' place. You my bitch and I did what I had to do. You can't talk to me like that. I'ma boss."

She looked like I slapped her again. "And you can't talk to me like that either. I'm a boss too. Your B ain't bigger than mine."

"Talk to you like what? You always talking that Carl shit. I didn't like it and I said something. You got slick and started talking about you made me. I let you know you didn't. You got outta line and I slapped you."

"You told me to get out of your house. This is my house too. I invested just as much as you did into GMT."

"See, Kianna, this is the problem. It's like you need to be validated or something. Yeah, you helped build GMT. But make no mistake about it, I got us the plug. I fucked Lace and got the money clean. You had the information and I used it. I never denied that you helped build GMT, but my face is on this team. Everybody looks to me. I know that none of this shit would be possible without you, but you act like all this would be possible without me. You didn't make me. You helped polish me. There's a difference."

She took a moment to let my words play in her head. And then her eyes cleared like the sky after a storm when the sun comes out. I had put her boss ass in her place and she liked it so much that she got on her knees, pulled down my boxers and started sucking my dick. Although my shit got hard, I didn't feel shit. Whatever spell Kianna had on me was broken. I now saw Kianna for what she was. My bitch. She did what I said, when I said. No questions. So when she pushed me on the bed and tried to climb on my dick, I stopped her.

"Nah, keep sucking."

Anger flashed in her brown eyes.

I stared back at her like that shit didn't faze me. When she realized I had bossed up, she went back to sucking my dick. I held my nut back for over an hour, losing track of time because I was busy thinking of my next move. Kianna stopped sucking a couple times, complaining of her jaws hurting, but I didn't care. I told her to keep sucking. When I finally let her swallow my kids, she looked relieved.

"About time! Now can a bitch finally get hers?" she asked, flexing her jaws.

I got up and started putting on my clothes. "Later. I need to run some shit by you. First of all, I just found out I got a son."

She blinked a couple times like she was confused. "What? A son?"

"Yeah. The somebody I used to know is Desiré. I dealt with her before I met you. I ran into her after we fought and met my son."

She looked skeptical. "A son, Drayez? Really? How do you know he's yours?"

I wanted to say, "Because Desiré ain't like yo' scandalous ass", but I didn't. "Because I ain't no fool. He my son and I don't know how much longer I'ma be doing this shit. I wanna make a power move and get the team back eating."

She looked like she wanted to question what I was saying, but didn't. "Okay. What do you want to do?"

"I wanna meet Carl."

Kianna looked like she just woke up from being knocked out. "Are you crazy?"

"Where else I'ma find somebody with enough dope to feed the team?"

"Baby, think about what you're saying. Carl is our competition. Damn near our enemy. You killed his brother and I was his bitch. I don't think this is a good plan."

"I already thought about it. Finding somebody to give me twenty keys of food is damn near impossible. You said Carl got longevity. He love money. I'ma propose that we bring our teams together and take over the whole state. Shit, the whole Midwest."

She wasn't buying what I was selling. "I don't know about this, Dray."

"Why not? It make sense to me."

"Because… Carl is… I don't think he will do it."

"But you don't know. You think he will turn down millions of dollars? If my biggest competition came to me wanting to cop, I would do it to put the nigga in my pocket. Make myself bigger. Nextel merged with Sprint. Chrysler with Dodge. TBT ain't bigger than none of them. But if Carl ever wanna get on that level, he needs us."

She was at a loss for words. She looked stuck.

I continued to watch her. Then something clicked. She didn't want me to meet Carl for her own reasons. It was written all over her face.

"Why don't you want me to meet Carl?"

The tears surprised me. "I don't want to be around him or near him or do business with him. He beat my ass and left me. Fuck Carl!"

"Yeah, he beat yo' ass and left you, but you built yo'self up stronger. Don't you want him to see you shining? Don't you wanna show him that you don't need him? This is the best move for the team. You have to set yo feelings aside and make a business decision. Unless it's another reason you don't want to see Carl. Is it another reason? What is it?"

"Because I still love him!"

There it was. The truth. And it didn't even affect me because I knew it all along. She never got over Carl and she didn't want to. She didn't fall in love with me because there wasn't enough room in her heart for two people. If she still wanted to be my bitch after I damn near killed her, why wouldn't she want to be Carl's? Kianna was never mine. She gave me what she wanted me to have. The rest was Carl's.

"About time you kept it real with yo'self."

"What do you want from me, Drayez?"

"I want you to set up a meeting with Carl."

***

Even though TBT got money in Milwaukee, Carl lived in Chicago. He didn't shit in his own backyard. That's how he stayed off the Feds' radar. In a lot of ways, I was a hybrid of Carl. I had his plug, his bitch, his hedge fund manager. And according to Kianna and Lace, I had his aura. Why not meet the man I had so much in common with? Only seemed right. And I was excited about the meet. I wanted to see how he would react to meeting me.

I drove, Damo was my passenger, and Kianna was in the backseat where bitches belonged. I wasn't mad at her. I finally recognized her for what she was and put her in her place. She had a part to play. Plus, I planned on walking away from GMT after I made this last deal. After putting everything in place, I was turning everything over to Damo. Desiré was right. I had achieved everything I wanted. I had money, power, and respect. Even fear. None of that satisfied me. But spending time with Desiré and my son was the closest thing I'd felt to satisfaction in a long time. I didn't want to spend the next thirty years in prison talking about the money I spent, bitches I fucked, and the good times. I wanted to tell those stories while I was still free. And I damn sure wasn't ready to die. I was only twenty-six. I had millions of dollars. It would be a waste not to be able to spend my hard-earned money. So this was it.

When I got off the highway, I followed Kianna's directions to Carl's club, Triple Time. The lot was filled with foreign cars, so my 750 fit right in. I hopped out, dressed fresh in Ferragamo with my GMT chain sparkling. Damo was fitted in Gucci, his GMT chain on deck. And Kianna looked like a bag of money in the Dolce dress and red bottoms. Strapped to her thigh was a seven shot 380. Me and Damo carried Glocks. No way we was going in there naked.

When the security saw Kianna, they showed her respect like she was Mrs. Obama. Triple Time was packed with bad bitches and money getting niggas. I seen a lot of niggas wearing some kind of TBT emblem on their clothes or jewelry. Our GMT chains stuck out like a nigga in the Trump administration. And I loved it! Carl was sitting at a table in back of the club with a couple TBT members. He looked how I imagined. He was forty-four years old, but could easily pass for a man in his mid-30s. Skin high yellow like he was mixed, hair cut low with thick brushed waves. His only facial hair was a little-ass mustache. He didn't wear jewelry; just a big-ass watch. The tailored suit told that he was past the days of jeans and sneakers. And when he spoke, his voice was smooth as velvet.

"GMT in the building!" Carl said coolly, watching us with sharp, calculating eyes.

His team sized us up as we approached the booth. I ignored them, keeping my eyes on Carl. They were soldiers, not on my level. I was a boss. Carl was my equal.

"What up, Carl?"

He took his time looking at me from head to toe. Then he smiled. "It's a real pleasure to meet the young nigga that's putting a dent in my pocket. And now that I see you, I can see why Kianna chose you," he said before looking to Kianna. "You did good, Ki-Ki."

Kianna's face showed no emotion. Good bitch.

Carl kept staring at her, want and desire in his eyes. "I been looking for you, Ki-Ki. Did your sister tell you?"

"Listen, Carl," I cut in. "She with me now. I know y'all got history, but she my present. I wanna keep this between us."

He looked at me like a proud father watching his son hit a game winning shot. "Y'all have a seat. Mind if I call you Dray?"

I nodded as I took a seat. "That's cool."

"I gotta be real, Dray. When Kianna called and said you wanted to meet me, I was shocked, for two reasons. The first being that my lady had a new nigga and this nigga wanted to meet me. Second, this new nigga that's putting a dent in my pocket got the audacity to want to meet me! I thought you was crazy or suicidal. You know how deadly the game can be. But now that you're here, I can see that you not crazy. You're ambitious. A young boss and deep thinker. Remind me of me. I believe strongly in first impressions, and had yours not been impressive, that 750 you pulled up in wouldn't have made it back to Milwaukee. I hope you don't take that as a threat, because that's not what it was. I told the truth because I respect you."

"Nah, I don't take that as a threat. I knew that was a possibility, and it was a risk I was willing to take. But I hope you weren't gon' rest in that and think that my death wouldn't be avenged. Since we being honest, let me keep it real. I got a hit squad not too far from here. Some niggas you know. Trav n'em. I told them if I didn't come out of here to burn it down. And you know Trav can bring it."

He smiled. "So that's what Trav is up to these days. You got a good one there. I hated to let him go. But here's a jewel. A general should pick his army well, both for skill and loyalty. Once a weapon is made, it can't be allowed to turn back on its user. Power must be delegated carefully. The blood of generals killed by their own lieutenants fills many rivers. Many victories have turned into defeat at the hands of fucked-up lieutenants."

Carl had just hit me with some wisdom. It sounded like a warning about Trav. He let him go for a reason, but I couldn't dwell on it now.

"I hear you, Carl. But I'm not here to talk about Trav or armies. I wanna talk business."

"I guess we should get on with it, Dray. What's on yo' mind?"

"I need a new supplier. I don't know if you heard, but Diego got knocked. That was my man. Even though you my competition, I know you smart. This is an opportunity. How often do rivals set aside beefs and come together to do great things? Not often enough. Too many egos. But I'm settin' mine aside because I got a team to feed. Loyal soldiers need loyal generals. I love GMT. I built it and I wanna see it shine. The way I see it, this is a win-win. We can take over all of Wisconsin. A few more power moves in different states, and we can take over the Midwest. I'm proposing a TBT/GMT merger. We can be the Chrysler/Dodge of the streets."

Carl's face was blank, but his eyes showed that he was evaluating everything I said. And then he smiled. "I hear you,

Drayez. Since you've come into my club, you haven't disappointed me yet. I can't remember meeting somebody for the first time and thinking so highly of them. But before I respond to your proposal, I have a question. And this is serious; make no mistake about it."

I stayed quiet, waiting.

"A little over a year ago, my brother came up missing in Atlanta. He disappeared and his body hasn't been found. I did some digging and found out your team was in Atlanta around the time he went missing. I guess y'all made an impression because people remembered GMT. Now tell me it was a coincidence that GMT was in Atlanta when my brother came up missing. Tell me, Drayez."

Carl leaned forward, staring knowingly into my eyes like he knew I killed his brother. For a moment I wondered if Kianna told him. But that would've been stupid on her part because Carl would've killed us all. He was fishing. So I met his knowingly look with a look of innocence.

"I didn't know you lost yo' brother. I was in Atlanta about a year ago partying for my nigga's bachelor party. And yeah, we did it big. We always do. But I never met yo' brother. Us being in the ATL at the same time was a coincidence."

Carl gave me a long stare. I didn't blink while sneaking a hand near my waist. If he flinched, I was popping his ass. No questions asked. If I died tonight, he was coming with me.

"Okay, Drayez." He smiled. "Call it a coincidence. Now as far as business goes, I like it. But I will agree to the merger only on one condition."

I relaxed, feeling my insides grow warm. "Name it."

He looked at Kianna like she was the love of his life. "I made a bad decision when I let her go. My ego got too big and I acted like a fool. My one condition is that you give me my girl back."

I looked to Kianna for a hint of how I should move, but her face was blank. She didn't smile, look upset, or nod her head. And there was nothing in her eyes. I had never seen her face so emotionless. She wanted me to make the choice and didn't want to influence my decision. The team needed this deal, but Kianna knew too much, mainly that I killed Cartier. GMT could go on without Kianna, but did she want to be with Carl? Did he want her back to kill her? Was I sending her to her death? But Kianna had lied about plenty of shit. Cartier being in our room, burning Lace's face, Donovan hitting her, and being in love with Carl.

"I owe this to the team, Kianna, but it's on you. What you wanna do?"

"Drayez, we built this together. I—"

"Leave, Drayez," Carl cut in. "Leave right now and let her stay. Find a hotel to stay for the night and I'll get with you in the morning to make plans for the drop."

I looked to Kianna for a sign. She still wore the blank look. No hints. No clues. No emotions. Nothing.

So I got up and left.

Chapter 24

I had just hung up the phone from Facetiming with Desiré when there was a knock on the door.

I immediately got on point. Was Carl trying to set me up, or is this how he wanted to do business? I wasn't sure, so I grabbed my pistol and crept to the door. Through the peephole I could see Kianna standing in the hallway. *Fuck is she doing?* I wondered, unlocking the door. I hoped she wasn't mad that I left her because I didn't feel like arguing.

"Kianna, what the—"

She forced her way into my room, kissing me and making me swallow my words. I pushed her off.

"What the fuck you doin'?"

"I needed to see you one last time."

I checked the hallway before locking the door. "We made a deal. What if Carl finds out?"

"He won't."

"So what are you doing here? You mad that I left you?"

"No. You did what you had to do. It was a business move. It was best for GMT. I get it and I'm not mad. I didn't come to talk, Drayez. This might be the last time I ever see you and I don't want to spend it talking."

She pulled the dress over her head and let it fall to the floor. She wore a red bra, no panties, red bottoms, and the 380 strapped to her thigh. She looked sexy as fuck. Before I could decide what to do, she closed the distance between us and kissed me. I dropped the pistol and went with the flow. My boxers came off so fast that I didn't remember taking them off and we fell onto the bed, me on top. My dick was harder than a nigga in jail watching Beyoncé do a strip tease. Her legs wrapped around my waist, the 380 digging into my side. I grabbed it from the holster and threw it on the bed. When I pushed my dick inside, she gasped, biting my bottom lip.

"Yeah, Drayez!" she moaned. "Fuck me like it's the last time."

I went deep into her guts, long-stroking and digging her out. She wanted more and rolled me over, never missing a beat as she rode me hard. I sat up to suck her titties and that made her ride faster. I grabbed her ass and squeezed, pulling her into me. That's when I felt something drip onto my forehead. I ignored it and kept sucking her titties until I felt it again. I looked up and saw Kianna's face wet with tears and sweat. This wasn't like her. The only woman I knew to cry during sex was Desiré.

"You good?"

She stopped riding, wrapping her arms around me, face in the crook of my neck. "I love you, Drayez."

Get the fuck outta here! The words stunned me. Why was she telling me this now?

"I didn't want to love you. I tried to hide it, Drayez. Tried to fight it, but it kept growing."

I tried to figure out why she was telling me this now. The deal was already made and I wasn't going back on it. This was about the team.

"I'm not telling you this because I want you to change your mind. I'm telling you this because I want you to know this is hard for me."

I felt the cold steel press against my temple. Nah! This wasn't happening! My hands were still palming her ass and I couldn't get to the gun before she pulled the trigger. If I flinched, she would kill me. I had to stay calm and buy myself some time.

"Carl doesn't want to make the merger. He thinks you are the head of the snake. If he kills you and takes me, he knows GMT will fall apart. He wants to eliminate the competition. He also can't accept the fact that I was yours. The world isn't big enough for me to have two lovers. This is why I didn't want you to meet Carl. I knew it would come to this. That's why I couldn't help you make the choice. It wasn't up to me. Your life was on the line. If we would've left the meeting without making the deal, I would have remained loyal to you. I would have remained your bitch and GMT."

While she was talking, a million thoughts ran through my head. It couldn't be over. I just wanted to make this last deal. I was looking out for the team. Why didn't Carl want more money? I answered my own question. Because money isn't everything. There are more important things in the world than money. Like principles. Morals. Integrity. Faith. Family. Love. And time. Time is more valuable than money. It was as clear to me now as it was when I was watching the doctors work on Draya in the emergency room. Van's words played my mind. He said there would be a time in my life when I wished I could go back and do it all over. He was right. I wanted to hit the reset button. Time is the currency of life and my time was running out. I had to do something. Draya needed me. Junior needed me. Desiré needed me. Tikka needed me.

"I'm sorry, Drayez. You are my creation. I have to be the one to take you out."

I made my move. I heard the boom. I felt a burning pain and seen a flash behind my eyelids.

To Be Continued...
Blood on the Money 3
Coming Soon

Submission Guideline

Submit the first three chapters of your completed manuscript to ldpsubmissions@gmail.com, subject line: Your book's title. The manuscript must be in a .doc file and sent as an attachment. Document should be in Times New Roman, double spaced and in size 12 font. Also, provide your synopsis and full contact information. If sending multiple submissions, they must each be in a separate email.

Have a story but no way to send it electronically? You can still submit to LDP/Ca$h Presents. Send in the first three chapters, written or typed, of your completed manuscript to:

LDP: Submissions Dept
Po Box 944
Stockbridge, Ga 30281

DO NOT send original manuscript. Must be a duplicate.

Provide your synopsis and a cover letter containing your full contact information.

Thanks for considering LDP and Ca$h Presents.

Coming Soon from Lock Down Publications/Ca$h Presents

BOW DOWN TO MY GANGSTA

By **Ca$h**

TORN BETWEEN TWO

By **Coffee**

THE STREETS STAINED MY SOUL **II**

By **Marcellus Allen**

BLOOD OF A BOSS **VI**

SHADOWS OF THE GAME II

By **Askari**

LOYAL TO THE GAME **IV**

By **T.J. & Jelissa**

IF LOVING YOU IS WRONG… **III**

By **Jelissa**

TRUE SAVAGE **VIII**

MIDNIGHT CARTEL III

DOPE BOY MAGIC IV

CITY OF KINGZ II

By **Chris Green**

BLAST FOR ME **III**

A SAVAGE DOPEBOY III

CUTTHROAT MAFIA III

DUFFLE BAG CARTEL VI

By **Ghost**

A HUSTLER'S DECEIT III

KILL ZONE **II**

BAE BELONGS TO ME III

A DOPE BOY'S QUEEN III

By **Aryanna**

COKE KINGS V

KING OF THE TRAP II

By **T.J. Edwards**

GORILLAZ IN THE BAY V

3X KRAZY II

De'Kari

THE STREETS ARE CALLING II

Duquie Wilson

KINGPIN KILLAZ IV

STREET KINGS III

PAID IN BLOOD III

CARTEL KILLAZ IV

DOPE GODS III

Hood Rich

SINS OF A HUSTLA II

ASAD

KINGZ OF THE GAME VI

Playa Ray

SLAUGHTER GANG IV

RUTHLESS HEART IV

By Willie Slaughter

THE HEART OF A SAVAGE III

By Jibril Williams

FUK SHYT II

By Blakk Diamond

THE REALEST KILLAZ III

By Tranay Adams

TRAP GOD III

By Troublesome

YAYO IV

GHOST MOB

Stilloan Robinson

KINGPIN DREAMS III

By Paper Boi Rari

CREAM II

By Yolanda Moore

SON OF A DOPE FIEND III

By Renta

FOREVER GANGSTA II

GLOCKS ON SATIN SHEETS III

By Adrian Dulan

LOYALTY AIN'T PROMISED III

By Keith Williams

THE PRICE YOU PAY FOR LOVE II

By Destiny Skai

CONFESSIONS OF A GANGSTA III

By Nicholas Lock

I'M NOTHING WITHOUT HIS LOVE II

SINS OF A THUG II

By Monet Dragun

LIFE OF A SAVAGE IV

MURDA SEASON IV

GANGLAND CARTEL III

By **Romell Tukes**

QUIET MONEY IV

THUG LIFE II

By **Trai'Quan**

THE STREETS MADE ME III

By **Larry D. Wright**

THE ULTIMATE SACRIFICE VI

IF YOU CROSS ME ONCE II

ANGEL III

By **Anthony Fields**

FRIEND OR FOE III

By **Mimi**

SAVAGE STORMS II

By **Meesha**

BLOOD ON THE MONEY III

By J-Blunt

THE STREETS WILL NEVER CLOSE II

By K'ajji

NIGHTMARES OF A HUSTLA II

By King Dream

THE WIFEY I USED TO BE II

By Nicole Goosby

IN THE ARM OF HIS BOSS

By Jamila

MONEY, MURDER & MEMORIES II

Malik D. Rice

Available Now

RESTRAINING ORDER **I & II**

By **CA$H & Coffee**

LOVE KNOWS NO BOUNDARIES **I II & III**

By **Coffee**

RAISED AS A GOON I, II, III & IV

BRED BY THE SLUMS I, II, III

BLAST FOR ME I & II

ROTTEN TO THE CORE I II III

A BRONX TALE I, II, III

DUFFLE BAG CARTEL I II III IV V

HEARTLESS GOON I II III IV

A SAVAGE DOPEBOY I II

HEARTLESS GOON I II III

DRUG LORDS I II III

CUTTHROAT MAFIA I II

By **Ghost**

LAY IT DOWN **I & II**

LAST OF A DYING BREED

BLOOD STAINS OF A SHOTTA I & II III

By **Jamaica**

LOYAL TO THE GAME I II III

LIFE OF SIN I, II III

By **TJ & Jelissa**

BLOODY COMMAS I & II

SKI MASK CARTEL I II & III

KING OF NEW YORK I II,III IV V

RISE TO POWER I II III

COKE KINGS I II III IV

BORN HEARTLESS I II III IV

KING OF THE TRAP

By **T.J. Edwards**

IF LOVING HIM IS WRONG…I & II

LOVE ME EVEN WHEN IT HURTS I II III

By **Jelissa**

WHEN THE STREETS CLAP BACK I & II III

THE HEART OF A SAVAGE I II

By **Jibril Williams**

A DISTINGUISHED THUG STOLE MY HEART I II & III

LOVE SHOULDN'T HURT I II III IV

RENEGADE BOYS I II III IV

PAID IN KARMA I II III

SAVAGE STORMS

By **Meesha**

A GANGSTER'S CODE I &, II III

A GANGSTER'S SYN I II III

THE SAVAGE LIFE I II III

CHAINED TO THE STREETS I II III

BLOOD ON THE MONEY I II

By J-Blunt

PUSH IT TO THE LIMIT

By **Bre' Hayes**

BLOOD OF A BOSS **I, II, III, IV, V**

SHADOWS OF THE GAME

By **Askari**

THE STREETS BLEED MURDER **I, II & III**

THE HEART OF A GANGSTA I II& III

By **Jerry Jackson**

CUM FOR ME I II III IV V VI

An **LDP Erotica Collaboration**

BRIDE OF A HUSTLA **I II & II**

THE FETTI GIRLS **I, II& III**

CORRUPTED BY A GANGSTA I, II III, IV

BLINDED BY HIS LOVE

THE PRICE YOU PAY FOR LOVE

DOPE GIRL MAGIC I II III

By **Destiny Skai**

WHEN A GOOD GIRL GOES BAD

By **Adrienne**

THE COST OF LOYALTY I II III

By Kweli

A GANGSTER'S REVENGE **I II III & IV**

THE BOSS MAN'S DAUGHTERS I II III IV V

A SAVAGE LOVE **I & II**

BAE BELONGS TO ME I II

A HUSTLER'S DECEIT I, II, III

WHAT BAD BITCHES DO I, II, III

SOUL OF A MONSTER I II III

KILL ZONE

A DOPE BOY'S QUEEN I II

By **Aryanna**

A KINGPIN'S AMBITON

A KINGPIN'S AMBITION **II**

I MURDER FOR THE DOUGH

By **Ambitious**

TRUE SAVAGE I II III IV V VI VII

DOPE BOY MAGIC I, II, III

MIDNIGHT CARTEL I II

CITY OF KINGZ

By **Chris Green**

A DOPEBOY'S PRAYER

By **Eddie "Wolf" Lee**

THE KING CARTEL **I, II & III**

By **Frank Gresham**

THESE NIGGAS AIN'T LOYAL **I, II & III**

By **Nikki Tee**

GANGSTA SHYT **I II &III**

By **CATO**

THE ULTIMATE BETRAYAL

By **Phoenix**

BOSS'N UP **I , II & III**

By **Royal Nicole**

I LOVE YOU TO DEATH

By Destiny J

I RIDE FOR MY HITTA

I STILL RIDE FOR MY HITTA

By **Misty Holt**

LOVE & CHASIN' PAPER

By **Qay Crockett**

TO DIE IN VAIN

SINS OF A HUSTLA

By **ASAD**

BROOKLYN HUSTLAZ

By **Boogsy Morina**

BROOKLYN ON LOCK I & II

By **Sonovia**

GANGSTA CITY

By **Teddy Duke**

A DRUG KING AND HIS DIAMOND I & II III

A DOPEMAN'S RICHES

HER MAN, MINE'S TOO I, II

CASH MONEY HO'S

THE WIFEY I USED TO BE

By Nicole Goosby

TRAPHOUSE KING **I II & III**

KINGPIN KILLAZ I II III

STREET KINGS I II

PAID IN BLOOD **I II**

CARTEL KILLAZ I II III

DOPE GODS I II

By **Hood Rich**

LIPSTICK KILLAH **I, II, III**

CRIME OF PASSION I II & III

FRIEND OR FOE I II

By **Mimi**

STEADY MOBBN' **I, II, III**

THE STREETS STAINED MY SOUL

By **Marcellus Allen**

WHO SHOT YA **I, II, III**

SON OF A DOPE FIEND I II

Renta

GORILLAZ IN THE BAY **I II III IV**

TEARS OF A GANGSTA I II

3X KRAZY

DE'KARI

TRIGGADALE I II III

Elijah R. Freeman

GOD BLESS THE TRAPPERS I, II, III

THESE SCANDALOUS STREETS I, II, III

FEAR MY GANGSTA I, II, III IV, V

THESE STREETS DON'T LOVE NOBODY I, II

BURY ME A G I, II, III, IV, V

A GANGSTA'S EMPIRE I, II, III, IV

THE DOPEMAN'S BODYGAURD I II

THE REALEST KILLAZ I II

Tranay Adams

THE STREETS ARE CALLING

Duquie Wilson

MARRIED TO A BOSS… I II III

By Destiny Skai & Chris Green

KINGZ OF THE GAME I II III IV V

Playa Ray

SLAUGHTER GANG I II III

RUTHLESS HEART I II III

By Willie Slaughter

FUK SHYT

By Blakk Diamond

DON'T F#CK WITH MY HEART I II

By Linnea

ADDICTED TO THE DRAMA I II III

IN THE ARM OF HIS BOSS II

By Jamila

YAYO I II III

A SHOOTER'S AMBITION I II

By S. Allen

TRAP GOD I II

By Troublesome

FOREVER GANGSTA

GLOCKS ON SATIN SHEETS I II

By Adrian Dulan

TOE TAGZ I II III

By Ah'Million

KINGPIN DREAMS I II

By Paper Boi Rari

CONFESSIONS OF A GANGSTA I II

By Nicholas Lock

I'M NOTHING WITHOUT HIS LOVE

SINS OF A THUG

By Monet Dragun

CAUGHT UP IN THE LIFE I II III

By Robert Baptiste

NEW TO MONEY, MURDER & MEMORIES

THE GAME I II III

By **Malik D. Rice**

LIFE OF A SAVAGE I II III

A GANGSTA'S QUR'AN I II III

MURDA SEASON I II III

GANGLAND CARTEL I II

By **Romell Tukes**

LOYALTY AIN'T PROMISED I II

By Keith Williams

QUIET MONEY I II III

THUG LIFE

By **Trai'Quan**

THE STREETS MADE ME I II

By **Larry D. Wright**

THE ULTIMATE SACRIFICE I, II, III, IV, V

KHADIFI

IF YOU CROSS ME ONCE

ANGEL I II

By **Anthony Fields**

THE LIFE OF A HOOD STAR

By Ca$h & Rashia Wilson

THE STREETS WILL NEVER CLOSE

By K'ajji

CREAM

By Yolanda Moore

NIGHTMARES OF A HUSTLA

By King Dream

BOOKS BY LDP'S CEO, CA$H

TRUST IN NO MAN

TRUST IN NO MAN 2

TRUST IN NO MAN 3

BONDED BY BLOOD

SHORTY GOT A THUG

THUGS CRY

THUGS CRY 2

THUGS CRY 3

TRUST NO BITCH

TRUST NO BITCH 2

TRUST NO BITCH 3

TIL MY CASKET DROPS

RESTRAINING ORDER

RESTRAINING ORDER 2

IN LOVE WITH A CONVICT

LIFE OF A HOOD STAR